The First Book of

Carrie

D. Antoinette

Acknowledgements

I would like to give glory and honor to God for blessing me and giving me this gift. Without Him, I am nothing.

To my daughters, Nikira (Toots) and Nevaeh (Mackie), thank you for being two of the most amazing human beings that I have ever known. I am honored to be your mother. God thought very highly of me when he blessed me with you two!

To my Mother, you may not know this but you are my role model. You are the smartest, bravest, strongest woman that I know. And thank you for believing me and never giving up on me even when I gave up on myself.

To my brother, my first child, Michael, you have grown to be a fine young man and I am so proud of you.

To Tirell, thank you for holding my hand and walking me through this process. I am very grateful. You are a true friend.

To Disturbed (An awesome rock band), thank you for the most amazing song, Down with the Sickness. I listened to this song A LOT while brainstorming the concept of this book.

And finally to the Brooks Sisters: Saundra, Wendy, Kathy, Pearl and Roxanne, thank you for being the inspiration behind my book.

I'm sorry if I missed anyone. I would literally have thousands of pages if I thanked everyone who has touched my life. Believe me; I appreciate each and every one of you.

God Bless:

D. Antoinette

Dedication

This book is dedicated to my beautiful daughters, Nikira (Toots) and Nevaeh (Mackie): You are the reason(s) why I get up and try hard every day! It is my hope that I can prove to you two that I deserve to be your mother.

And the Brooks sisters: Saundra, Wendy, Kathy, Pearl (my mom) and Roxanne: Thank you for being the inspiration for the story because without you all, I wouldn't even have a story to write.

And to my Daddy: Rest in Peace. I hope that I have made you proud!

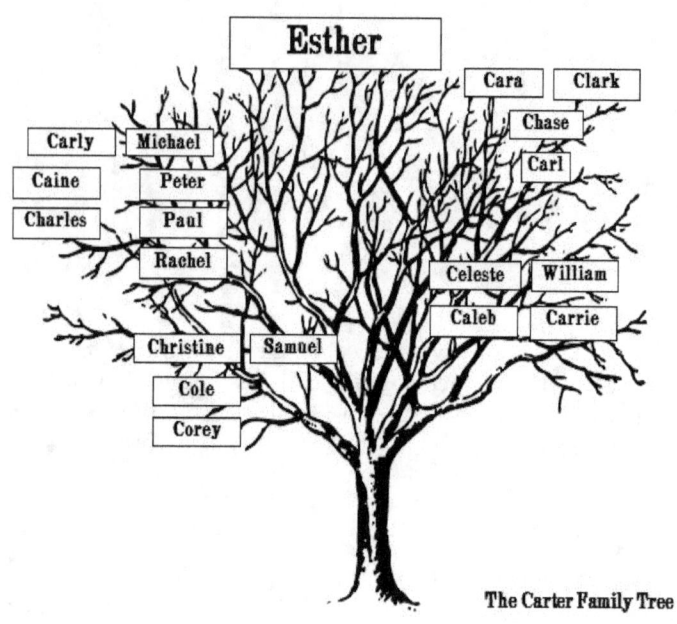

Esther

Cara   Clark

Carly   Michael   Chase

Caine   Peter   Carl

Charles   Paul

Rachel   Celeste   William

Caleb   Carrie

Christine   Samuel

Cole

Corey

The Carter Family Tree

So it begins...
Five years earlier...

Celeste, this is what is best for Carrie. You would want her to be protected and so she shall be, Cara reasoned with Celeste using mental telepathy.

The sisters all could share thoughts with one another. That was one of the realities of being their kind.

Cara hated driving. Flying was much faster, but she couldn't just leap out of the car and literally fly with the hospital staff in the car with her. Actually, she physically could and she had honestly considered doing it, but for Carrie's sake, they were going to retrieve her in the most humanly way possible. There was a greater goal to be accomplished; today was only the beginning. The sisters had greedily anticipated this—all save one.

Carrie, Celeste's only daughter, was all that mattered. Exposing her too early in advance of transition could possibly traumatize her. Besides, all would be revealed in due time. Carrie was of age now.

Many of their kind changed in their early adolescence. Cara herself had. Now that Carrie was in middle school, her time was coming.

Soon.

You can't have her! I won't let you! Please, I beg you! Don't do this! Let Esther be! Leave Carrie alone! Celeste screamed in her head, desperation pouring out of her.

Celeste knew her sisters were getting closer to her house. She could smell them. The air was thick with the scent of her siblings. The sin, the evil, the passion…all of this excited her.

Celeste eyes grew wild with rage. She was barely able to choke out a smile at her young daughter, who was completely in the dark about what was about to happen to her mother and to her. Carrie turned on the living room TV and sat on the love seat. Celeste closed her eyes as she paced the room, hoping Carrie didn't notice that her eyes were changing from green to black.

In an attempt to block all that was happening, Celeste focused mentally on closing the curtains without physically touching them. In a futile effort she attempted to close her mind to her sisters. No matter what she did, she couldn't stop them from coming. Celeste could feel her power draining. Moving objects mentally always sapped her energy. The effort was physically taxing. She could feel her eyes fading from black to white, as they always did when she exercised her power.

Celeste! Carly chimed in, *Stop being so damn dramatic! It's only a child, remember. You've told me that many times before! How can this be any different? Ohhhh, because it's you? YOU'D BEST GET OVER YOURSELF!*

It is said that revenge is a dish best served cold, Carly continued to mentally rant. *Some would say it's even better than sex!*

Carly giggled, enjoying every moment of this. Truth be told, Carly had been waiting for this moment since Celeste left their sisterhood and decided to raise Carrie as a human. Carly drove her Range Rover with their other sister, Christine. The hospital staff followed behind in the hospital van along with Cara. Carly had the biggest smile on her face as if they weren't about to break up a family, her own sister's family.

Christine surveyed Carly as she drove. Christine may have been the only one out the three who was not enjoying this. If she had her way, Celeste would still be a part of their sisterhood, and this would not be happening. The fact that Carly was enjoying this annoyed the hell out of Christine; however, she also knew Carly was a total bitch, so Christine didn't hold Carly's behavior against her.

Celeste, dear sister, please be reasonable, Christine interjected before Carly could continue to gloat. *What did you expect? You knew this day was coming. Carrie will be turning soon; and since you no longer wish to be a sister to us, we must do what is best for Carrie and us.*

What's best for Carrie is to be with her mother! Celeste screamed. *I will tell her about her lineage and our history before she turns, but this is my daughter! I will explain everything to her! Please, don't do this! I am begging you, do not do this!* Celeste tried to appeal to Christine and Cara.

There was no need to try reason with Carly because she was...well...Carly.

Celeste was now near tears as she continued to pace the floor. She was moving even faster now, trying to calm down. Her feet barely touched the floor. Celeste's body was a live wire. She wanted to physically fight her three sisters. She did agree to these terms, but she never, ever thought she would have to pay, and so soon. She didn't plan well for this day, mistakenly believing that she had more time.

Carrie, her beautiful, sweet Carrie, was channel surfing, still very unaware of what was about to happen. Celeste wished she could pray because she needed divine intervention. She didn't want her sisters to take her daughter, but she couldn't stop them, either.

She is the key and we need her, Cara scolded Celeste. *You of all people know that better than anyone. This is what has been planned and ordered. It's already done.*

I smell you, Celeste! Carly piped in. *I smell bubble gum and watermelon lip gloss. Oh, wait...that's Carrie! We are going to have sooo much fun while you're away. You used to be so strong, Celeste. Now you are just pathetic. It's sad, really.*

This isn't over! Celeste warned.

Of course not! This is just the beginning, Carly sang as they all pulled up to take Celeste to a mental hospital.

And Carrie would be one of them...

My Family Is Crazy

Present Day
Carrie, 17 years old

"My aunts are crazy!" I finally admitted.

That was the first step of any recovery process, acknowledging the problem. I remembered reading that somewhere.

Now, how to fix it? If I could fix my aunts, and make them crazy-free or even less zany, then maybe I could fix my mother. My mother was hospitalized when I was in middle school because she was, well, crazy. It was something that my aunts didn't really talk much about, probably because they might have been unsure of what to say to me.

How could anyone explain to their seventeen years old niece that her mother was insane? *"Sorry kid, but it's true. There is a crazy gene and it was passed on from our mother to your mother and we are hoping it skips you."* If I could fix my aunts' and my mother's psychosis, then maybe I could stop mine from ever happening.

I was trying to be proactive in my own life. I was afraid that once I became an adult that I would turn out like my aunts, or, even worse, end up in a mental institution like Mother. They were all beautiful and all equally insane. How else would one explain my aunts, all extremely beautiful living alone, on a farm?

It also made me wonder about my own sanity. Was derangement really hereditary? Was there a crazy gene? Or maybe it was my family's farm sucking the life out of everyone who ever lived here?

Maybe if I just got away from the farm, I would be ok.

No…better stick to plan A, curing the madness.

That was my only hope of saving me. I was having this internal debate as I stood in front of Baltimore City High School as I waited to be picked up by my aunts.

"SCARY CARRIE," a classmate of mine called as she walked pass me with a group of girls. I just hung my head and kicked a pebble around trying not to appear fazed by the name calling. I allowed my hair to fall to cover my face. The last thing I needed was for these girls to see that my feelings were hurt.

This was my life. I was tormented twenty-four hours a day, three hundred and sixty-five days a year. After seemingly endless years of teasing, you would think I would be used to it by now, but, surprisingly the taunting hurt more now than it had in the past.

The girls all giggled and carried on an idiotic conversation about me and my family.

"Her mother is crazy, right?" one girl asked. She must have been new to our school or new to the city for that matter. It was common knowledge that my mother was insane.

Or at least it felt like everyone knew she was.

"If she was my daughter and dressed like that, I would be crazy too," another girl teased and laughed.

Now, I would be the first to admit, well the second, because Aunt Carly would be the first, that I wasn't the best dresser. But I was sure I wasn't the worst. I looked down and examined my outfit. I had on a purple t-shirt with a white cat on it with the word, "Pppuurrfect!" appearing as the cat's thoughts and cut-off jeans shorts that came to my knees with some white decks. I was totally clueless about fashion, so maybe I was the worst, but I had more important things on my mind. I didn't have time to worry about the normal teenage problems: boys, clothes, peer pressure, drugs…

Nope, I had real problems: demented mother, odd aunts, and me possibly joining that insane classification.

"Yes, her mother is completely out of her mind!" another girl answered.

As the girls kept walking out of my earshot, another added *sotto voce*, "Careful, she's a witch."

"I hear that her aunts worship the devil," yet another clueless classmate of mine added. "That's why they are soooo beautiful. They sold their souls to the devil when they were young, and now they don't age. My Uncle Louis told me. He said they all went crazy and killed their sons and buried their bodies on that farm they own."

They giggled conspiratorially like a bunch of little schoolgirls. That was exactly what they were stupid little schoolgirls. I still pretended that I couldn't hear them. I lowered my head even more and focused on my pebble.

"Scary Carrie should have been sold her soul! She needs all the help she can get, looking and dressing like that," someone else added. They all laughed.

"I heard they adopted her to appear normal and that before she turns eighteen, they are going to eat her."

Another girl added, "I heard she drove her mother crazy! That Carrie is like some demon seed." They all looked back at me and shook their heads in disapproval and kept walking.

I watched them until they were out of sight. I paced the front of the school from one end of the building to the other in the scorching sun. I was on the verge of tears. I wished I had the courage to stand up for myself. No, that was not true. I wished I was like those girls. I wished I was normal. I wished my mother wasn't crazy, I wished my aunts weren't so…them.

I looked down at my Mickey Mouse watch. My aunts were running late and it was so unlike them. I never waited to be picked up from school before. They were usually waiting for me in front of the school. I tugged at my book bag. It felt extremely heavy as if I had the weight of the world on my back.

"Hey, Care Bear."

I was startled out of my thoughts by Noah Green. He was my best friend, my only friend and I was possibly in love with him. He was pure perfection with his pale skin and his jet black hair. His eyes were a piercing blue. He could place anyone under his spell

14

with one glance, and I was. He was lean and muscular due to his swimmer's body and he had a smile that could melt butter. Why he was my friend, I would never know. Maybe he was a sucker for losers.

"Hey, Noah." I stopped playing with the pebble to look at him. He had on a black tank top and jean shorts.

He looked amazing.

He *was* amazing.

"Last day of school, awesome, right?" He smiled.

My mind was elsewhere. I wanted to talk to him but I just had a revelation and I was on the road to recovery. Before I could answer, he ended our conversation and I was so disappointed, even though I was not in the mood to talk.

"Well, talk to you later." He said as he looked across the parking lot. "Your aunts are here. I'll walk you." My eyes followed his gaze to my Aunt Cara car. She was driving one of her many cars. Today was the black Mercedes with the wood and crème interior. Aunt Christine was in the passenger seat.

I looked back at him. "MJ won't mind, will she?" That was his girlfriend. And of course she and I weren't the best of friends.

He smiled. "We are just walking together. I don't think it's illegal."

I smiled back at him but I also scanned the school grounds. I didn't want MJ popping up out of nowhere. We walked to Aunt Cara's car in silence. "Thanks, Noah."

"Sure, and I hope your mother is doing better. Please tell her I asked about her the next time that you see her," he said with genuine concern.   Noah greeted my aunts, he said, "Good afternoon, Ms. Cara, Ms. Christine."

I smiled at Noah as I jumped in the back seat and I waved goodbye.   Aunt Cara pulled off, neither of them acknowledged Noah.   I sighed and went back to my original thoughts about Mother.

The overall consensus was that Mother was crazy. Actually it was more like a three to one vote. I was the one vote who thought she was healthy and my aunts were the majority vote in favor of lunacy. I was concerned about my mother's mental health at times that much I would concede. She did scare me sometimes when I would visit her only because of the foolishness that came out of her mouth.

I couldn't help but to think, that if you actually believed what you said was the truth, did that make you crazy even if your thoughts were delusional? My mother was crazy to everyone else but to me, she was savable. I liked some of her colorful views and different takes on reality. And I missed her. She was my mother, crazy or not, I still loved her and wanted her to be well.

When I was growing up, the thought of Mother being crazy never entered my mind until my aunts put it there. Though I will be the first to admit, Mother's behavior was questionable at times, she was never textbook insane. She never harmed me, herself, or anyone else. She wasn't a danger to society. She just had some screws loose, but she wasn't crazy enough to be hospitalized at least not in my professional opinion.

Something was a little off about Mother. She told me that she could smell me and my aunts at the entrance of the home she resided in for the mentally handicapped. That was highly unlikely especially because her room was on the fifth floor. When we would visit her, she would have her back to us or she would be reading a book and greet us without looking up.

She even knew if one of my aunts were missing. She claimed she was able to tell who was there and who wasn't based off our smells. I thought that talent made her extraordinary, not weird.

Noah's comment about Mother's health made me want to see her. As we drove to the farmland, I asked, "Aunt Cara, Aunt Chris, can I see my mother, please?" We were in Baltimore City. We lived on the outskirts of rural Howard County and we were going to go past the hospital anyway, so I asked if we could make a detour.

Aunt Cara, my understanding aunt, agreed without hesitation. Aunt Chris agreed but with reservations. Wordless communication was exchanged between my aunts as I observed from the backseat. This much I knew because Aunt Chris made about eight different facial expressions. One very clear emotion that was visibly expressed was anger. Nonetheless, I was satisfied that Aunt Cara won the staring contest.

"Good afternoon, Cara, Christine, and Carrie. Where's Carly? She didn't feel like pretending today?" Mother called from her crossword puzzle book not bothering to look up.

My mouth gaped in surprise. "Ma, are you a psychic? You do that every time and you are always right." And I was amazed every time. Was she psychic? And if so, did that make her mentally ill because she could see things that others couldn't? I didn't think so. I thought her psychic ability made her special. Though I often wondered if she could smell us, how did we smell? What exactly did she smell? So I made sure I took a bath every day, just in case. I didn't ever want her to say I smelled bad.

"No, not a psychic, just psychotic according to my loving sisters." She looked up at my aunts. I noticed that her eyes were darker than their usual brilliant green color. *Can medicine have that side effect?* I wondered.

No, a voice that sounded very much like Mother's whispered.

What? What was that? It sounded like Mother's voice responding faintly to a question I asked in my head.

Okay, Carrie. You're not crazy, I thought to myself.

I looked at Mother as she stared at me silently. Obviously she didn't say anything. I must have imagined the whole thing. Yes, that was exactly what happened. *I imagined that whole exchange.* Case closed. My sanity was still intact.

"Hello, Celeste," Aunt Chris sneered, standing closer to the door than to Mother like she was trying not to catch the crazy as if it was a disease. But she was already crazy, just like Mother and other two aunts. I was the one that needed to be cautious.

"And you seem very lucid today," Aunt Cara commented from the hallway. She had not entered the room and by the looks of things, she didn't plan on doing so, either.

Maybe she felt as if Mother was contagious too. "Not a compliment, Cara. And I thought you were supposed to be the nice one." Mother looked back down in her book to finish her puzzle.

I laughed as I inched forward to where she was sitting in her rocking chair in front of the stationary thirteen inch TV that was jammed into the wall. She was being her old witty self.

"It's still true, on both accounts," Aunt Cara responded.

My mother was still amazingly beautiful despite being locked away in an insane asylum as she called it. Her distinct features had not been tarnished. Her long flowing black hair was as long as ever, her emerald green eyes still glowed, and her teeth were still as brilliant as diamonds. The only feature that had suffered was her complexion. She was once the color of honey like the rest my aunts, but now her once sun-kissed skin was dull and pale like mine. She looked thin and fragile, her curves were sunken in.

"Ma, when was the last time you ate?" I sat on the bed next to her. Though we weren't in a regular hospital, it sure did feel like one, with the bland colors and the universal furniture that institutions like that used, and of course, the smells. It smelled of medicine, antiseptic, bowels and death. Not a good smell. Aunt Carly would pass out. Not that my aunt had a weak stomach and couldn't handle it, but she had a low tolerance for things not being in perfect order. This hospital was not in perfect order.

"Thanksgiving. I ate for the first time in," she paused, then added, "years."

"Ma, stop playing! That was almost nine months ago, try again," I teased. "You need to eat and sleep. When was the last time you slept? You look tired." There were dark blue bruises under her eyes.

19

"Can't really remember, I think it was almost twenty years ago." Again she had to think about her response.

At first, when Mother talked like this, it was cute and animated now I just wished she would stop. She was not helping her case with my aunts or the outside world when she displayed her fanciful thoughts.

Aunt Cara must have read something in my face because she interjected, "Stop scaring the poor girl, Celeste," my aunt berated Mother. "She came to see you, and the least you can do is to be more hospitable."

Mother was livid, "Cara, I could sit here and pretend that I'm not all high off the numerous medications that I'm sure you convinced the hospital staff I needed. And I can pretend that you guys are visiting me at the Ritz Carlton while I'm on vacation, but in reality, I need to find a seven letter word for 'bitter' for this puzzle.

Oh, wait, I got it…Celeste!" Mother snapped.

"That's it," Aunt Chris announced. "Cara, Carrie, let's go. Celeste has had about all the excitement she can stand for today."

I was heartbroken, but I got up to leave. I wanted to spend time with my mother even if she was acting weird. She was still my mother and I loved her. I hated seeing her like that. I hated having to defend her to my aunts and to other people. Why couldn't she just get better? I promised myself right there, I would fix her.

"But we just got here." I countered. I wanted to start undoing her illness, today!

"True but Christine wants more time with Peter so she can influence him to commit an unspeakable act," Mother said, with her eyes closed. She scribbled words in her book ferociously. Her face was flushed with excitement.

I eyed Mother suspiciously. Could she really read minds? Was she really a psychic? Did she really know what Aunt Chris was thinking?

"Unspeakable act?" I questioned. I turned toward my Aunt Chris, who was beyond upset. Her facial expression of anger was undeniable.

Mother started mumbling. It was unintelligible gibberish but I could have sworn I heard her say *red rum*…

"What are you saying, Mother?" I stood in the middle of the floor and tried to decipher her crazy talk. I didn't get much other than the red rum reference. I didn't know much about language or speaking in tongues but red rum was the word murder backward.

Was Mother talking backward?

Wasn't that considered to be demonic?

Mother continued scribbling words down. She had yet to open her eyes. "Red rum?" I turned to face my aunts for confirmation. Maybe she needed a doctor, or better yet, a priest. Neither one of them looked pleased. "What's…"

"Good-bye, Celeste." Aunt Chris barked, grimacing from where she stood. I reluctantly started to walk toward them again.

Mother needed us to help her, not retreat. I didn't dare look at Aunt Chris as I made my way to exit. I could feel the heat radiating from her body. Aunt Chris was angry, maybe even angry enough to fight Mother, a serious brawl. Aunt Chris had an issue with anger, and maybe she could benefit from a hospital stay herself.

There was no need to try to melee with my Aunt Chris when she got upset. I knew I wouldn't win. Crazy people were strong and Mother at that moment was acting crazy so maybe Mother could take her.

I wouldn't mind seeing that, I thought.

As if they all could hear me, Aunt Cara smirked and Aunt Chris looked even more furious. *Did I say that aloud, only meaning to think it?* I panicked.

Oh, no.

"See ya, Ma," I whimpered. "I love you and I hope you get better." She never opened her eyes and she never stopped writing. "What's wrong with her?" I asked Aunt Chris.

"A LOT!" Aunt Chris fumed.

"Celeste, stop that and say good bye to Carrie," Aunt Cara ordered Mother as if she was instructing a child.

Mother ignored my aunt's request, but she finally opened her eyes and stopped writing. Maybe she was really abnormal and not vibrant like I hoped.

"Christine, Peter will not do what you wish. He has a stronger will than you originally thought." Mother looked at my frozen frame as I stood near Aunt Chris. Then Mother cut her eyes back to Aunt Cara, "You can't bring her back. She will never walk this earth again and you won't use Carrie to do it. I'll see to it, even if it kills me."

I was confused. I was about to ask what on earth were they talking about but before I could blink, Aunt Chris was out the room and Aunt Cara was ushering me toward the door.

I had never seen Aunt Chris with any man, yet alone talk about one. And what did Mother mean by, *you can't bring her back*?

So it was true. My aunts were witches or devil worshippers! I knew it!

I didn't bring up the horrible visit with Mother after we left the facility. For what? I wasn't going to get a straight answer. But I did stress to my aunts that I wanted to go alone to visit Mother from then on. Aunt Chris was against it and expressed so, Aunt Carly didn't care either way, but Aunt Cara agreed saying that the only stipulation was that I get a ride to and from the hospital, and I was allowed two hours per visit. I agreed to those terms because I wanted desperately for Mother to return to her proper mental state; I was sure that, if nothing else, I could love her back to normal.

So from then on, my aunts took turns coordinating my visits with Mother. Some days were great. Mother and I would talk and laugh and play games, and then some days were awful and scary. She would speak in tongues or backward, and sometimes she was so drugged up that she never even looked at me or woke from her slumber.

Commonality, was that too much to ask? This instability went on for a long month; the high highs and the low lows.

One of Mother's nurses said inconsistency was commonplace of someone with her mental health. Commonplace? Was the nurse delusional? I questioned.

Mother's condition deteriorated rapidly over the summer break. It was now August and anyone could see that Mother was slipping away. Her once luxurious hair was now thinning in some spots and balding in others, her frame was brittle and gaunt, her emerald green eyes were clouded, and her creamy complexion was now whiter than before. She became transparent. This woman barely got out of bed. She barely took baths, barely got dressed, or barely ate. Mother checked out a long time ago, this was just her shell.

I didn't talk to her much; I just sat by her as she lay in the bed and slept. I would bring a book to read, or do one of her beloved word puzzles, watch TV, but mostly I would just watch her, afraid that she would die right in front of my eyes.

Till one day, I had it! I decided I would march into the room and demand that she get up.

"MA, GET UP NOW!" I screamed at the top of my lungs.

She didn't wake up, she didn't even budge. There was no reaction, other than the nurses charging into the room telling me to keep the noise down or I would have to leave. And with that, I gave up on my road-to-recovery campaign.

"Why can't you be normal, like everyone else's mother?" I cried. "For my birthday, can you just be normal? Please?" I collapsed in the rocking chair beside her bed.

"Normal?" she murmured from under her hospital-issued covers. "What's normal?" She turned to face me, her eyes, were not as cloudy, her face not so hard, her complexion still needed some work but not so bad.

"Well," I said through my tears, "do the opposite of what you are doing right now. That's normal."

She closed her eyes, still facing me. "All relative."

"No, normal is a uniform term, Mother," I spat.

"You would like to think it is, Carrie, but it isn't."

I kind of had to admit, I agreed with her thinking. The word normal was open for interpretation. However, this was the most she had said to me in two months. I continued to argue with her, just to hear her husky voice, just to hear her form sentences and have complete thoughts; my normal mother.

"Mother, everyone would agree, you are not acting like a normal person."

"So what's the definition of normal, then?" she asked as if she was naturally curious. "My nurse takes anti-depressants every day. Normal? Her son lies to her and steals the pills and money from her purse. Normal? The receptionist plays the lottery every Friday on a full moon because her psychic friend told her so. And this is defined as normal behavior?"

I stared at her for what seemed like forever. I was shocked, I was in awe, and, most importantly I was glad that Mother was starting to act like my mother in those last ten minutes. A smile crept onto my face. "So has the receptionist won anything?" I couldn't resist asking.

She smiled, too, and showed me her dazzling white teeth. "NO!" She laughed a musical laugh. "And the sad thing is that she continues to go to her psychic for advice." She screamed and jumped up because she was so tickled.

"Now that is crazy! If she's so psychic, why hasn't she won?" I screamed back.

We continued to laugh. Normalcy, this was nice.

"So I guess I let them off the hook." She propped herself up on her bed.

"What?"

"Your aunts, my sisters, now they don't have to come visit me. No more sympathy left for the loony sister." She made her eyes cross and her head dance to illustrate the word crazy.

"Ma, you were acting strange. It was so unlike you."

She looked like she was about to argue, but she pressed her lips together. "Well, I'm sick. What do they expect? They put me here. I'm playing the part," she snapped at me.

I never knew the whole story behind Mother being institutionalized. I was all of twelve when my aunts told me that I had to move to the family farm in rural Maryland with them because Mother could no longer take care of me. At the time Mother and I lived in a house in the city, away from my family's huge farmland. Then one random day I was forced to move with my aunts because Mother was sick.

"Ma, do you think about Caleb much? Is that why you are here? The grief of losing him was too much?"

That was the story I was told. My aunts made it clear that Mother was unfit because of Caleb. Caleb was my brother; and although I never met him or any of my aunts' sons, for that matter, because they all died before I was born. I still felt like the madness was all connected to them.

People in Maryland said that my family was cursed because there no one to carry on the Carter blood line. Mother said that was a good thing because they were right. And to drive the point further home, there were no males in my family.

I was the only surviving member of the second generation. All my male cousins died before the age of twenty, so I was sure it was probably a generational curse and I would be the next to die. Before Mother went all psycho, she assured me that I would live a long life.

Mother thought for a moment. "I think of Caleb all the time. He is always in my thoughts." She paused. "As are you, but he is not the reason I am locked up."

Aunt Chris said Mother never got over losing Caleb, and that was why she was sick. Aunt Cara said that the burden of life just become too much for her. Aunt Carly simply said the bitch was crazy, 'nough said.

"So tell me, what's the real reason why can't we be together?" I was seventeen, soon to be eighteen in a matter of weeks. I felt I could handle it. I was old enough for the truth now. "Why can't you get yourself together and come home? I want my mother back!" I pleaded.

"There are things," she sighed heavily, "things I can't make you understand right now. There are secrets that I can't tell you. You will only get hurt if I say anything now and you most likely wouldn't believe me. You would think I was…crazy."

I opened my mouth to protest, but she continued. "You would have loved your brother. He was much like you. He was smart, very smart, kind, too kind, athletic, everything a mother would want in a son. I knew, Carrie, I knew I would lose him."

She looked as if she was going to cry. I had never seen my mother cry before, ever. She added, "He was determined, yes, almost as if he could fight it, as if he would beat it." She clenched her fist in her hand. "But no one in our family can escape it, not me, not Cara, Christine, not Carly, not their sons, not Caleb; I'm so sorry, but even you cannot escape it."

I was scared now. The crazy lady had returned, but I was intrigued by the conversation so I had to ask, "Escape what, Ma?"

The curiosity was killing me. Maybe I could succeed in fighting what was coming to me with the proper preparation.

She looked me in the eyes and said, "Their demons. No one can escape their demons."

As my senior year approached, I was actually happy that I would have a routine with some normalcy. But surprise, surprise, my aunts decided that I should be home schooled for my final year of high school.

Where was this idea when I was in middle school, before I got use to torture?

I was never popular in school. In fact, I was an outcast. Even the socially handicapped didn't want me to hang out with them. I was social kryptonite. However, getting off the farmland, from under my aunts' watchful eyes for eight hours a day was almost worth it. I would just suffer in some other hell hole until I was forced to come back to the farm and suffer some more.

"The Baltimore City School System is on the decline, and you should have the best education we can afford," Aunt Cara encouraged as we sat in the large, open kitchen in the main house and discussed my future educational arrangements over a continental breakfast. I ate; my aunts did not.

"Which is a lot," Aunt Carly added as she poured me a cup of apple juice.

Is this really happening? Maybe I am going to die soon. What other reasons do they have to explain this change?

Maybe they wanted to kill me and chop me up and give me to their god as a sacrifice.

I took a deep breath and closed my eyes. *Carrie, calm down; you're not crazy, so stop thinking like a crazy person. These are your aunts and they love you even if something is wrong with them.*

So maybe they just want you to join their cult, which, if it came down to your living or dying, is something you can live with.

I opened my eyes to find that my aunts both were fighting back laughter.

"May I be excused?" I asked. I was growing increasingly uncomfortable. Aunt Cara gestured with her hand that I had permission to go. As I was leaving the kitchen, I heard an outburst of laughter.

This is funny to them?

I went directly upstairs to call Mother about this new development.

When I told her, of course she wasn't surprised. Crazy understood crazy. I was nothing like them and I hoped that with a lot of prayer and work I would never be.

"Are they afraid that I will be like their sons?" I asked Mother.

"Yes. And no," Mother replied.

Their sons? Why would I be like their sons? Then again, why wouldn't I be like theirs sons? I was damned too, right?

Mother said we all had demons, including me, whatever that meant. What was our demon? Why our family? Was it something horrible someone did a long time ago, and now my family had to pay the price, over and over? A curse?

Each of my aunts had two sons. All of my cousins died before the age of twenty, and they all died before I was born. I had no idea what they looked like. I had not seen any pictures of my cousins. Where were their obituaries? Oddly enough, my aunts never talked about their sons. We never went to visit their graves. It was as if they never existed. Was that crazy, to grieve as if a person or persons never existed? Mother was right, words like *crazy* and *normal* were relative terms.

I would never bring this up to my aunts; that would be a sign of disrespect. I was raised to never question adults, especially my mother and aunts. Besides, I'm sure that I wouldn't get a straight answer because I never got a straight answer about anything I asked my aunts.

Is the sky blue?

Maybe. Insert the name of any one of my aunts as the one who answered.

There were no pictures in the house of anyone, living or otherwise, but I wondered why they wouldn't want to honor their dead sons' memories. I was not a parent and I didn't know

31

anything about being a parent, but I knew the love I felt for Mother. If something happened to her, I would want to honor her presence in some way.

Mother used to wear a bracelet with a locket on it, inside of which was a picture of Caleb. She no longer wore it because she gave it to me. When my aunts came to forcefully take her to the hospital, she gave me the locket right before they came crashing through the door.

"Keep Caleb safe," Mother said. "You two are all I have." She firmly placed her beloved piece of jewelry into my hand.

"Don't let your aunts know you have that," she added.

Just as she placed the locket into my palm, my aunts and the hospital staff came rushing in and took Mother away.

A tear ran down my face as I watched.

She went willingly, as if she knew that it was her fate. "I love you, Carrie," she called as she let go of my hand. "Never forget that."

I nodded as I watched the men dressed in scrubs escort Mother from our open front door to the back of a white van. I slid the locket into my denim shorts.

Caleb, I got you, I thought. *This is what Ma wants.*

Aunt Carly looked at me from the corner of her eye and then looked at Aunt Chris, who then glanced back at me. They both seemed uneasy. I assumed because of the weight of the situation. I didn't realize they were crazy too. Aunt Chris shook her head no, and Aunt Carly rolled her eyes.

Aunt Chris ran upstairs so fast she almost didn't appear to move. Aunt Carly just watched me and looked around aimlessly.

"Celeste's taste is questionable. This house is homely," Aunt Carly said with repulsion.

Aunt Chris came downstairs with a box that she said she found under Mother's bed, but I knew she was lying. I played under Mother's bed all the time. It was so high that I needed to use the stepstool that came with it just to sit on it.

There was nothing under her bed, not even a pair of shoes. Mother hated shoes.

"So, Celeste is too busy missing Caleb to care for you properly?" Aunt Chris asked. That was the first and only time I had heard any of my aunts mention my dead brother's name.

"What? No!" I answered. I was taken aback.

Aunt Carly was on the attack also. "She obviously didn't teach you about respect, either. Christine wasn't talking to you."

I was confused as hell. *Didn't Aunt Chris just ask me a question?*

I was about to be even more disrespectful and defend Mother when I noticed what was inside the box Aunt Chris claimed she found.

She had evidence of Caleb's existence. Inside the box were his pictures, awards, articles, papers, anything that pertained to him. I knew nothing of this box. I felt betrayed by Mother for having kept it from me, for not allowing me to experience Caleb with her, through her eyes and her heart. And I felt betrayed by my aunts, who took Mother away from me because of him.

"No, she is a great mother," I weakly argued.

"Please, let's get out of here before the bad taste follows us home," Aunt Carly said as she left out of the front door.

"I am home," I whispered.

33

"Sorry, sweetie," Aunt Chris started, "you have to come with us. Your mother simply isn't well enough to take care of you at this time. Maybe she can after she gets herself together, but not right now." She grabbed my hand. "Come," she instructed, and I did as I was told.

As we walked to the car, I looked back at my two-bedroom, one-bathroom modest row home, determined not to cry. I didn't want to show my aunts any signs of weakness. Mother hadn't spent that much time with my aunts; as a result, neither had I. I really didn't know much about them other than the fact that they were emotionally impaired women. I didn't want my aunts to think I was weak or that Mother had raised me to be weak. I had never seen my mother cry, not that day, not ever. I wanted to be strong like her and strong for her. I left with my aunts, in silence.

The family farmland was about a half-hour drive from my home in the city. Being there on the farm just felt different. The energy that surrounded that place was overwhelming. There was always this feeling that someone just died, as if the farm itself was in mourning. It was a sad place. It was a place of mystery that held a lot of secrets and history, but mostly, held a secret history. I never felt welcomed.

There were acres upon acres of beautiful scenery. It had to have been over one hundred acres that my family owned. Anyone should have felt more than comfortable on the farm, but something was just not right about it, and I was able to pick up on that even at twelve.

As we drove up to the carport, I was mesmerized by this one tree. It was the first thing I noticed, and I could not take my eyes off this horrific eyesore. It took away the true beauty of the land.

It was possibly the scariest looking tree in existence. Standing over two hundred feet, its trunk looked like the deformed body of a huge, headless, hunched-over giant monster. Even the bark looked like dried wrinkled skin. The branches extended out like veins, and the blood-colored leaves were always wet, making the tree appear as if it was bleeding.

I named it the "blood tree." It stood right in front of the main house, directly in front of the room that eventually became my bedroom.

As we walked to the main house, I asked, "Why does that tree look like it is bleeding?" I didn't know any better, and since I was now living there, I felt I had a right to know.

Aunt Carly looked back at me and smiled. "Because it is. It has a lot of blood on its hands."

Aunt Chris shot her look. Then she looked at me and kept walking, her expression unreadable. I avoided that tree at all cost.

Frankly, it scared the shit out of me.

That was the last memory I had of my house, my home, my normal mother, and my somewhat normal life. Now I lived with my aunts, but it felt nothing like home, more like a prison with the blood tree as my guard. I understood completely what Mother meant about being locked up. I was in a maximum security prison, no visitors, restricted play time, and no outside contact.

What had I done to deserve such punishment?

There had been many instances in which I tried to give the Caleb locket back to Mother, but she refused and instructed me to take care of him. Which was crazier, pretending that a dead person was alive, or pretending that a dead person never existed? The jury was still out, but I did feel a personal responsibility to care for the locket as if it was a real person. It was the least I could do for Mother.

So I carried Caleb with me wherever I went. I have not been without him since Mother gave me the locket.

Knock, knock.

"Yes?" I called. I was sitting on my bed, looking out my window, trying to avoid looking at the blood tree. That was nearly impossible.

"It's just me," Aunt Cara answered. "Are you ready to go visit your mother?"

"Yes, ma'am."

"Come. And please wear that blue sundress that Carly picked out. It will please her."

I hated dresses, but I agreed. "Sure," I replied, which made my aunt smile. "Aunt Cara, I was wondering, how often I'll get to see my mother once I start home school."

Aunt Cara deliberated. "I need to discuss that with your aunts, but I don't see why we can't keep our current agreement."

"Okay."

As I put on the blue and orange sundress Aunt Carly picked out for me to wear, I glanced at the blood tree. It demanded attention. The wind blew, and one of the branches waved at me. My heart skipped a beat. Even in the daytime that tree was still frightening. I looked at the ground around the blood tree. It was red, as if it were stained by blood.

A bleeding tree…and my aunts don't see anything wrong with that?

Nothing grew around the blood tree nor lived in it. No birds flew around it or perched on its branches, and none of the rabbits or foxes that wandered on our land would go anywhere near it.

"It's just a stupid tree," I said and refocused on getting ready to see Mother and finding suitable shoes to wear with the stupid dress. As I looked at the beautiful sunny sky, I could have sworn I saw a drop of blood fall from the leaves.

No way!

"Carrie! Come on." Aunt Cara called.

I ran downstairs to my aunt, scared halfway out of my mind.

"Oh, I see Carly got her way," Mother commented as I entered her room.

"Excuse me?" I was still spooked by the blood tree and wasn't prepared for the playful banter.

"Carly wanted you to wear that dress, and you did, so she got her way. I remember you hated wearing dresses, unless that has changed." She was sitting in her rocking chair, doing her puzzles, being herself again.

How on earth did she know that Aunt Carly dressed me today?

Maybe they talked on the phone?

I thought I heard Mother say, *Doesn't Carly dress everyone?*

Was I hearing things again? She hadn't opened her mouth, I was certain. I was staring right at her. *Maybe I imagined that.* I pondered over the statement Mother didn't make but I surely heard when I noticed something even more incredible.

"Ma, you got out of the bed!" I rejoiced.

"Yes, it's four in the afternoon," she replied. Mother looked so much better, like her old self almost. She pulled her long black hair into a ponytail and wore a blue t-shirt and sweatpants. She was never as flashy as her sisters. She was a minimalist, and I loved that about her. I guess that was why I felt the way I felt about fashion.

"So, you ready for school?" Mother asked.

"Yeah, Ma. It will be so hard to adjust with not having to get up and physically having to put on clothes. And I wonder if the kids will like me?" I joked as I sat on the edge of her bed beside her.

She laughed and I smiled at the thought of her actually getting better. "Your aunts are...something," she responded.

I was suddenly distracted by the image of the bleeding tree. I just couldn't get that image out of my mind. Mother noticed my distress. "Carrie, are you all right?"

"I don't know. Ma, what's the story with the creepy tree in front of the main house?"

"You mean your blood tree?" she asked.

My blood tree? "I hate that thing."

38

"I remember the first time you saw the blood tree; you were five and screamed like crazy for hours. You made the mistake of touching it."

What? My earliest memory of the tree was when I was twelve. "I don't remember that."

She looked as if she quickly remembered something and started humming in an obvious attempt to distract me. It didn't work.

"Ma, I don't remember that. What is it that you are not telling me?"

"Many people don't remember things about their lives till they're about six, anyway," she said offhandedly.

"Mother?"

Not true. I had one hell of a memory. Something was wrong with this story.

Why don't I remember touching that awful thing? I must have died and they brought me back to life and erased my memory of it. No way would I ever go near that tree.

"That tree is one of a kind, the only one in existence," she stated. "It has a story, and maybe you should try to find out what the story is before you condemn it."

"It's a tree. You must tell me the story of that hideous thing. I've never seen a tree the shape of a deformed monster before."

"A monster?" she asked.

I was more confused now than when I walked in. Of course, she must have seen it before to know what I am talking about.

"It bleeds, Ma." That was my strongest argument to prove that something was wrong with it.

"Most living things do, Carrie."

"I'm sorry, Ma, but plants don't bleed. And especially not a tree, for goodness' sake. Nope, can't say that in the history of the world plants ever bled."

"You haven't lived long enough to know otherwise," she answered coolly. I didn't know how to respond to that. Moments like this, when Mother displayed her most colorful views, I questioned her sanity.

I decided to change the subject, well sort of, from creepy tree to creepy aunts. "Why are my aunts taking me out of regular school?"

"You know why," she said flatly.

"I know you said that they are afraid that I will be like their sons. Is it that because I will die like them?"

She thought for a minute and replied, "No, not die."

My interest was piqued. "Ma, please tell me. Tell me about Caleb. Tell me about all of them before I go crazy. What's up with the unsolved family mystery?"

She closed her book and started rocking back and forth in the chair. "Caleb Carter was different from Carl, Corey, Chase, Chance, Cole and Caine. He lived the longest," she said with reverence. "He died when he was twenty. My nephews died in their teens. He was so strong. Caleb was much stronger than any of us ever imagined."

"Okay…what killed him, then? What killed all of them?" I needed answers, the sooner, the better. She was taking too long to tell her story.

Mother was pensive. "He died because it was his time, Carrie. He couldn't handle the stress of it all. None of our boys could. That's why they all died. Men are not as strong as women. Even Caleb, as strong as he was, was not strong enough."

My heart raced. "Will I be like them?" I asked.

"I'm not sure I know what you mean, Carrie."

"Will I die at twenty or before then?" My voice cracked. I wasn't prepared to die anytime soon, but still I needed to know if it was a possibility.

"No." She answered almost too quickly, as if she were lying.

"How do you know this?"

"Trust me, I just do. Psychic, remember?" she answered. Mother pointed to her head to illustrate her mental abilities.

"So the men in our family can't handle being men in our family?"

"Yes, it's the bloodline. Men born into our family can't handle…it and die because of …it."

"Did you love Caleb at all?" I asked.

Mother looked offended. "What type of question is that to ask?"

"Sorry, Ma." I knew that she loved him. It was pouring out of her eyes every time she spoke of him. "Did my aunts love their sons?"

That was what I really wanted to know. None of my aunts seemed to suffer from the same longing as Mother did.

She was silent. She probably debated whether or not to answer me honestly. She pressed her lips tightly together before she replied. "Yes, they loved their children."

Children? *I thought they all had boys? Why say the word children instead of sons, or boys?* "I thought they had all boys."

Her eyes grew big. She quickly gathered herself. "Yes." She stopped short of saying more.

"But you said 'their children?'"

"Just a word, Carrie, nothing more." She closed her eyes as though she was done with this conversation. She began to rock in her chair again. She appeared to be drifting asleep. She was hiding something else from me. That I was sure of.

"So, you never did answer my question. How did Caleb die?" I pressed.

"I told you." She didn't open her eyes as she turned away from me.

"No, you didn't. People don't just die without reason, Mother. There had to be reasons for all of them to die. Were they sick?" I could feel my temperature rise. I was growing increasingly more impatient with all the riddle talk.

"Sick, another of those funny words people like to use like *normal* and *sane*." She smirked. "Sick like me? Sick like physically ill? What type of sickness, Carrie?"

"Any." I tried to calm down. I almost raised my voice to my mother. I already disrespected her once today. I knew better; however, my blood was boiling at this point.

"They were both," she responded.

"Both what?"

"Sick like me and physically sick."

"What about me?"

42

She turned back to me. Her face had little life left in it. Her natural glow had dimmed. She was pale again. She looked at the door to her room. It was open, but no one was there. "Carly is here. It is time for you to go," she said stoically. She was no longer my colorful, treatable mother; she was back to being crazy once again.

I asked, "Ma, what about me?"

She turned back to face me again. "Yes, you will be sick like me, too." She sounded defeated.

"Why?" I was on the brink of having a breakdown. "Just tell me!"

"I told you." She turned to face the door once more.

"What? Told me what, exactly?"

"It's because of your demon. We all have them, and some of us die because of them, but you, me, and some others, we are the unfortunate ones who live long lives because of them. I'm so sorry for passing this on to you, Carrie.

"Really, it's my own fault. I was being selfish. I wanted to be a mother, and I knew." She paused. She appeared to be in physical pain. "I knew that if I had a son I was sentencing him to death and if I had a daughter, I was giving her a life of grief, but I did it anyway. And there is nothing that can be done about it."

I got up off the bed to get closer to her. Her eyes were growing darker right before me. "Ma, what is going on with your eyes?" I whispered, afraid that the hospital staff would hear me. I didn't want them to hear me ask Mother a crazy question.

When I got close enough to touch her, I hesitated because I was scared. She was on some poltergeist-type trip.

43

"Ma?"

Where was the button that summoned the nurse? Or maybe I needed a priest to call. *Do they have holy water here? Can a priest cure crazy?*

"Carrie, this is the last time you are to see me in this place." Her eyes were now black, and she was scaring the shit out of me.

"What?" I breathed. I didn't know what to do.

"I have passed my demons on to you and your brother, and I am sorry," she continued.

"Ma, tell me what to do! Let me help you!" I wept.

She ignored my request and continued talking as if I hadn't said anything at all. "Caleb is dead and you would be better off if you were as well."

I paused. I was completely shocked by her words. "You wish I was dead?" I started to feel faint. I was under the impression that Mother loved me. She'd never talked like that before. I stumbled back, gripping the bed for balance.

"It's one thing for me to carry this burden, but to pass it on to my children... Blasphemy!" Her voice was still very stoic.

"Talk to me, please!" I pleaded. "What is going on? Are we cursed?" That would explain her scary black pupils and the odd behavior our family exhibited.

Mother took a deep breath. Her reaction was unexplainable. She expressed excitement in her dead black eyes.

What had turned her on?

I looked around for something that might have triggered that reaction. Maybe she smelled something sweet or pleasing. I followed her lead and took a deep breath. I didn't smell anything that I believed that would make her react that way. I smelled the same stale air that was always filled with death and despair.

I was torn over what to do. I wanted to help her, but I was also afraid.

"No, this is far worse than a curse. A curse is easy. Curses can be lifted. Damned...yes, that is what we are. We are DAMNED! I have done some awful things in my lifetime, but having children...that was by far the worst thing I could have ever done. Making my children pay for my transgressions."

"I'm a terrible mother!" she screamed. Her eyes were still black as night. The machines Mother was hooked up to started beeping uncontrollably. She started to shake.

The hospital staff came in and pulled me to the side so they could sedate her.

Do not come back Carrie. I will not be here. My time here is over.

I heard Mother's voice in my head just as I had before. Only this time, I was sure it was my mother and not just me being crazy or paranoid.

"No, wait!" I called above the commotion of hurried people in white coats, who were moving the furniture so they could get to her in order to calm her down. She sat still as they pumped her full of medicine. Beeping noises were still coming from the machines. More people charged in. I balled up in the corner of the room, too scared to do anything else. She shook her head, and her eyes changed back to green.

I couldn't believe what was happening. I was terrified. I wished I had the courage to do something, *anything*. I prayed for the first time in my life. *Lord, please help her.*

It's okay, Carrie; you'll be fine. I know it. I will always be with you. Mother said in my head.

What? I shook my head as if I was trying to shake away her dismissal. I studied her as the staff continued attempting to tranquilize her down.

So Mother really can communicate with me without speaking. Is that even possible?

Yes! She answered. *I have been doing it for a while now. It's almost your time. Soon you will have extraordinary powers.*

Just as Mother predicted, Aunt Carly appeared in the doorway.

"Carly, take her away and don't ever bring her back. She'll just be disappointed," Mother addressed Aunt Carly above the commotion.

I turned to my aunt. "Fine," Aunt Carly said with about the same amount of emotion you would expect to get from a blank sheet of paper. The fact that my aunt seemed to expect the chaos in Mother's room was odd. She didn't even look remotely startled. Aunt Carly carried on as if it was a regular visit and nothing eventful was happening.

"NO! I won't let you do this, Mother!" I protested. I was still in the corner. I was too afraid to come anywhere near Mother.

Mother sighed as if she was about to take her last breath. "You have no choice," she said. She closed her eyes. I suddenly felt a slight push by an invisible force. "It is already done." Her voice trailed off.

I looked around. No one was beside or near me. And there it was again. I was being moved toward the door. Was no one else

46

aware of what was going on with me? Did no one else see that? I was moving, but not of my own accord. I slid closer to the door. I planted my feet, but that did nothing. There it was again. I didn't dare speak this aloud because I was in a crazy house, and I would get the bed next to Mother.

Staff members still surrounded Mother and continued their attempt to stabilize her. The beeping noises from the machines started to slow down and became less frantic. She looked up at me, and her pupils were white, void of any color, not green, not even the spooky black, but all white.

"Ma!" I called as I tried to walk back to her bed. I was still being forced toward the door by the invisible presence.

Aunt Carly pushed me out of the hospital room in full stride. She didn't appear to be exerting any force; however, she pushed me so hard I hit the cement wall adjacent to Mother's room. She grabbed the upper part of my arm as one would a toddler's and escorted me out of the hospital.

Once we were in Aunt Carly's Range Rover, I addressed her extreme and unnecessary force. "You must have wanted to do that for a long time," I snapped as I caressed my arm. I had red bruises from the impact from hitting the wall.

"Oh, I can't stand that place, the colors and the smells. It's a disaster," Aunt Carly said in disdain.

"No, I was talking about swinging me around like a rag doll," I answered.

My aunt looked at me out of the corner of her eye as she drove us home. She was surprised by my response.

"Carrie," she said.

47

"Yes?"

"You must really be pissed, huh?" She was trying not to smile, which irritated me even more.

I knew needed to apologize to my aunt for my rudeness. "Sorry, Aunt Carly, it's just that, well, I didn't know you were a former body builder. You don't look that strong." Aunt Carly looked like a regular woman, not Arnold Schwarzenegger. She looked like the rest of my aunts and Mother. The Carter women were slender with all their curves in the right places; none of them weighed more than one hundred forty pounds. They all had hourglass figures, the body type that every woman including me desired.

"No, it's quite all right; I was never a body builder, just stronger than I look, that's all. When you live on a farm with three women and no men, you have to take care of things yourself," she mused. "Nice dress by the way."

"Sure." I snapped. I wasn't in the mood for fashion talk.

"Carrie, you are quite nasty today. Maybe you are spending way too much time with your old Aunt Carly," she joked.

I shot her a look that could kill. "Maybe." I definitely wasn't in the mood for my aunt being my aunt.

She repeated, "Maybe." We were almost at the family farm. I wanted to be alone. "Your behavior... is this about your mother?" my aunt asked.

I stared at her blankly. My aunt was about as observant as a brick. Yes! It was about Mother. Surely Aunt Carly heard Mother say to her that she didn't want to see me again.

"Well, maybe I should tell Noah not to ask but so many questions today; your patience is rather used up. No, I'll tell him you want to be alone. You do, don't you?" She was out of her truck just as fast as I was. *Did she put the car in park? How did I miss that?*

"Noah is here?" I asked her.

"Yes, awaiting your return, but if you want, I will tell him that you aren't up for company…"

"No." I answered quickly. "It's quite all right. I'll talk to him myself." I couldn't breathe. The hill was steep, my hormones were in overdrive, and to top it off I was sweating, too.

"I'm sure you will." She walked up the hill to the main house with such ease that she appeared to glide. My aunts were so graceful; dancers would be lucky to have an ounce of their grace. I, on the other hand, though having a head start, struggled to walk up the steep hills and through the deep valleys of the land. My aunt beat me to the house with not so much as a speck of dirt on her. I was still playing catch-up when I almost tripped over something.

A root from the blood tree? A rock? Maybe I was too focused on Noah, who was sitting on the stairs to the main house, and I just tripped over my own damn feet and stumbled right into the blood tree. One of the branches grabbed my arm as I reached for the tree's trunk for balance. I touched its skin-like bark. Instantly I felt electricity pulsing through my body. As the blood tree held my arm, I heard screaming and growling coming from it. I felt pain and hurt, misery and despair. I tried to let go, but the tree's grip grew stronger, and drew me in closer. The branch pushed me into the strained earth. I moaned in pain.

49

"It has a story, and maybe you should try to find out what the story is before you condemn it." Mother's words from earlier echoed in my head.

The energy from the tree continued to flow through my body as I tried to free myself from its grip. Images poured into my mind. Boys, men of all ages who all looked alike. I innately knew them somehow. They all possessed jet black hair, green eyes, and honey-colored skin. They screamed in pain as I watched them die. I cried out as well. I felt what they felt. Something was eating them alive, snatching their souls from their bodies. There were so many of them.

Oh my GOD! Caleb?

Caleb was in pain, screaming and growling. He was lying in bed with Mother at his side and my aunts watching over him. I reached out for him.

Caleb!

My vision abruptly stopped when Noah touched me. The tree released me.

"Care Bear, are you all right?" he asked as he led me to the main house.

That was a trick question. I wasn't sure. Doctors probably wouldn't find anything physically wrong with me, but that didn't mean that nothing was wrong with me because something was definitely wrong with me.

Do I tell him? Do I tell him I saw the men in my family wither away in pain as I touched the blood tree? Do I tell him my mother communicated with me with her mind? Or that I think she might have pushed me without touching me?

As I was thinking of something to say, Noah interrupted my thoughts, "Carrie, you're bleeding. Look at your hand."

My hand that touched the tree was covered in blood but I knew it wasn't mine. He rushed me over to the side of the porch where we kept the hose to water the lawn. Ironically, there wasn't much to water because nothing grew even remotely close to the blood tree. He turned the cold water on and rinsed off my hand. I was still focused on the images that had been engraved in my mind.

So many deaths.

So much pain.

"Carrie?" Noah sounded confused. "You don't have a cut or a scratch on you. I don't understand." My hand was strained red. He examined my hand more carefully, trying to make sense of the blood on my hand.

"It has a lot of blood on its hands." I spoke the very words Aunt Carly said to me when I first moved here. I looked at Noah for the first time since touching the tree. Noah cut the water off and looked at me as though I had just spoken a foreign language to him.

"Carrie, trees don't bleed. There has to be a good explanation for this."

I found myself quoting Mother this time, "Most living things do."

"It's a tree, Carrie. Trees don't bleed," he stressed.

"Maybe we haven't lived long enough to know otherwise." I answered coolly.

One Crazy Dream

Noah didn't stay long. Mainly because I totally freaked him out. I was scared shitless as well, if that was any consolation. I could tell he was really frightened by the way he looked at me before he left. I hoped he was frightened enough to stay away from me. Maybe that was for the best.

Did I imagine the whole thing?

As Noah was leaving, he started walking toward the blood tree, but decided against it and continued his gait in the direction of his car.

Part of me was relieved because I didn't want him to experience the same thing I just had. Another part me was anxious because I wanted him to touch the blood tree to see if he was going to have the same experience.

After I watched Noah safely get into his car and leave the farm, I concentrated on blocking the last twenty minutes out of my mind. I just wished Aunt Carly was aware of my plans.

She stood at the door as I entered the main house. She probably had seen the whole exchange between Noah, me, and the blood tree.

"Noah didn't stay long," she commented. She wore an emerald green off-the-shoulder dress that had all these tattered layers made into the design. Her dress had a long train that I tried to avoid at all cost. She was determined not to move, and I was determined not to trip over her dress. I bumped into her as I tried to pass her.

"No, he didn't. Whoops…sorry Aunt---'

I felt the same electricity that went through me when I fell into the blood tree. As the energy flowed through me, I had more visions. Only this time, I saw Mother and Aunt Carly arguing. I couldn't quite make out what they were saying, but it was a heated exchange. Aunt Carly was crying, something I didn't think she was capable of. I also noticed that they were dressed differently, like from time period other than the present.

Aunt Carly caught me before I hit the floor and led me to the kitchen table. Another wave of electricity circulated between us. I saw Aunt Carly holding a baby girl and kissing a man. Then I saw her standing over one of her dead sons on his death bed. I saw her look at my mother with abhorrence as she passed her and Aunt Cara. "I'll do it myself," Aunt Carly said as she was fighting back tears. Afterward, I saw her digging in front of the main house beside a little tree shrub that had one lonely apple hanging from it.

53

"Carrie, Carrie? First day with your new feet?" Aunt Carly was annoyed. She rolled her green eyes at me. I was mesmerized by her even though she was irritated with me.

I tried to focus. "Aunt Carly..."

Again, what was I supposed to say? *That I had a vision? That I saw her sons die? Tell her that I saw her and Mother arguing, in another century? That I saw her holding a baby girl? Do I tell her I saw all of this when I touched the blood tree and when I fell into her?*

I rubbed my arm. "No, I'm sorry. I was distracted."

She rolled her eyes again. The movement filtered into her hair. Her hair was wild and curly, but every curl was perfectly placed. She walked out the kitchen without another word. I just sat at the kitchen table, too scared to move.

What is happening to me?

I went to bed early that night with a lot on my mind, and ninety-nine-point-nine percent of it I couldn't explain. Every time I closed my eyes I kept seeing the images that the blood tree bored into my brain. I was able to witness the deaths of my dead cousins somehow. And Caleb's...

I saw how my brother died.

Mother's words came back to me..."*That tree is one of a kind, the only one in existence. It has a story, and maybe you should try to figure out what that story is before you condemn it.*"

I wondered whether I should talk to the blood tree.

The idea of talking to the blood tree was actually making sense to me. That further proved I was losing my mind.

I laid in my bed, thinking. I wanted to clear my mind and pass out because I didn't want to think anymore. I heard a voice

54

coming from outside, or so I thought. I got up and looked out the window and saw nothing but the blood tree. The wind blew and one of the branches waved at me….again.

I jumped back from the window. I reminded myself, "I'm not crazy; I'm not crazy; I'm not crazy," over and over again.

I was sure I heard a woman's voice again coming from outside. "I'm not crazy! I'm not crazy! There is no one outside."

I was panicking. My heart was racing. I closed my eyes. "I'm asleep; this is not really happening." This was all a bad dream, a very weird, scary dream. I opened my eyes and heard the woman's voice again.

"Carrie," the woman's voice whispered, "I've come for you."

I crawled to the foot of the bed and peeped out my window once more. This time there was a woman outside standing next to the blood tree.

Oh, my GOD! I'm not crazy! I'm not crazy! I'm dreaming! I'm dreaming!

The air that night was heavy and stiff. I felt my throat closing up. I grabbed it. I was sweating profusely. My hair was damp from my panicked state. "Please, God, I know I'm not very religious, but please, please help me." A dark figure flew in my window. I balled up on my bed. *This is the end,* I thought. The figure morphed into Mother.

HOLY SHIT!

I was paralyzed with fear. "Ma?"

I am not crazy; I am not crazy; I am not crazy...

She faced me. Mother was stunning. She was fluid like water. She wore a black flowing gown that, when the breeze hit it, became a part of the darkness. Her dress matched her black long flowing hair that hugged the curve of her back. She wore no shoes; her feet looked amazing. She looked like an angel. Her eyes were bright green, and her complexion was sun-kissed again. I couldn't make out her all the features, just her piercing green eyes.

I was still anxious.

This was obviously a dream, right?

I'm not crazy!

I'm not crazy…

"Ma?" I called again. Excitement and fear mixed in my tone.

"No need to fear, Carrie," she responded. "It is me."

"Ma?" I crawled closer to her to make out her face better, but it was still a challenge due to the darkness. "What is happening to me? Tell me, please." I pleaded. My sanity was in question. I needed to know if there was any hope for me. I concluded my aunts weren't going to be any help based on how they have treated Mother. I would be joining her in the mental hospital if my aunts knew what I was going through.

Mother placed her bare feet on the hardwood floors for the first time since she entered my room. She tip-toed and sat in my wooden chair in front of my window. Her face was flawless. Her teeth glowed in the darkness. The inside of her mouth looked endless as a bottomless pit.

"There are things that I will try to explain the best I can. Though you will not believe these things at first, you will accept them soon enough."

I nodded my head in agreement. "Tell me what is happening," I choked out. "I need to know the truth."

She began. "Before Christians gave it a name, before mankind's existence, even before time itself, there was always a balance of good and evil. In the shadows of the void of space, good and evil existed even before there was a universe. No one can fully explain their origins.

"They are the oldest known entities. You can't have one without the other. The balance must be maintained at all times."

I studied Mother's face as well as her words. I was clueless about her facial expression as well as the history lesson, but I listened intently.

She continued. "There are things in life that you can't explain. No, correction, you can explain them, but most humans would rather not. Just like the world needs Martin Luther King, JFK, and Gandhi, the world also needs Ted Bundy, Charles Manson, and John Muhammad."

I interjected, "What? Why are you saying this? The world doesn't need evil people. And what does this have to do with me, you, my dead brother, my dead cousins, and your weird sisters? What does this have to do with me hearing voices and seeing things? I'm going crazy, and you want to talk about evil men?"

She closed her eyes. "The balance must be maintained at all times, baby." She opened her eyes, they were black.

Even in my dreams, her eyes totally freaked me out and I was still praying this was a dream.

She continued, "I know things about you, Carrie, and not just because I am your mother. I know them because of what I am, what you will be. I know things that I could use against you, things I could use to influence you."

She rose up from the chair and she began to float.

"I know you love Noah and would die and kill for him." She closed her eyes and sniffed the room. "You wish I was more like Cara."

She flew over to the window and licked the sill. "You wrote in a diary of yours when you were fifteen that you were jealous of Caleb and thought I loved him more than I love you, even till this day."

It was all true, every word she spoke. I would kill for Noah, I did want Mother to be more like my aunt, and I did feel that Mother loved her dead son more than she loved me, her living daughter. But how did she know this? I didn't share any of that with anyone, not even Noah.

Why did she lick my window? She must be batshit crazy. And so was I. There was no other explanation.

"How? Influence me how?" I asked.

"To do bad, hurtful, evil things, Carrie."

"Exactly how? How can you make me do bad things?" I was not a weak-minded person, not even with my desire to be accepted in society.

She closed her eyes and eased back in the chair. When she opened her eyes again, they were back to green, "A long time ago, there was an angel named Lucifer. He was the most beautiful angel and the most beloved angel of them all. It was obvious that he was God's favorite. The entities began whispering in his head and poisoning his mind.

"The dark spirits not only told him that he was great, but they told him he was even greater than God. They told him he could do and be all that God was. He didn't believe them at first, but they kept planting the seeds of ambition, greed, and envy. The seeds were buried so deep and rooted so profoundly in his mind that the entities knew they now had a home in his thoughts. They spoke louder in his ear, 'Better and greater than He who created you.'

"They whispered this to him more and more. And when he finally spoke the words he had been hearing in his mind, aloud, God banished him from the heavens. When he hit the Earth, the ground trembled and the skies cried. But he was not alone. There were others who followed him—angels who had believed what Lucifer was saying, that he was greater than God and that they could be, too.

"They wanted no more to live a life of servitude and righteousness. They wanted to follow their own will. So they did. Disguised as men, these fallen angels, now demons, killed, lied, fornicated, and more.

"They lay with beautiful women, and some of these women bore children. The women noticed quickly that their children were different, more than human. They were aggressive and strong, combative and smart, beautiful and evil."

I whispered, "Evil?"

She looked me in my eyes and affirmed, "Yes, evil. The children, if they lived long enough, underwent change when they came of age, no longer innocent, no longer children. They could hear humans' thoughts. They could smell sin and, even worse, were attracted to it. Humans were attracted to them, too— mentally, spiritually, emotionally, but especially physically. Their offspring were beautiful with long hair and beautiful green eyes.

This physical change happens when the demon takes over." She pointed out her features.

"Our demon isn't compatible with men. Men are carriers of the gene, but they don't survive the change. When we started to see the change happen in men, we watched them die because of it."

"What about Caleb?" I asked.

"Caleb knew what was happening to him because I told him. He thought he was stronger than his demon, but no man is."

Tears flowed down my face in a long, endless stream. "So that's the mystery? I have a demon; I am one? And that's why I'm going crazy? And the demon killed all the males in our family?"

"You are the descendent of angels and humans. You are half human and half demon. You are about to change soon."

"Something is happening to me. I heard you in my head. I touched the blood tree, and I started to have these horrible visions."

"Your blood tree? You talked to it? It has many stories to tell," she said.

I looked out the window. "It's a tree. Trees don't talk."

"And they don't bleed, either. But that one does."

"Are we possessed?" I was going to google a priest in the morning. I was getting rid of my demon. Wasn't there a ritual that could be performed to rid oneself of one? Wasn't that the premise of the movie, *The Exorcist*?

"No, that's Ezekiel; only he can possess you."

"Who?" *Who in the hell was Ezekiel?*

She explained, "If you were possessed, then you could have an exorcism and rid yourself of your monster. No, my dear, this is who you are. The demon is in our genetic makeup. We cannot change that fact nor get rid of it."

"Why is this happening? Do you know what you are saying? I'm not evil. I DON'T WANT THIS!" I shouted. "I don't accept. I WON'T!"

She sighed, "You have no choice. I tried to deny my demon and look where it got me, committed to a mental institution. My sisters banished me, told everyone I was crazy because I wanted something else. They made me leave you with them because I desired a different life for me and my offspring. They wanted and still do want something else, something that I cannot allow."

I figured my aunts were evil. I knew that much. They were just too perfect. My aunts were gorgeous, fashionable, financially stable women and no man desired them? I knew something was up but I didn't know it was because they danced with the devil. I was not them. I was not perfect. I was human and I knew that humans had a choice. I was going to choose.

"I can't be evil." I did do some things that weren't so nice, but that didn't make me evil. Or did it? No matter. I was declaring myself, right there, in front of my demonic mother.

I was choosing the other team, the better team, the team that always won.

"Define a good person, Carrie," Mother demanded.

"What do you mean, define a good person?" I thought for a moment. What made a person good? Good deeds? Good deeds defined a good person. I answered, "Mr. Kip, he volunteers his free time to help feed needy kids and helps them to find shelter." He was a good person. I felt good about the choice of Mr. Kip. He lived on the closest piece of farmland to ours. He was a quiet, reserved man who even helped me from time to time. When I locked myself out of the main house, he let me crash at his house until Aunt Chris got home. He had taken in homeless children and provided them a place to stay. He was the definition of a good person.

Mother laughed a dry laugh, "Mr. Kip has molested and raped every one of those 'strays' he took in. And don't let me get started on what he does with them after he is done."

"Oh, my God! Mother, how do you know this?"

"I know him. I hear his thoughts. I put some of those evil thoughts there."

I was sickened by both my mother and Mr. Kip. I had been in that man's house numerous times by myself. I thought I knew him. I would have never guessed he was a deranged individual. Maybe I never truly knew him as a person. And Mother, what did her actions say about her?

"I'm not all that you think I am, Carrie. You don't know the whole story. I'm both good and bad. And unfortunately most times the bad side wins. I'm only half-." She stopped short of her explanation. "Name another good person," she ordered.

My mother was evil. The woman I knew was only one part of Celeste Carter. Would I be like that in time? Would I be evil?

"No one else, Carrie? Any more good people?"

"Pastor McDaniels?"

"Is this the best you can do? These are people you name as good souls?"

My family didn't go to church. I just assumed Pastor McDaniels, the pastor of the church closest to the main house, was a decent person. He was a pastor. He represented goodness and righteousness, right? He was a man of God.

"Carrie, Pastor McDaniels is stealing from his church, sleeping with everything that has a pulse. You got any more good souls?" she challenged.

I was lost. What defined a good person? Mother found a flaw with everyone I named. Good people did bad things, I concluded. But I wondered did the bad outweigh all the good one had done?

"Just because no one knows of your transgressions doesn't make you any less accountable for them. It's not as black and white as you think, Carrie."

"Yes, it is. And what is your part in all of this, Mother?" I asked acidly. "You are bad person. All these years I thought you were crazy. So you're not crazy, you're just evil, and your sisters are evil as well." I accused.

I wanted nothing to do with Mother or my aunts if it meant we were all on a one way trip to hell.

Better to sever all ties now.

"Yes, I am a bad person. I can admit that. Many of the people you named, I have influenced. I have caused great pain to mankind and only now I am remorseful." I narrowed my eyes at her she continued, "Cara, Carly, and Christine are just doing what they were told. They don't know how to be any other way. We are all evil, and you will be, too. As you age, the more you will

63

embrace your demon, the less human you will feel, and the more havoc you will want to create. It's in your nature, our nature."

"I would rather be crazy than evil, Mother," I said, remembering all of my pain over Mother's fake illness. All that time lost and wasted. She abandoned me, and for what?

"I wish it were that simple," she commented.

"I. Don't. Want. This."

Mother voice softened, a little. "You have to have evil in order to have good. You need both, or how else will you know the difference? I'm sorry, Carrie. Truly." She got up from the chair and started to float. Her pupils were black. "I've tried to atone for the things I have done, and I hope I helped you. I've tried, Carrie."

She paused. "There is something else. There is a life that can be had without all this, and I intend on finding it. I believed I had it once, and I will have it again."

I was confused by her words. She looked out of the window; in the distance a dark figure came into view across the County's clear sky. Whatever it was, it was coming fast.

"Ma?" I knew something bad was going to happen as the ominous figure came into view and blackened the whole sky. There were no stars, no moon, just darkness. "Ma, when did Caleb die?" It was something I always wondered about.

"When he turned twenty," she said.

"The blood tree showed me Caleb, all of them, and they were all dressed differently from different times. Oh my God, how old are you?" I never thought to ask before but in my vision, Mother, and my aunts were all dressed from different time periods too.

"Old. Timeless," she answered.

She looked out of the window again; the black form was still coming. The figure split into three separate entities. The figures were hard to see without the help of the moonlight. The shadowy shapes entered my room and faded into the walls like moving artwork. Mother positioned herself in front of the open window, and the three shadows came from off the walls and grabbed her. They all leaped out the window and flew across the sky. Then, in an instant, they were all one body as they blanketed the sky. I could hear Mother as if she was still in the room with me. "Keep Caleb safe. I love you, Carrie. I did this to help you. I will come back. I will stop this. I will save you."

"From whom? No, don't do this, Mother, please, not twice in one day. Don't go! Save me from whom, Mother? From whom?" I cried.

"Me." Her voice faded.

"Please, come back, Mother!" I begged. "Please! Tell me more. Tell me how old you are. Tell me about Caleb, my dad, tell me everything." My pleas went unheard. The room grew darker and eerily silent. I sat on my bed and cried. I looked out my window to see if I saw my mother or the black figure that took her. Nothing was out there, nothing except the blood tree. Red drops started to trickle to the ground as if the blood tree were crying with me.

Knowledge Is Power

When I woke up the next morning, everything was picture perfect. It was weird. Even the blood tree wasn't as menacing. The sun shone brighter than it had since the beginning of summer vacation. The birds were chirping at my window, and there was even a rainbow in the sky.

However, my dream was still haunting me. The image of Mother, the story she told me about demons, the aberrations that came to steal her away...

I had to figure out some things on my own. I jumped out of the bed and examined my room. No mysterious figures flying around, no evidence of Mother's visit. It was just my plain purple, pink, and turquoise room. My room hadn't changed much since I was twelve, with the exception of my toy chest being replaced by a bookcase and desk. My room was very plain, just like me.

I called Noah. It was a week before Labor Day, so I knew he would be available unless he was with Melissa.

"Hey, Care Bear."

"Noah, I need you to meet me at the library downtown."

"Okay, is everything all right?"

"No, but I need to look for some answers before I lose my mind completely." I hoped it wasn't too late.

"Sure. Sure. Do you want me to come get you?"

YES! "No, I can walk to the main road and catch the bus. I don't want my aunts to try and stop me."

"Okay." He paused. "You know what? I want to look up lunar eclipses. The one last night was amazing."

"There was a lunar eclipse last night?"

"Damn, Care Bear, yeah! Everyone saw it. How could you miss it? The whole sky was black; I couldn't see ten feet in front of me. It was totally awesome!"

Noah continued to talk, but all I could think about was my dream and how the aberrations blanketed the sky as they took Mother away. The sky was an endless sea of darkness.

"Carrie? *Carrie?* Hello, earth to Care Bear."

"Yeah, I'm here. Just meet me at the library."

"Okay, Care Bear, in one hour. "

I quickly washed up and got dressed, opting for a white t-shirt and denim capris. I pulled my impossible thin and stringy black hair into a ponytail. I didn't feel pretty, but this wasn't the day for that.

67

"Going somewhere?" I was almost out of the house unnoticed when Aunt Carly caught me at the door. She looked breathtakingly beautiful, but that was always the case. She wore a long white dress. If I didn't know any better, I would have thought she was getting married today. Her hair was twisted into a loose bun. If the wind blew hard enough, it would unleash her beautiful curly black hair. Her green eyes were the prettiest shade of green to exist. Her bare feet were the most beautiful feet I had ever seen in my life.

"Yeah, I'm going to help Noah with his school work. You know he just didn't get a *Tale of Two Cities*. I tried to tell him, 'Noah it's the same city.'" I was babbling. I sounded about as convincing as Pinocchio. Surely my nose had grown two feet.

You're lying. But why are you lying to me? My aunt's voice cooed in my head. She looked at me as if she could see right through me. I also noticed her lips didn't move.

Why are you lying to me, Carrie? What are you hiding from me? Tell me, she whispered seductively in my mind.

She was in my head. Was she in my head? Was I just paranoid? Or crazy? It was as if she was physically walking inside my brain. Her voice echoed through the halls of my mind.

I felt her trying to open up the doors to my secrets. At every turn I was one step behind her, closing a door she just opened. I shook my head, trying to physically block out that thought. *I'm not crazy; I'm not crazy…*

She looked curiously at me. "Noah and the library? All right, I will tell your aunts, and please—"

"I have it. Thanks, Aunt Carly. I promise not to be long."

68

Have what? "Have—" I already knew what she was going to ask me.

"My cell phone. You were going to tell me to make sure I have my cell, right?"

She looked disturbed. "Of course. When you come back, which will be in three hours, please take off that dreadful outfit. People will think we are poor." Whatever it was that had her spooked, she was over it now if she was critiquing my attire. "Did you see the eclipse last night?" she added.

"Excuse me?" I couldn't hide the troubled look on my face. I hadn't mastered the poker face as my aunts had.

"The eclipse. There was one last night. The sky was so clear. No way you missed it," she purred.

My dream, the shadows covering the sky, I tried to focus on the conversation but my mind started to wonder. I saw the vision of Aunt Carly and the baby girl. Then I saw her arguing with Mother. *I'm not crazy!* I closed my eyes trying to think. "I was asleep," I finally answered.

She smiled. "I hope you had sweet dreams, then." She turned away from me.

She knew something. Maybe she knew I was going crazy. I didn't want to risk her finding out. I bolted out of the door.

"So what's up, Care Bear?" Noah asked me. He looked like a prince from a fairytale. He looked so dreamy in his V-neck white t-shirt and his khaki shorts; his hair was disheveled, but it suited him.

I loved his bedroom hair. His deep blue eyes were glowing. His lips were pink and full. When the air conditioner blew, I could smell his cologne. I was in love with my best friend. I could admit that.

Carrie Greene... that has an awesome ring to it. I smiled at the thought.

He stood in the massive lobby of the library when he greeted me. "I'm going crazy, Noah!"

"Okay." He looked concerned.

"I could tell you all the details, but you will really think I was crazy. I swear I'm not, but something is wrong with me."

"Okay." He looked even more concerned.

"Please stop saying 'okay' like that. Just trust me." I needed his support and friendship now more than ever.

"Okay, Carrie, but you have to tell me something."

"I have to do some digging. My mother told me the names of my cousins--"

"You have cousins?" He was shocked.

"Had. I had cousins. All males and all are dead."

"SHIT! That blows. Remind me to never marry you. I don't want to be next."

My face fell. All the air had been sucked out of the library. Why did I care, anyway? We were just friends. He was just teasing me, right? Why couldn't I take a joke?

"Care Bear, I was joking. Can't take a joke anymore?"

"Yeah, Noah, there is a lot that I'm not comfortable with..."

"Say no more. I won't bring it up again. Now, tell me about your cousins."

I love you. I smiled. "I want to see if their deaths made the papers. If there were enough of them, I don't see how they couldn't. Something bad happened to them. I know it. I need to figure out what the family mystery is." I conveniently left out me touching the blood tree and seeing their deaths. And I certainly wasn't going to tell him Mother told me I was evil. *No,* I thought, *he doesn't need to know everything.*

"What about asking your aunts?" he asked.

"They won't give me a straight answer. They never do."

"Oh, yeah, Care Bear, don't take this the wrong way, but your aunts are kind of weird."

Evil was the correct word. "You're telling me. I live with them."

He smiled at my joke. I could tell he was unsure how to act given my earlier reaction to his joke. "Beautiful, but weird. How about asking your mother?"

Do I tell him the real reason why we were at the library? We were close, but if the shoe was on the other foot and he said he had a dream about his mother saying he was a demon and he heard voices in his head, I would have security escort me safely to the bus stop.

I simply said, "She's crazy, remember? Let's just start looking. I want some real answers and not the BS ones my mother and my aunts give me."

"Cool. What year?"

"I don't know." *DAMN!*

"Well, it had to be before you were born, so at least eighteen years ago, right?"

71

"Okay." That was a good start.

I started toward the periodicals.

"Oh, no! We'll be here for days if we do it that way. Let's look on the internet first," he recommended.

"You are so smart." *And I love you even more.*

"Yes, this is true. C'mon." He pulled me toward the computers lined up against the wall designated for quick searches. "Okay," he said as we stood at the computer station, "what were their names?"

I had to think to remember, "Try Carl Carter, Cole Carter, Caine Carter…"

"Your family sure does have a thing for the C alliteration."

"Yeah." I giggled. "I guess you are right." He knew what alliteration was. He was perfect for me.

He typed *Carl Carter* into the computer and clicked on the search button. "We got over five thousand hits on Facebook alone," he commented.

"Considering that Carl is dead, I don't think he has a Facebook page."

"Maybe we if we try something more local," he suggested.

"Like?" I asked.

"Let's try the paper or a news channel, something that would note that Carl was from Baltimore."

"Yes," I chimed in, "and that he is dead."

"Ok, let's google it."

So Noah typed in: *Looking for an article or obituary about Carl Carter from Baltimore, mysterious death.*

Over 200 search results returned. We skimmed through most of them; they were either too recent, or the Carl Carter was married with children when he died. We eliminated those because my cousin died in his teens. We were down to our last three possible Carl Carters.

"I don't know about this one," Noah started. "This article was written in the *Baltimore Gazette*. I never even heard of that paper."

"Me either, but click it anyway," I urged.

"But the name is hyphenated, it says Carl Carter-Coolidge."

"Would you just click it?" I ordered. *Nothing beats a failure but a try.*

The *Baltimore Gazette* article read:

> Carl Coolidge, sixteen, died of a mysterious illness. It is believed that it is the same illness that took the life of his brother, Chase Coolidge, earlier this year, and his cousin Corey Carter two years prior. This mystery illness has the medical community baffled.
>
> "We're thinking that it might be genetically linked because this disease has plagued only this particular bloodline, and no one else has contracted the disease," stated Dr. Stanley McCoy of Mercy Medical, who treated two other

victims. "We are, however taking the necessary precautions so that no one else catches the deadly disease."

Symptoms of the mystery illness include a very high fever, aches and pains, a heavy *cough, and paralysis. The young men who died from this disease had been placed on bed rest a week prior; and within a week or so, their condition worsened, and they died shortly afterward. Carl Carter was on bed rest for two weeks before he succumbed to the sickness.*

There are those who believe that this disease has taken on a more sinister meaning, "They're evil," Minister Harry Cross said in a statement. "Plain and simple. I've tried to pray over them, heal them; I even tried an exorcism, but nothing would stop the fiend from growing inside of them." Minister Harry Cross has been the pastor of the Church of Jesus Christ for twenty years, but has been living in the Howard Town community all his life. "There is a reason why this illness has targeted only one family," he answered. *Though others do not agree with Minister Cross entirely, many have asked the Carter-Coolidge family, Clara, Carla, Cecil, and Christina along with Cecil's son, Caleb, to leave Howard Town.*

"I'll feel better once they are gone," one resident commented. The resident did not want to be identified.

The Carters were not available for comment when this article was printed.

The tension was so thick I could hardly breathe. I felt as if I was in a horror film and I just found out that I was related to the killer trying to kill me.

"This can't be right. I think this is just some made-up news article. You know, like a gag, a tasteless joke," Noah said. "Look at when the article was written, 1930. This can't be your family, Carrie."

I couldn't speak because deep in my heart I knew it was my family. Sure, the names were off just a little and the article was written in 1930; however, it was indeed about my family.

In my mind I'm going *Clara=Cara, Christina=Christine, Carla=Carly*, and *Cecil=Celeste*. A child could have made that connection. And as if I needed any more confirmation, the article mentioned my brother, Caleb, by name. This was a real article. I knew what I read was true. When I touched the blood tree, I saw their deaths as if I was there.

I saw the pain they were in. The illness, my vision, it all fit. I shuddered at the thought of Caleb wailing and screaming in pain. Noah said something else, but I was too distracted to notice, something about the clergyman that was interviewed for the article. I felt sick and was just about ready to throw up when--

"You didn't tell me you were going to be here." I heard a familiar high-pitched voice coming from the opposite side of the computer. I hid behind the fairly large outdated computer monitor. I didn't want her to see me. As if my day couldn't get any worse, there in her glorious perfection was Melissa Jones, AKA MJ, also known as Noah's girlfriend. I literally wanted to die.

"I wasn't planning on being here. Care Bear, I mean Carrie, needed my help with a school project," Noah answered honestly.

"Carrie?" She turned up her nose as if the air suddenly became foul. "You're here with Scary Carrie?"

I peeked up from my hiding spot to see Melissa and her BFF, Frances, known as Frankie, standing in front of Noah as though he were on trial for committing a crime. "Hey, MJ. Hey, Frankie." I did at least manage to greet them without making a complete fool of myself. Now, I was wishing like crazy that I had dressed better. Melissa and Frances were dressed as if they belonged in a Ralph Lauren clothing ad. I sank back down in my hiding spot behind the monitor.

Please, please go away.

Melissa huffed. One thing for sure, she didn't like me. Besides the fact that my family was considered everything from witches to cult leaders to whatever else your imagination could cook up, she didn't like the fact that Noah spent time with me, a considerable amount of his time. Not that I was competition either way, but how did it look for the future prom king to spend his time with another girl other than the future prom queen? And did I mention I was an outcast and no one liked me? It would have been better for Noah to be seen with a beautiful popular rival of Melissa's; that made more sense, but no, he was here with me, plain, weird, crazy, Carrie Carter.

"What project? We are in the same class and all our projects were reading projects that could be done alone," Melissa growled. She twirled her blonde locks that fell to her shoulders. Frances stood there in silence. She was there for support only, not that Melissa needed any.

"Care Bear, I mean Carrie isn't not coming back to Baltimore City High this year. She has a history project to do for her new school," he answered as he flashed the screen quickly to Melissa. Then he closed out the article.

I was so grateful; the last thing I needed was for anyone, especially Melissa, to read about my bizarre family history. As if they needed any proof that the rumors about my family were somewhat true...

"He's lying." I heard Frances whisper to Melissa. "He's trying to protect her. Everyone knows that Scary Carrie is in love with your Noah Greene, MJ."

Why is she so freaking dramatic? Frances, however, was right about two things: I was in love with him, though I didn't know that everyone knew that, and he was lying about the history project. But Noah knew if he told MJ the truth about our fact-finding mission, she would use the information to hurt me, but she was wrong about his lying to protect me, I think. Well, maybe he was lying to protect me.

Okay, she was dead on in her assessment.

I peeped from behind the white monitor that was the size of Texas to get a closer look at Melissa. I was drawn to her. I felt this need to be close to her. *Where was this feeling coming from?* I stared at Melissa, gawking almost; I couldn't explain why, but I was compelled to look at her. I was looking past her ice blue eyes and her perfectly tanned skin. I was looking past her button nose and her thin lips and I was looking past her freckled, chiseled face. I wasn't seeing any of that at all. I was looking at something else, something non-physical about her. I couldn't put my finger on it, but it even had a smell, a sweet smell, like a freshly baked apple pie.

"Seriously, Noah, you have got to get over feeling sorry for her," she said with even more disgust than she displayed earlier. "I mean, really—" She stopped short of what she was saying when she noticed me staring at her. I got up from behind the computer to meet her on the other side of the massive wood table. "What exactly are you staring at, freak?" she demanded of me.

I was uncertain of what I was about to say, but I could feel my lips moving; before I realized it, I was speaking.

"You are here to see Matthew Shaw? You were here to see Matthew Shaw? You are sleeping with Matthew Shaw?" I couldn't believe that I was saying this, but as soon as I heard my own voice, I knew this to be true, even though when I started speaking, I sounded more as if I were asking a question rather than making a firm factual statement.

"Carrie, what the hell!" Noah yelled, obviously surprised.

Melissa and Frances were speechless. The shock was written all over their faces, hell, the shock that was written on mine. This was definitely a Kodak moment. I touched my lips to make sure that they were mine. I tilted my head to be sure my thoughts were my own. They were. *What in the hell is going on?*

Frances recovered first. "See, this is exactly how rumors get started." She nudged Melissa, who still couldn't believe I had this information; she was so careful, so methodical in her planning, but here it was, I knew, an outsider, an outcast knew something damaging about Melissa Jones. "Noah, don't listen to Scary Carrie; she's making this up," Frances babbled on.

I faced them with the confidence I wished I had all school year, the confidence I wished I had all my life. Melissa and Frances, the beautiful ones, the perfect ones, and I knew, I knew that they were not that beautiful or perfect. "No, I can say with absolute certainty that Matt Shaw is upstairs in the men's bathroom, cleaning himself up."

Everyone looked up at the cascading staircase as if Matt would appear. He didn't. He was still washing up after his sexual encounter with Melissa. That moment would have been perfect if he had appeared. *How do I know that? How do I know any of this?*

"You can't even lie to me." Noah said. I wasn't sure if it was a statement or a question. It just hung out there, and for the first time today, the library seemed to be silent, moving in slow motion at the weight of our conversation.

"Noah…I…" Melissa started. "I…Carrie's lying." She sounded defeated. I rendered her speechless. One point for me and none for Team Melissa. That felt great. I couldn't help but feel empowered.

Then as icing on the cake, Matt was now coming downstairs. I could hear him whistling.

"Hey, Matt," I called. For the first time in my entire life, I felt cocky. It was an awesome feeling.

Matt jogged over to where we were having our confrontation. He smiled, "Hey, Noah, Frankie, MJ, Sherrie."

I corrected him. "Carrie." *Butthole!*

"Yeah, that's cool." He tried to be polite. He was the proverbial bad boy, tall, dark, and dangerous. He had many bones in his closet.

How do I know that?

He tousled his black hair. "Funny running into you guys here, I was catching up on some, umm…"

"Reading?" I helped.

"Yeah, that." He was so stupid. If there was an award for stupidity, he would win, hands down, every time it was handed out. He did, however, have a charming, warm smile. I could see how Melissa was attracted to him, but he was no Noah.

"See you guys at Tonya's party. Well, maybe not you, Sherrie. Later." Matt exited. He was clueless as to what was going on, and, as I stated before, he really was an ass.

Noah packed his things. I forgot that I was there with my Noah. I needed to say something. I never meant to hurt him, just mortally wound that evil dog Melissa. Noah was an unfortunate causality of war. "Noah, I'm sorry," I tried to soothe him, but he then turned his anger on me.

"Why didn't you tell me this before, Carrie?" His voice was razor sharp. *Did he just call me Carrie? Again? He almost never calls me Carrie. He is upset with me.* He was a shade of red that can only be described as the color of a stop sign.

"I didn't know." Which was true, I didn't know, that I knew what I now know, but how would I explain that?

"You seem to know quite enough. I thought we were friends? I thought you cared about--- so is this why you dragged me to the library—to bust Melissa? To embarrass me?" He flung his book bag over his back.

"NO!" He had it all wrong. I didn't know that this was going to happen. Now that it had, I started to wish it hadn't. *What do I tell him? What do I say to him? I wasn't even sure what was going on with me.* I went to grab him to, I don't know, hug him? Tell him I loved him? Tell him I was going crazy? It didn't matter, he pulled away from me.

He pulled away from me?

"Oh, give it up, Carrie." Melissa had completely checked out, so Frances was now the mouthpiece, and she took my focus off Noah and back on them. "You thought that if you tried to break up Noah and MJ, he would want you. But your plan backfired. Noah and MJ love each other." Frances spat.

Was this chick completely delusional? Noah crossed in front of Frances and Melissa without saying goodbye to them or to me. "Noah." I called but he was soon out the door without turning to acknowledge me. I was going to follow him, but I was suddenly drawn to Frances the same way I was drawn to Melissa, but stronger. Her scent excited me even more. "You don't want me to tell everyone about your father, do you?" I said to Frances.

The color left Frances's face. She looked dead. What did I know about her father? *Think.* I knew he was evil. He stole money from his company and cheated on his wife with his secretary. He was a...rapist. He raped his daughters. He raped Frances. OMG! He raped Frances! *How in the world did I come up with that?* I have never even met her father.

She held her heart as if to stop it from leaping out of her chest, a tear dropped from her eye, "Please, don't," she whispered.

"You never know, these things do have a way of getting out." *Where was all this confidence, and, might I add, arrogance, coming from?* I didn't even sound like myself. I liked it. I loved it. I collected my things. I won. Check and mate.

"I hate you," Frances mouthed through her chalk white lips, but I heard her. She had her other hand wrapped around Melissa, who was now leaning on the computer table for support. Melissa was crying, and so was Frances; it was a beautiful sight. The bliss I felt was unexplainable.

"I know," I said, smiling. She did hate me. "But now at least you have a real reason." I smiled even harder as I walked away.

The More You Know

"Hey, Noah, this is like one hundredth time I've called. I'm so sorry, I really am. I swear I never wanted things to end like that. I didn't mean--would you just call me back? Let's sort this out," I pleaded on Noah's voice mail. He was avoiding me and was extremely good at doing so.

"Trouble in paradise?" Aunt Cara asked from the hallway.

I quickly slapped the phone shut. "I don't want to talk about it. If that's okay?"

"Sure, of course. I was your age once, a long, long time ago. I remember those feelings, thinking that no one cared or could understand. Noah Greene, the love of your life."

"Love of my life?" So everyone did know that I was in love with him.

Aunt Cara smiled. She was beautiful. Her long black locks were loose, dancing around her face and down her back. She wore an ankle length orange, red, and yellow dress. She was as mesmerizing as a flame. She was a walking work of art. "Noah has been the only boy you have talked about since… well, since I can remember." she explained.

True. He had been the only person to ever really talk to me in life. The only person who didn't whisper when I walked past; he was never mean to me. He was always nice and sweet. He didn't care that Mother was a lunatic or that my aunts were equally as odd. No, he saw past all that and accepted me.

I needed Noah. I needed him so that I could feel normal. "I don't feel like talking about it, Aunt Cara. I'm sorry."

She was very understanding. "But if you need to talk or want to talk about Noah, let me know. I may be able to help," she offered.

I nodded my head yes so she could leave and so I could call Noah for the one hundred and first time to apologize.

"Carrie, love, please put on some decent clothes," Aunt Cara added. I had on a tee shirt and capri sweats. I knew what she meant, *"Carrie please put on some clothes that Aunt Carly would approve of."* She was just about to leave me alone when she took a deep breath, "Carrie?"

"Yes ma'am." I put my cell phone down. I tried not to sound annoyed, but I was sure she could tell I was.

She walked into my room. Actually, she glided. It was as if her beautiful bare feet never touched the floor. She looked at me with a curiosity that I couldn't explain. Her amazing green eyes seem to glow. "Are you all right? Are you feeling well?"

I looked at her as if she were crazy. She stood over me as I sat on my twin-size bed. "Yes, other than Noah," I said slowly. I was not sure how to respond.

She stared at me for what seemed like an eternity. I felt like I was shrinking under her gaze. *Maybe she knew I was going crazy too. Maybe she talked to Aunt Carly... I guess I'll be joining Mother in the mental hospital soon.*

She took another deep breath, shaking her head. "Carrie, is Noah okay?" she asked very methodically.

"I don't know," I answered. "He's hurt." I didn't know what to say. I couldn't tell her about the library scene because I was unsure of what happened my damn self.

"Well, I hope he feels better," she offered as she combed her manicured hands through my hair. She took one long, last look. She was concerned about me. She knew something. She licked her fingers that she played in my hair with then she smelled them. Then she winked at me. After she did that, I became concerned about her.

As she was leaving my room, I'm not even sure why, but I felt the need to share what I learned from my experience at the library with Melissa and Frances. "Aunt Cara."

She turned back to face me. "Yes, dear."

"It's no secret that the people in Baltimore don't really care about our family. Most of it is people just being...stupid. Our family is being condemned because of rumors and lies. And the sad thing about that is the same people casting stones at us have done horrible things too. Things you can't even imagine."

She smiled at my observation. "Yes, honey. People do commit terrible, horrible acts. And I can imagine. But don't worry, things will work out; they always do," she said, turning to leave the room. "And this will all seem like one bad dream," she called out as she got farther down the hall. "People have a need to feel better than everyone else, but sin is sin and judgment is judgment. It will all work out." Her voice was like a gentle caress in my ear.

Yes, it will all work out... I thought.

I did change my clothes to a floral blouse with a bone colored skirt and Old Navy ballerina slippers. At least I tried. *I should get an A for effort, even by Aunt Carly's standards.* I reasoned.

It had been days since the scene in the library, and somehow I was now the talk of the BCHS student body. Scary Carrie—that was what the natives called me—got the best of the Witches of Eastwick, that was what I called MJ and Frankie. To my surprise, I was kind of popular now. Word had gotten out that David took down Goliath. My classmates were calling the house to ask me for the rundown.

I had known most of these teens all of my life, and never once had any of them called me except for a group class assignment, and most times not even then. A social call? What was that?

Well, I summarized that it was a bunch of nothing. As much as I wanted to be popular, now I wished the phone would stop ringing. I didn't even know how word gotten out. The only

86

person I wanted to talk to was mad at me. He wouldn't even talk to me or accept my apology. I wanted nothing more than to hear his voice.

"Carrie, OMG! I can't believe you got in MJ's face like that." That was Tonya Belle. She was a lesser part of the Witches of Eastwick.

"How did you get this number?" I asked. Since I become popular overnight, Aunt Chris put a land line in my room the very next day. I never needed a phone in my room before. My aunts got tired of teenagers calling and hanging up on them. They were still frightened by my aunts, but not frightened enough to stop calling.

"Toby gave it to me."

"Who?" I had no idea who that was.

Tonya continued. "Frankie told Kim, who told Will, who told Bobby, who told Michelle, who told Lisa, who told Toby, who told me that you gave MJ the riot act. That MJ was speechless and she was so scared of you. I just can't believe someone finally stood up to her crap. I did almost… this one time… when we were in the tenth grade---"

"Frances is telling everyone this?" *Why?*

"Yeah, she said that MJ had it coming. You know she's jealous of you?"

"Who? What?"

"Keep up, Care Bear. MJ is so jealous of you. Everyone knows that Noah likes you. That's why she started that whole Scary Carrie thing. No hard feelings, though, right?"

"Did you just call me Care Bear?"

"Yes, everyone knows that Noah gave you that nickname; it's so cute, by the way. He has had this thing for you since like pre-K. Get with it, Care Bear. I called to get the scoop from you, but you sound like you need the scoop yourself." She giggled. "So I heard you aren't coming back to school. What a shame; you are really hot now. Oh and by the way, Matt said MJ was horrible in bed. HORRIBLE! Did you know that they slept together like ten times? She's such a whore. I knew she was a skanky skank. Come over tomorrow for my back-to-school party; it's so on."

Did I sound like this? Like a talking head? "I don't know, Tonya."

"Parentals will be there and absolutely no alcohol. Your aunts would approve, right?"

I sighed. "I guess."

"Cool, see ya there. It starts at nine. You got my address, right?"

"No, you didn't want me to have it."

"Oh."

"Yeah, we had that group project for Mr. Pierce's class."

"Yeah."

"You said you would rather go to hell than to give me your address. So I failed that project," I jabbed. And personally, I was still waiting for her to cash in her one way ticket. *Tramp!*

"Bummer." I assumed that was her form of an apology. "Totally, give me your cell number. I'll text it to you. Cool?"

"Umm…."

"Don't worry, MJ is licking her wounds; she won't be there, but Matt will, and he's kind of digging you now. You will come, right?"

"I'll have to see, Tonya."

I gave her my cell number. I can't tell you why, but I did. *Did I just get invited to a party?* I had to ask myself. I had never been to one nor had one, so I was actually kind of excited, not that I really wanted to go. I had more important things to do, like patching things up with Noah and finding out more information about that newspaper article that Noah and I read about, plus I needed to figure out what was happening to me.

I felt as though I was having an out-of-body experience. I was able to see things about people that weren't pleasant, like Frances's nasty father, and Melissa whoring around with Matt. I wasn't looking for these insights, but they just came to me.

I felt less and less like myself. Sure, I still looked like me, with my dewy light skin, my thin black hair, my blank eyes, and my petite shape, but I didn't feel like me on the inside. Not to mention I was hearing voices in my head, not the "the dog made me kill those people" type voices, but more like my voice telling me things about people and seeing the evil in them.

I heard my aunt in my head trying to get information from me subconsciously. Remarkably I was able to shut her out. I heard Mother's voice too as if she was guiding me, somehow.

And then there was the blood tree showing me visions. I was lost. This new sense of being was frightening, and all this was happening so close to my birthday. I was sure that was the reason why I was felt differently. I was also sure that time was running out for me.

All of my cousins were dead before eighteen; only my brother lived to twenty. If this was a generational curse, I planned to fight it, just like Caleb had; but unlike Caleb, I was claiming victory. I needed to know how to kill this creature that was taking over my body.

First, I was going to Noah's to fix things and see if he wanted to help me look up some more articles and then help me interview people who were familiar with my family. As if they could read my mind, two of my aunts were waiting for me at the front door.

"Are you going to Tonya's party?" Aunt Chris asked with a blank face. All of my aunts had this uncanny ability to talk to someone, void of emotion while barely moving their lips. It was unnatural.

Maybe they were all ventriloquists by trade?

Not likely.

Aunt Chris was looking exceptionally stunning today. Of course, she did every day, but I was drawn to her today. Her presence was magnetic. Her skin was radiant, her green eyes were endless. She wore a purple halter dress with no shoes, and even her feet were perfectly manicured. My aunts, and even Mother, seemed to have a problem with shoes. Maybe shoes were connected to the craziness. I always knew shoes were evil.

"Oh, look at you!" Aunt Carly beamed. "You didn't even need my help. I'm so proud of you." Aunt Carly was the official fashionista of the family and she always looked heavenly. I was flattered by her acknowledgment of my effort.

However, I was not lost to the fact that I was being cornered. I was caught. Not that I was sneaking out, but I didn't tell any of my aunts my plans for today. That wasn't a crime last time I checked. And of all things to ask, was I going to the party? I had a better chance of winning the lottery.

"I'm not sure, Aunt Chris. I've never been to a party before." I had a theory that I wanted test, so I was sure to keep my thoughts light.

I focused on Noah and the library. I wanted to see if I could feel my aunts' presences in my head. I was sure they were probing for information because they were prying more than usual. They wanted to know what I was up to. I didn't like the feeling of having my aunts in my head, but if they were looking for something, they weren't going to find anything of consequence. This theory, of course, was solely based on whether they even had some type of mental ability and whether I had the mental capacity to keep them out.

"You haven't asked to see your mother recently. You do not wish to see her?" Aunt Chris asked me with pensive eyes.

True. I haven't visited Mother since she flipped out, but she came to me in a dream, and that was even weirder. Mother told me in my dream that she would no longer going to be in the hospital. I believed her. Sure, it was a dream, but it felt so real. I knew for a fact that Mother moved on.

Hospital visit popped up in my head. Aunt Chris stared at me, much in the matter in which I stared at Melissa in the library and like Aunt Cara stared at me earlier. She was looking past me, trying to get into my head. Her eyes even looked peculiar. Not the same

91

emerald green that I was used to seeing. Her eyes were a hint darker. Again, I was drawn to her. I stared into her eyes as if they were calling me. I couldn't help myself. I felt compelled to tell her everything that my mind was hiding. I had to fight this power she had over me. I couldn't let her win.

Keep it light, Carrie. Keep it light, I ordered myself. I blocked out my thoughts as much as possible.

I am going crazy. I am a loon. But somehow, doing this thinking exercise made me feel somewhat sane. I also felt I had no choice if I wanted to keep all my secrets truly secret.

Both of my aunts stood there waiting to find out what they wanted to know by reading my thoughts, or by me telling them what they wanted to know. "It's just that, well, Aunt Carly probably has already told you how the last visit ended, and I just…I wanted to get over what happened before I go back there. I was bothered by what my mother said to me."

"What did she say," Aunt Chris asked cautiously, "that had you bothered?"

Should I tell them the truth? Should I say she expressed that we were demons and therefore evil? And it is our job to destroy mankind's souls? They would have me committed just as they did Mother for loving her dead son, but the opportunity to be so open with my aunts was rare. We never discussed feelings or curses, dead sons, or my crazy mother, so this was my only chance, my one shot. I had to take it.

"She said that we were cursed. Well, worse than that, she said we were damned. She told me to never come to visit her again and she wished she never had me because then I wouldn't be cursed or damned." I waited for them to respond.

Please take the bait. I couldn't cross my fingers, so I crossed my toes.

Aunt Carly twisted her lips trying to think of something either clever or something superficial to say. Aunt Chris examined me with a long look. She tried to get in my head again, but I was ready her. I felt her trying to read my mind. "Carrie, I would be lying if I said life was easy, but it's not; it's hard."

Let me in, Carrie. Let me see what's going on, Aunt Chris encouraged mentally. I heard her and felt her presence in my head, very invasive.

"Especially if you are a Carter." Aunt Carly regained her composure. "I should have said something to Christine and Cara after I picked up you that day, but, Carrie, you were so…defeated. I really didn't want them pestering you about how your mother treated you. Crazy or not, Carrie, your mother was wrong for saying those horrible things to you." She was actually being apologetic? Was that possible for Aunt Carly, sympathy? Was she possessed?

I can't see anything. Can you, Carly? Aunt Chris asked Aunt Carly using her mind.

No. She hasn't changed yet, has she? Aunt Carly answered using her mental ability. Both of them were staring at me.

Aunt Chris responded, *No, look at her. She's still looks the same. Let me try something else no human can resist. Keep her talking.*
They hadn't opened their mouths, yet I could hear them mentally conversing. So there was a crazy gene, and I obviously inherited it.

"I don't think my mother is crazy at all." I knew she wasn't crazy, she was evil. There had to be a difference.

"Your mother is…" Aunt Chris started. *DAMN IT! She's strong. I can't break down her mental walls. She's blocking me from her thoughts. Can she do that already? Do you think she knows?*

"When you love someone, Carrie, it's easy to accept their flaws. You can forgive them or see past them." Aunt Carly placed her hand on my shoulder. "Your mother isn't well, and maybe it is best that you take a break from seeing her every day." *WOW! I got nothing, Christine. I don't think she knows yet. She would have said something. That's a huge fucking secret to keep.*

"Okay." I said as I was leaving and at the same time trying not to disclose that I could actually hear what my aunts were thinking. It was hard to concentrate on keeping a poker face, since my aunts were so good at reading minute changes in anyone's face and voice, but I believed I did a good job. At least they haven't seen past my guise that I could tell.

"Carrie, may we ask where you are going?" Aunt Chris asked. *She actually asked me?*

"I want to apologize to Noah." I was going past Noah's house. He couldn't avoid me forever. And then we—and I was being hopeful when I said we—were going to do some more research on my wicked family.

Aunt Carly must not have noticed any deception. "Okay, that's why you are dressed up," she said as winked at me. "Go get 'em, girl!"

I blushed. She wasn't possessed any more. She was scaring me with all the loving and caring talk.

94

Aunt Chris wasn't an easy sell. "Back at a reasonable hour, then. I trust we do not need to talk of improper relations?" *Nothing, Carly! Think of something to say to keep her talking.*

"Umm, no. Nothing improper about our relationship." I felt rather uncomfortable with the thought of my aunts questioning me about sex. Why are they prolonging this conversation? *Please, brain, think of Noah and nothing else.*

"I told you, Christine, they are not at that stage, yet." Aunt Carly chuckled and Aunt Chris backed off.

"Not too late, Carrie," Aunt Chris called, closing the screen door behind me. I nodded as I stepped off the porch. My aunts stood in the doorway for a moment while I made it down the steps. I looked back to see if they were inside of the house.

They were.

Before they could think of some more non-essential conversation, I decided to run. I had to get off the farmland as quickly as my feet could carry me.

As soon as my feet hit the pathway, I ran. I ran from my aunts and the blood tree. Yet, somehow I was now connected to it. Before I touched it, I was able to ignore it somewhat; but now it was as if the tree were calling me.

The visions hadn't gone away, either. They were as vivid as the day I touched the tree.

I stopped directly in front of the tree. "Why are you doing this?" I asked in frustration. "What do you want from me?"

It has a story, and maybe you should they to figure out what it is before you condemn it.

"Fine, tell me your story. What do you want me to know?"

95

The wind blew, and the blood tree extended one of its hand-like branches and reached for my hand. I hesitated; the wind blew again, and the branch brushed against the back of my hand and wrapped itself around it. The wet red leaves stained my skin as the tree shared another vision.

This time, I saw myself lying very still in my bed, as if I was dead. My aunts were standing over me, watching. The wind blew again, and the tree branch released my hand. I grabbed my heart. It was beating so loudly I thought my aunts could hear it from in the house.

"I knew it, I'm going to die," I whispered.

I walked away from the tree. "So you wanted me to know I am going to die? Uh? Well, I'm not! I'm not going to let them kill me like they did my cousins and Caleb!" I affirmed in anger. But mostly I was fearful.

I was at Noah's in what felt like a matter of seconds. The bus ride to his house seemed extremely short.

Noah lived in town, in a normal neighborhood with normal neighbors—a luxury I didn't have, but desperately desired. When I approached the door, Noah's mother was already standing there.

"Hello, Mrs. Greene," I said, "is Noah in?" Noah's mother was a typical, normal suburban housewife. She smiled as I came onto the front patio. She seemed not to fear my family, but I did always wonder how she felt about me and my friendship with her son.

"My, my, if it isn't Carrie Carter; I haven't seen you in ages," she purred through her door. I think her family was originally from the South, maybe New Orleans. She had a heavy southern drawl not typical of a Baltimorean.

"Oh, and look at you; you look very nice. But I'm afraid Noah's not feeling well today and asked that I not let anyone up to see him," she said, frowning.

Noah's mother was being polite; what she really meant was that he didn't want to see me. I fished around in my pocket for his letter that I wrote. "Mrs. Greene, I had a feeling that Noah might not be feeling well enough to see visitors, so can you pass this along to him, please? I need him to know that I am sorry," I forced out, "and I want us to be friends again." I was so disappointed it was hard not to cry right then and there.

She took the letter I wrote while on the bus, just in case he didn't want to see me. *I'm glad I came prepared.*

"Of course. I'm so sorry you two had a fight." I felt that she wanted to say more, but she just smiled. I excused myself and continued with my agenda. As much I wanted to smooth things over with Noah, I needed even more to find out what was going on with me.

The blood tree showed me that I was dying. Maybe the same thing happened to Caleb and my cousins. Maybe they felt confused and disoriented and then powerful and amazing only to get gravely ill and die. I wanted to save myself. I needed answers, fast.

I ended up at the library downtown at a computer station looking up the same article as before. I jotted down names and I was hoping that some of these people were still alive and in the immediate area. It was a long shot, but at least it was a start.

"Pastor Harry Cross." The internet made finding people so easy it was scary. There were three pastors by the name of Harry Cross that showed up during my research, but only one of them still lived in the area, so he won the prize of a visit from me today.

The search engine led me to the Archangel Michael Lutheran Church, a couple of blocks away from the library. I located the church in a matter of minutes after getting directions.

The church was a massive building with beautiful stained-glass art featured on the windows. I used all my strength to open the unlocked doors. A loud BOOM filled the lobby and echoed through the sanctuary as the doors slammed shut. I looked around because a thunderous noise like that would have startled anyone, even the dead.

As I started toward the sanctuary, a little elderly white woman materialized. "Hello, dear, can I help you?" she inquired.

I had to strain to hear her because her voice was so weak. "Yes, I'm looking for Pastor Cross." I met her in the in middle aisle of the sanctuary.

"Come, dear, he's in his study." She led me through the frosty sanctuary. The air conditioner must been set to Arctic Tundra. I shivered as we travelled through a long corridor to the back of the church. We stopped at a closed wooden door. "Harry." She knocked then opened it. "You have a guest."

Pastor Cross sat at a large black desk, reading. He looked up from his glasses. He appeared to be just as frail as the woman who led the way to his office. "Who is it, Ingrid?" he asked. He sounded irritated; I was an unwanted disruption.

"Here she is. You can ask her yourself." She turned and exited the room. She was all too trusting. How did she know I wasn't there to rob the church or something? That was not the reason why I was there, but this was still Baltimore City. The murder rate was always in the top three among major cities, and it made me wonder if they kept a gun in there or if they were relying strictly on God for protection.

I crossed the large office and stopped at the front of the desk, "Pastor Cross, my name is--"

Do I really want to leave my real name?

"—Carrie Greene, sir."

It was my fantasy to be married to Noah.

That would never happen. So what was wrong with pretending now?

He stood and gestured for me to have a seat. "What can I help you with, Ms. Greene?"

"I am doing a history project about religion in Baltimore because there is a huge religious presence in the city's history, well, in the state of Maryland." I was trying to find something that would fit why I would be asking him about my aunts and the newspaper article from 1930.

He looked baffled, and rightly so. "What you are looking for, maybe you can find it in history books. You may have better luck going to a Catholic church, since Baltimore was once a safe haven for Catholics. I'm not sure how much help I will be."

"Actually—"

Stop, slow down, you are going to scare the man.

"—I am looking for a more personal account. Pastor Cross, I came across this article in the *Baltimore Gazette* about the Carter-Coolidge family---"

He went from friendly to furious in zero point eight seconds. "Miss Greene, if you came here to make fun of the small town minister, well, I got news for you. You won't have my help!"

"No, sir, it's not like that. I have experienced some of the same phenomena with a certain group of women, and I would like your take on it. Please, sir, it would help me to have a better understanding. I'm not looking to make fun of you, Pastor Cross, or anyone, for matter. I desperately need your help," I begged.

He relaxed and eased back in his seat. He searched my face. I hoped he saw I meant him no harm. He looked around in his desk drawer and pulled out his own newspaper clipping.

"Clark Coolidge, may he rest in peace, came to our little community, sometime in 1912 with his wife, Clara, and their sons, Carl and Chase. Clark was the first to die. He took ill and never recovered. Clara's sisters—" He pointed to the newspaper and handed it to me. There they were, my aunts, looking exactly the same as they did today. They haven't aged, at all.

I almost vomited.

OH, CRAP!

"Christina and Carla Carter came and helped Clara out when Clark first got sick, and they stayed after he died, too, to help Clara with his businesses. He was a very fortunate man, at least as far as his businesses were concerned. Are you all right, young lady?"

NO! I felt as if I was going to pass out. I angled myself so I didn't get too dizzy because I couldn't breathe.

Oh, God!

I managed to get out a barely audible yes. "Please continue, sir."

"Clark's death didn't make the papers. People just thought he was sick, and I believe he was overcome by some illness, human illness."

"Did, they, the Carter women, do something to Clark?"

"I can't be sure. I'm going to guess that it wasn't the same illness that killed the boys. Chase, Carl and Caleb died from something else."

My face lit up. "You knew Caleb?" More sickness washed over me. My stomach started doing flips. If he knew my family in 1912, that meant Mother and the aunts were how old?

He answered, "No, not really. His mother came into the picture later, but his death did make the papers. What exactly do you want to know, young lady? No one has asked me about the Carters in over sixty years." He was curious about my curiosity, as he should have been. Why would a teen-aged girl ask about some evil women from over sixty years ago?

I didn't know how to come out and ask, mainly because it sounded crazy in my head, but I asked anyway. "I read the article, and everyone believed that they were evil. Can you tell me why?"

"They are evil; those Carter women are evil. In one family, all of the men died mysterious deaths in exactly the same way except Clark. All the men born in that family those women manage to kill somehow. And the women never age."

"Something is going on, there. I don't believe that there is a fountain of youth, so how else can you or anyone explain that? It's more than just that. They look different, act different from us, humans. It's more than any of that, much, much more, I'm afraid."

If I wasn't who I was, going through what I was going through, I would have thought Pastor Cross was crazy or just old and senile, but he was lucid and sharp for his age. And, sadly, he was also correct.

"Why do you think Clark died from something different, from the other men in the family?" I inquired.

"Well, it had a lot to do with how the corpses looked. The boys looked more like the women when they died, their hair turned jet black, eyes turned green. They were beautiful, just like the women. Clark looked like regular old Clark when he died. He was dark, gaunt, and ugly. Clark was a man, an old man when he died. Chase, Carl Chance, and Caleb died in their teens. They gave Clark a regular burial. No one knows what happened to the boys' bodies."

I do, I thought.

It has a story, and maybe you should try to figure out what it is before you condemn it.

That was its story. That was what the tree was trying to tell me.

I saw them die one by one. The bodies were in the yard. The tree was stained with their blood and maybe others.

"It has a lot of blood on its hands," Aunt Carly once told me.

"I'll do it myself." That was what Aunt Carly meant when she said that to Mother. She was going to bury her son by herself in the yard, under the blood tree.

"Is it witchcraft, demonic possession, a cult thing, maybe?" I asked.

"No, young lady, it's more than that; each of them is born to change into a monster. I witnessed Carl die, saw the madness in his eyes and watched his eyes turn from brown to green. He was about as brown as milk chocolate when he was living; when he died, he was the color of gold, and his skin glowed. I had never seen anything like it before in my life, or since. He was growling, hollering like some type of animal. I have never heard a human make that kind of noise; it was gut wrenching."

I was going to die just like the blood tree showed me. Maybe the demon made you crazy and then killed you. Maybe there was no stopping this. Caleb died trying. I wondered if I should even try to fight it. Maybe if I went peacefully, it won't be so bad or hurt so much.

Pastor Cross continued talking. "Those Coolidge-Carters are not even human, not even close. They don't eat, sleep, or do things that humans need to do to survive. They don't have to, they do it to fit in. I spent a whole summer over at Clara's and Clark's; Clara never ate. I've even seen one of the sisters recently. She looks just the same as she looked back then, as if she is still in her twenties, still unbelievably beautiful."

He crossed his arms. "They are wolves in sheep's clothing. Possession, umm… twice; the other sister asked for her son to have an exorcism before he died. Unfortunately he still changed into that monster. The creature just laughed as it was performed. It's not possession; it's who they are. They are evil." He inspected me closely. "Now I'm going to have to ask again, why are you curious about the ramblings of this old man?"

"I don't think you are rambling sir, I believe you." I asked him, "Did you perform the exorcism on Caleb?" I assumed Caleb was the one that had the exorcism. He was the only one that fought his demon; at least, that's what Mother said.

"Caleb?" He looked at me dubiously as he went back to the desk and pulled out another article. This time it was the same article I looked up on the internet with Noah, complete with pictures: one with Mother and my aunts, another with just my aunts and a few other people in front of a church, and another of just Carl and Chase.

"Oh, dear heavens, no. As I stated before, I didn't know Caleb," he said. I looked up from the newspaper, puzzled by his response. "I was a young boy when Carl and Chase died. I used to play with them. My father, Harry Cross, Sr."--- he pointed to the picture of the people in front of the church, and singled out a white man with a blue and gray robe on---"performed the exorcism." He pointed to a little boy in the corner of the picture. "That's me."

He stared into my expressionless face. "I told you they never age, but as for me..." He showed me how time had been unkind to him with his papery skin, his turkey neck, and his clouded eyes. He was old.

Oh, God...I started to feel nauseous again.

He continued, "We told them to move from our town after the boys died. They did, but strange things started to happen. My father's church burned to the ground." He pulled out yet another newspaper clipping. "The church burned down to the foundation.

The firefighters put it out with their feet. A few of the parishioners committed suicide, including my mother, may she rest in peace. Our little town simply rotted away. It was like Sodom and Gomorrah. Howard Town was no more."

"OH, GOD!" I blurted out.

"Well, you are going to need Him if you are keeping company with them." He looked at me. "There's nothing you can do, young lady. If you are born into that family, there is nothing but death, misery, and pain. Nothing can stop it. They killed my daddy, too. He thought he could kill them, but how can you kill evil?"

He stood up. "I hope I helped you in some way and answered all your questions." He was ready for me to leave.

"Yes, thank you," I said as I stood up. I was able to regain my composure while he led me the same way back to the front doors of the church.

He did answer my questions, and I was grateful; however, now I had more.

Changing With The Times

I was seated at my vanity in my bathroom, feeling sick. I was hoping it was more of a mental thing. My heart was beating like a drum, my skin was clammy, I couldn't catch my breath, and my head was pounding.

"Geez, Carrie, calm down. It's just a party," Aunt Carly said, trying to relax me. Of course, she was helping me get ready for Tonya's back-to-school party.

"Aunt Carly, is this necessary? I mean, it's a house party; most of the girls are probably going to wear tee shirts and jeans anyway."

She closed her eyes for a brief second, "No, they will be dressed like whores and some with horrible make-up to match. You'll be the belle of the ball, I promise," she chuckled as she combed with my hair.

"How do you know that?" I asked as I turned to face her.

"Teenaged girls are all the same. Nothing is new under the sun. And I've seen it all, more than once." She turned my head back around so she could finish doing my hair.

"Aunt Carly, I know this is impolite, but I need to know, how old are you?" After seeing the photos that accompanied the article courtesy of Pastor Cross, I feared my aunt was old and now officially evil.

She was embarrassed. "Oh, Carrie, is it that obvious? I know I'm old, but I thought I was the cool aunt. Cara is the motherly one, Christine is the mean one, I am the cool one…"

"Aunt Carly, you are cool. In fact, you are one of the coolest people on this planet," I soothed her.

She was pleased. "Yes, this is true; I am cool. And Carrie, please, I don't feel comfortable discussing my age. It's something that some adults go through, a midlife crisis thing, I guess." She cleared her throat.

I turned around to face her, which annoyed her more, and she turned me back around. "Aunt Carly, you don't look old. You look like you are only a couple of years older than me." My aunt looked closer to twenty-one than eighty. After my conversation with Pastor Cross, I realized she was at least that. Eighty years old, that is.

"You always seem to know what to say." She braided my thin and shedding hair into this intricate masterpiece that was reminiscent of a Grecian princess, complete with a gold head band that she wove along with the design. "Now, are you ready to see your dress?"

My heart nearly jumped out of my chest.

"Really, Carrie," she said, displeased with my trepidation, "Get over it! It's just a dress."

I grabbed my chest to make sure my heart still had some function.

"You are getting ready for a party, not your execution." She added.

I tried to steady my breathing. "Well, this is my first party; and, to be perfectly honest with you, I don't feel well." I was not sure if I felt anxiety over the party or over what Pastor Cross told me yesterday. My aunt left my bathroom and came back with this very girly, spaghetti-strap, pink, blue, and gray bubble dress that stopped mid-thigh. It was perfect for a girl my age. It was fun, youthful, not too revealing, and not too sophisticated.

It was perfect for any girl except me. I had no need for dresses for social outings with friends because I had none. "Are you sure, Aunt Carly?"

She smiled. "Have I ever steered you wrong before as far as fashion is concerned?"

I shook my head no.

"Right," she affirmed.

"Aunt Carly?"

"Yes."

"I think I would like to go and see my mother tomorrow." I knew she wouldn't be at the hospital, but I wanted to see what Aunt Carly would say. And maybe she would be there. Who knew? Pastor Cross had let me have copies of his newspaper clippings. If Mother just so happened to be there, I would present the articles to her and see what she would have to say. I hid the newspapers in my favorite horse, Sprinkles's stall. My aunts would never think to look for any of my secrets there. I hadn't ridden or even visited Sprinkles in years.

Damn, I should stop neglecting Sprinkles, I thought.

"I have to talk to your aunts about that," Aunt Carly said off-handedly. She stood back to admire her work. "You're perfect."

"I don't look anything like you, or Aunt Cara or Aunt Chris, so I'm not perfect."

"Not yet, but soon," she promised. And after she took inventory of my look, I was out the door and on my way to the party.

"OMG! Care Bear, you made it!" Tonya announced as I walked through her front door. "And you look absolutely stunning!" She said in shock.

"Carrie will do just fine." I didn't want to be called Care Bear by anyone other than Noah.

She mindlessly nodded. She wasn't listening to me.

Aunt Carly could make a pit bull look like a beauty queen, but Tonya was right. Before I left, Aunt Carly made me stand in front of the full-length mirror in my bedroom, the same mirror I made a habit of avoiding. There was no need for me to look at myself; I knew I looked horrible; I didn't need visual confirmation. However, tonight I looked like a Greek goddess. She gave me flat gold sandals with braided straps that wrapped up my legs to wear. My makeup was minimal.

"You only need a lot of makeup only when you are old," Aunt Carly justified before I left. "When you are young, you don't need so much. Only whores wear excessive makeup. Now go and have fun." She always gave sound fashion and style advice, though most times I refused to listen.

"Thanks, Tonya. Nice place." After we exchanged a few more pleasantries, we stood in the hallway, silent. There was nothing else to talk about because we didn't know each other. She, just like everyone else there, didn't start liking me until I stood up to MJ. I would be all but forgotten by next week, if not sooner.

Finally Tonya said, "Hey go get a drink and make yourself at home." She ran into her living room to dance with her friends. A few of the other kids did speak to me, mainly because I stood at the front door, too scared to move. I felt like an alien observing some strange human ritual. Even though I was dressed the part, I didn't fit in. No matter how you look on the outside, on the inside you are who you are; I was still an outsider.

I noticed that Aunt Carly was right. These girls were dressed like whores, tramps, whatever. They had on miniskirts that should be illegal to wear outside. Some had on deep, low-cut blouses that exposed almost all of their breasts and their makeup was even worse. Even Tonya looked as if she was to go out on the corner to sell her body. I felt as if I had on a nun's garb rather than a cute, short bubble dress. I was overdressed.

The boys were dressed equally as horrible. My male peers looked as if they just rolled out of bed and came straight to the party. They looked greasy, dirty, and unkempt.

Why did I come here? As to further prove I had no business being at this party, I felt pressure on the back of my head.

"Why don't you come with me out back?" a familiar female voice said. It was Kathy Turner. She was a year older than me, and this was not her scene, either. I followed her like a lost puppy. Even though we were not friends, we did have something in common, not belonging to this crowd. She sat on the rail as I sat on the back patio swing.

"So", she started as she pulled out her cigarette, "I know why I am here, but why are you here?" She was just as surprised as everyone else that I actually came and so was I.

"Good question." I didn't feel threatened by Kathy; she was merely curious. "Can you believe I got invited?" *I can't.* I tried to smile, but it didn't feel like one.

"Really?" She took a long drag. Kathy was into the Goth scene. This picture perfect teen party was not her. "I heard about you and Melissa. Cool."

"Yeah, word spreads, fast." My stomach started doing flips again. I grabbed it.

"I never liked that pretty bitch anyway. Toby is afraid of that piece of shit, so she won't stand up to her. She is too afraid of not fitting in. I say, fuck it! Tell her to kiss your ass, but Toby has always been a kiss-ass." Kathy's dark lipstick was all over her cigarette. She noticed me staring at it. "Smoke?"

"No thanks. I didn't know that you and Toby were sisters." I really didn't know Toby. To be honest, I didn't really know Kathy. I knew of Kathy. I sure as hell didn't know Kathy had a sister in my grade. The only reason I knew of Kathy was due to her reputation. She gave the teachers a really hard time during her four years at BCHS.

"Yeah, I hope she gets over this *Leave it to Beaver* life crap. I had to come because Mom and Dad are so afraid she will be exposed to sex and alcohol. It's too late for that. Shit, I'm the one who gave Toby her first drink, hoping it would change her view of life, but it didn't. Now I'm here, in teenage hell. Which brings me to you; you a conformist now? You were so much cooler when you were on your loner vibe." Her dark polish was fading off her nails. *Aunt Carly would literally die if she saw that.*

"My aunt forced me to come, for the experience. My first and probably only party."

"Your aunt? I thought you guys were witches or some shit like that? I didn't know witches liked to party?"

My head was pounding. "No, demons, actually, and we are quite sociable," I said with a strained voice. I started to feel very ill.

"Cool." She wasn't even fazed or shocked at my revelation. She was either weird or just didn't care—maybe both. "Hey, man, you all right? Need something?" She asked. I was dying and she was worried about me maintaining my image.

"Yeah," I said, grabbing my head and bending over, "something to drink."

"I got you." Kathy disappeared. I sat on the porch swing feeling like death warmed up. If I died at this party, that would be the ultimate embarrassment, not that it would matter because I would be dead, but still embarrassing, nonetheless. I tried to find a corner to ball up in to pass out, but I couldn't. I was weak. I forgot how to stand, my legs gave out on me. I grabbed the side of the house for support.

I will never do this again," I thought as an affirmation. Parties were not for me, not if they made me feel like this.

"Whoa, someone had a lot to drink." I looked up. It was Matt Shaw. "Hey, Tonya told me you would be out here. Are you okay?"

"Never better," I mumbled.

"Ta da!" Kathy sang as she handed me a cup. "Drink up."

I took the cup and started drinking. I didn't think to ask what she brought me. "What is this?" I asked as I spit it out.

"Rum and Coke. You looked like you needed something heavy, but not too heavy." She pulled out another cigarette to smoke.

Then I threw up. "Oh, that is nice." Matt said as he retreated back into the house.

"Damn, girl, I thought you could handle it. It's not even a lot of alcohol." Kathy continued to smoke as she sat on the railing as if everything was fine.

Matt came back outside with reinforcements. I was a little relived. Kathy was a terrible caretaker. "What did you do to her, Kat?" Toby cried.

Kathy shrugged. "I thought she needed a buzz; hell, I do. This party is lame." She got down from the railing, picked up my drink, and gulped it down.

"Great! Just great," Tonya sneered. "She's totally wasted."

"What are you going to do?" Toby asked Tonya. "If her aunts find out…"

"I don't know!" Tonya yelled at Toby. "I strictly told her aunts that there would be no alcohol, and now her aunts are going to kill me." Tonya really started to lose it. "Toby, if anything happens to me, her aunts did it. I should have never invited her. Her aunts can erase your memory and make you drink pee and eat cats!"

This was just the type of rumor that people said about my family all the time. Maybe somewhere in that statement there was some truth. However, drinking pee and eating cats? That was just plain ridiculous.

"Relax," Kathy said very coolly. She looked down at me. "All she needs to do is sleep it off. Just put her in your bed and let her lie down for a while. She should be fine before the party is over. Amateurs." She picked up someone else's cup and started to drink it. Then she lit another cigarette. Kathy appeared to be a chain smoker and possibly an alcoholic.

"Matt, help me get her upstairs," Tonya ordered.

"What?" Matt asked. He had no intention of getting involved any further, which was why he retrieved Tonya.

"Just do it!" Tonya snapped.

"And what happens when she wakes up? How will we get her home?" Toby asked.

I was on the verge of passing out when Tonya answered, "Call Noah. He will come for her. Let him deal with it."

Yes! I prayed he would. Toby led the three of us into the house. The next thing I knew, I was lying on a twin bed with a flowery bedspread on it. I didn't know how long it had been since I passed out or how I got up there. I felt like someone was burning me alive, I was so hot. I tried to sit up, but couldn't.

"Hey, take it easy," a male's voice ordered. It was too dark to see who was speaking.

"Noah?" I whispered because speaking louder than a whisper would have caused my head to explode.

"No, it's me, Matt."

Matt, not whom I was expecting, but I was glad I wasn't alone. And where exactly was I? "Matt, what--how?"

"I came in and you were already done. I mean done! How did you get so wasted so fast?"

"I'm not wasted," I breathed. I wasn't. The only thing I had to drink was a sip from the cup that Kathy gave me. I was, however, sick and wanted to die.

"Man, Tonya and I had to carry you upstairs. I decided to stay in case you woke up. I'm missing the party, though."

"Thanks for staying, and I'm sorry you are missing the party." I grabbed my head, trying to stop my brain from leaping out. "How long have I been out?"

"Not long."

Matt came over from the corner of the room and sat on the bed beside me. I sat straight up. Thinking on his feet, Matt grabbed the waste basket and pushed it to my face.

After I finished throwing up, I mouthed a weak thanks. I was so embarrassed. It was one thing to be sick, but I threw up in front of a boy, this popular boy, twice. I was never going to another party in my life! All the preparation Aunt Carly put in to get me ready, my beautiful hair, my pretty dress, all ruined. I began to sob.

As if he knew what I was thinking, Matt soothed me. "It's okay. Carrie, you still look very pretty. In fact, I've never seen you dressed like this before. I like it." He smiled.

Matt proved in the minutes we were alone that he wasn't a complete jerk. I was surprised by his compassion and very thankful.

"Thanks." Matt pulled back a long strand of hair that escaped my braids and twisted it behind my ear. It was a very sensual thing for him to do and made me feel....awkward. I stared into his eyes and saw something that wasn't there before, something that led me to believe that he might be coming on to me.

"What?" I asked mainly to break his trance and kill the deafening silence.

He leaned in toward my face. I quickly turned away. He smiled and pulled my face back to face his. "You know I like you, right?" he asked in a way that made me feel very uncomfortable.

There was something in his voice that I never heard in a male's voice before. It was something I wished I heard in Noah's when he talked to me.

I just shook my head no. *No, I didn't know that you liked me! In fact, a couple of days ago you called me Sherrie in the library.* I thought of all that, but I settled for "I thought you were dating MJ."

He still had his hand on my face and leaned in again. I pulled away from him a second time. "No, that was just something to do."

Is that how all boys think? She was something to do? I didn't even like Melissa, but for someone to just belittle her like that was unsettling. "And me? Am I just something to do?"

"No, you would be a great conquest, a badge of honor."

Was that a compliment, to be a notch on his belt? I stood corrected. I'd been fooled by his display of compassion. He was a complete and total jerk. He had no redeeming qualities. He guided me with the weight of his body to lie back down. I followed, not because I wanted to, but because I felt I had no choice.

"Please, Matt, I don't want this, like this," I pleaded as he gently positioned himself on top of me.

I wasn't attracted Matt at all, but I felt if I wanted to get out of this situation without a confrontation, I needed to play up his ego. I was in no shape to have sex, even if I wanted to. I felt that my own body was turning against me and attacking me. My body was treating every organ like some foreign material that didn't belong there. Matt laid more securely on top of me, smelling like cheap beer and outdoors. "But you will," he said as licked my ear.

"Oh, God!" I squealed. "I'm about to throw up." He lifted up off of me. I just laid there, motionless. The thought of his tongue on me made me sick to my stomach. It was as if a snake's tongue touched me.

The sickness from that thought passed. He smiled and eased back on top of me. He undid his jeans. "This will be over in a few, so just relax and enjoy. You might like it." He grimaced. "In fact I know you will. They all do, eventually. Just ask MJ."

He was going to rape me. I shut my eyes really tight. I thought of my aunts with all my strength. I figured if this was going to happen and I wanted to stop it, given recent events, I knew my aunts could hear me. I started screaming my aunts' names in my head as if I was actually screaming aloud. What did I have to lose?

Aunt Carly! Aunt Cara! Aunt Chris! HELP! I screamed so loudly in my mind that I was certain I burst a blood vessel. He lifted my dress up. "Matt, no! DON'T!"

"You gay?" he asked in a very condescending way.

"NO!" I squeaked. Not that there was anything wrong with being gay, it was just not the lifestyle I had chosen. "It's just—I don't feel good; I told you," I whined. I was being truthful. I felt like shit.

"Don't worry, after this, you will feel much better." Then he kissed me on my neck with his chapped lips.

As I wept, I focused all my energy on my aunts. If I could hear them in my mind, then they could hear me in theirs.

Please, aunts! SEE ME! SAVE ME!

I closed my eyes and bit my lip. I started having hallucinations to escape the horror of what was actually happening. I focused really hard. In my mind I could see my aunts, all throughout the main house. *Aunt Carly was in her bedroom in the mirror, of course, playing with her hair. Aunt Cara was downstairs in her study, playing her violin, something she did when she needed to think; Aunt Chris was with some man named Peter in the doorway of the main house, having a deep conversation about love. In my mind, when I sent out my SOS, they all stopped when they heard my mental cry. Aunt Carly glided down the stairs into the study where Aunt Cara and Aunt Chris were already waiting. Aunt Cara placed her hand over her mouth,*

"No!" Aunt Cara whispered.

"That Matthew Shaw is a dead man!" Aunt Chris slammed her fist into the wall, punching a hole through it.

"CHRISTINE!" Aunt Carly yelled. "We are going to save her. Was it really necessary for you to do that to the wall?"

"Carly, you knew she wasn't feeling good, and still you made her go!" Aunt Cara accused.

"I thought it was just party jitters," Aunt Carly said nonchalantly.

"Anything for dress up, right?" Aunt Cara snapped. "WAIT! How can we hear her? It's happening!" Aunt Cara announced, then she paused. "It's been happening? Why didn't either of you say something?"

"We couldn't be sure. It could have been a fluke! And neither did you, Cara," Aunt Carly snapped.

"She blocked you!" Aunt Cara was grew angrier.

"We can fight about this later, but right now, we need to get our Carrie." Aunt Chris called things back to order.

"Oh, believe me, we will. Let's go, now!" Aunt Cara growled.

I saw all of that in my mind, but in reality I was with Matthew Shaw. He was about to put his unprotected penis inside of me when I screamed as loud as I could. No one came to my rescue because no one could hear me over the loud music. He smiled and positioned himself so he could just ease inside me when—

"What the hell is going on?" Noah yelled as he charged into the room.

"Noah!" I screamed. "Thank God! Matt is—"

"Hey Noah, my man, I'm a little busy, here." Matt gestured at the two of us as if we were about to have consensual sex and not rape.

Noah looked hurt as he observed the scene. "I see. Tonya called me like fifty times back to back saying Carrie was sick, but I guess—"

"No, Noah, I am sick, and Matt is trying to take advantage of me." I pushed him. He looked at me as if I was crazy. "I told you no." I'd gotten braver since Noah walked in. "Get off of me!" I ordered with more authority and another shove.

Exasperated, Matt got up and mashed my face. "You're a tease." He spat and pulled his pants up. "Man, she is not worth it." Matt walked to the door.

As Matt passed Noah, Noah punched Matt in the middle of his face, knocking him back a step or two.

"Man, you hit me over this whore?" Matt managed to say as blood poured from his split lip. He held it and ran out of the room.

Noah shut the door. "Hey, are you okay?" he asked. I sat up and fixed my clothes.

I felt like a princess whose brave knight had come to defend her honor, but hitting a creep like Matt wasn't necessary. "Yeah. You didn't have to fight with your friend over me."

"What, that?" He smiled. "Oh, Matt is not my friend, and I've wanted to punch him for a while now." He sat on the bed beside me. "Holy shit! You've got on another dress!" He pulled the covers back to see my feet, to get the full effect. "Man, you are beautiful my Care Bear," he said in awe.

I threw up again. I just barely made it to the trash can that time. I was going to die from embarrassment if my illness didn't kill me first. Noah didn't say anything. He just held my head and pulled my loose hair back. "Thank you," I said, blushing.

"No problem. What are you doing here, anyway, Care Bear?" He asked, concerned.

"I wanted to see you, plus Aunt Carly made me come."

"I never go to these things. I can't stand Tonya." He laughed.

"Yeah, I know what you mean. I don't think I'll be coming back, if I ever get invited back." I paused. There was something I needed to tell him. "I wanted to say that I am sorry for the library thing—"

"Let's worry about that later. Let's get you well enough to take you home. The last thing we need is for your aunts to see you like this. I'm going to get you some water, okay?"

I nodded in agreement and crashed down on the lumpy mattress. "Carrie? Are you all right?" he asked as he brushed my hair back off my sweaty forehead.

"I don't know." I tried to explain, but I was breathless. "I just need to rest. My head—"

"Okay, don't strain yourself; I'll be right back." He brushed his cool hand across my face again, a welcomed relief, I might add. Then he kissed my forehead.

I was in heaven. I could have died right then and there. I just laid as still as I possibly could, afraid that I would ruin the moment.

I simply said, "Okay." He could have said that he was going to gut me like a fish, and I would have agreed. All I ever wanted was for Noah to be with me like this, minus the vomiting, sweating, fighting, and sexual assault. Noah got up very cautiously from the bed.

"Noah," I breathed.

"Yes?" He turned back to face me.

"Thanks, you are great…" I started to give this whole speech on how awesome he was, but my body was shutting down. I couldn't think or talk.

Before he left the room and before I slipped into unconsciousness, Noah said, "When you love someone, you try to be there for them."

I was sure I was dreaming. *Did he really say that? And what was taking Noah so long with that water?*

My aunts came in through the lone bedroom window. *I'm dreaming about my aunts? Great!*

"I mean, really," Aunt Carly stated, "one window? I don't care how old this house is, they need to remodel. I hate squeezing into tight spaces with you two, especially since Cara put on a couple of pounds. Don't think I haven't noticed. You'd wrinkle my dress with all your weight gain!"

Aunt Cara ignored Aunt Carly's rant and they both stood over me while Aunt Chris examined the room. "She's in transition,"

Aunt Cara said. Her voice was filled with urgency. "She needs to be moved, now."

"Nothing happened. Matt is pretty pissed that Noah stopped him," Aunt Chris confirmed.

"Yes, we all know that, Christine. We can hear Matt's thoughts, but thanks for speaking them aloud for no reason," Aunt Carly snapped. "One window?"

Aunt Cara picked me up in her arms.

"Look at her, all of my work, ruined." Aunt Carly sounded as though she were going to cry.

"Carly, you are really pissing me off, so shut the hell up!" Aunt Cara said, looking me over. "I don't think I know of a case of a human showing evidence of having a demon before they turned."

"I can't say that I have either but she is Celeste's daughter. No telling what she is capable of," Aunt Carly added.

"Noah is on his way back up. Matt is going to stop him and try to fight him, this will be our only chance to leave unnoticed," Aunt Chris said as she placed her ear to the bedroom door.

"I'm sorry, well no I'm not but explain why are you saying this aloud again? For Carrie's benefit? She's in no condition to understand!" Aunt Carly snapped again.

"Noah," I said faintly.

"She can talk?" Aunt Chris asked.

"The dead does speak," Aunt Carly observed.

"She's strong, just like Caleb was," Aunt Cara announced. "This is amazing. Esther will be pleased."

"She is indeed the one." Aunt Chris announced.

"If only her mother was pleased with her and with us," Aunt Carly said. "She should be pleased."

"We will not speak ill of our sister. In time she will return to us and she shall be pleased. And we will be happy to receive her," Aunt Chris said.

"Speak for yourself," Aunt Carly sneered.

I whispered, "Noah saved me. I survived the party." I broke up their conversation.

"Yes, now let's go home, you need your rest, baby. And when you wake up, you will be all better," Aunt Cara promised me.

"And when you wake up, you will be perfect just like I told you," Aunt Carly said.

"Perfect," I whispered.

"Just like I said." Aunt Carly smiled.

"Honestly, Carly, for an evil ass such as yourself, you are vain as hell," Aunt Chris berated Aunt Carly.

Aunt Carly just smiled. "Perfect, Carrie." She brushed my hair back off my face. "Oh my! She smells like alcohol and boys." She wrinkled her face in disgust and walked away from me.

"Let's go!" Aunt Cara ordered, still carrying me.

And then we flew out the window into the night, across the moonless sky to our farm.

That was the second most amazing dream I've ever had.

Nothing. I felt absolutely, positively nothing. Was I dead? No. I didn't think I was dead because I had feeling. However, all I could feel was nothing. Not only did I not feel anything, nothing special came to mind either.

Were my eyes open? No. They were still closed.

Move your head, wiggle your toes. Do something! Still nothing.

Okay, Carrie, get it together. Center yourself and get your mind together. Where are you?

Oh, shit! Where was I?

Panic flooded my mind. I wanted to cry but I couldn't. I tried to move my mouth. It felt tight, as if I had been punched in it.

Was I in a fight?

I don't remember.

I can't remember.

FOCUS.

Please, remember something, anything, I ordered myself. Then a tidal wave of memories, recent and past, paraded through my mind. It was as if I was trying to get an old TV to focus. I tried to clear my head of the static. None of my thoughts or the images was lucid, at first.

Whispers echoed in my head…

"Sorry, Sweetie," Aunt Chris started, "you have to come with us. Your mother simply isn't well enough to take care of you at this time; maybe after she gets it together, but not right now…"

"But no one in our family can escape it, not I, not Cara, Christine, not Carly, not their sons, not Caleb; I'm so sorry, but even you can't escape it…"

"No, far worse than a curse; a curse is easy. Curses can be lifted… this, what we are, we are DAMNED! Damned souls. I have done some awful things in my lifetime, but having CHILDREN…that was the worst I could have done. Making my children pay for my transgressions…TERRIBLE! I'm a terrible mother…"

"Evil?"

"So, that's the mystery? I've got a demon. I am one? And the demon killed all the males in our family?"

"Evil?"

"Yes, evil."

"This physical change happens when the demon takes over…"

"This physical change happens when the demon takes over…"

"Demon takes over…"

"Demon takes over…."

There it was, the blood tree. It waved at me. Blood dripped from its branches. The leaves were drenched in it. I could smell the blood as I walked toward the tree. There was a pool of blood under it. I stepped in it and reached for one of its branches. A branch grabbed me, and I was sucked into the blood. I almost drowned.

I was transported to another place, in another time in the past. I saw Mother and Aunt Carly talking. They were dressed funny. My aunt wore a peasant dress and surprisingly looked like an actually peasant. She had to have been poor. Her face and hands were filthy. A look I have never seen from Aunt Carly before.

On the other hand, Mother looked like a million bucks. Actually she was dressed as though she didn't belong in my aunt's presence and vice versa. Aunt Carly sat in a rocking chair in a meager cottage holding a baby girl. It was the same baby from my previous vision.

"Honestly, your name is Celestial?" Aunt Carly asked Mother. "What a strange name."

"I am a foreigner, and we do have names different from those in the Americas," Mother answered with a smirk.

"Yes, but your name is odd," Aunt Carly countered.

A man walked in and kissed my aunt, then kissed the baby. "I'm sorry, please excuse my wife. She isn't used to meeting people of culture."

"Michael." My aunt was embarrassed. Then she addressed Mother. "If I offended you, I do apologize. Michael normally doesn't bring foreign women home from work." My aunt jabbed.

Aunt Carly's husband, Michael, sat in a chair across from my mother, beside his wife. He responded to my aunt's snide remark, "I explained to my wife that the big bosses were coming to visit the port to make sure everything was in order. My wife just couldn't, or wouldn't, believe that a woman owned the port."

Aunt Carly smiled. "It's just not common here. A woman's place is in the home." My aunt cooed at her baby.

Mother sat on a rotting sofa that was once white but was now old and discolored. She looked very uncomfortable.

"My father passed away, and his businesses became my mother's. She is a very smart woman. I wish you could have met her today. She would adore you," Mother said in a soft voice. "She does send her regards. She was unable to make the business trip. She's ill."

"My apologies," my aunt responded.

"I'll go; clearly I have intruded. Good day." Mother got up to go, relieved.

"No, please stay," my aunt's husband insisted.

"I have other employees to visit. Thank you, Michael, for opening your cozy little home to me. And please take good care of your wife. I have a feeling," Mother said, smiling, "that she could change the world one day." Then she walked out of the modest house and into the open air.

"She is not the one!" Mother suddenly snapped, talking to herself as she walked swiftly. "First off, she is too old. Secondly, she has children. Are you sure she is the one we are looking for? I don't think she can help us. I will look for others. Esther, please don't make me go back there. They're poor. She can't help us build an army and she can't bring you back."

I followed Mother as she talked to herself. She said the name Esther as if she was talking to someone by that name. *Is she using her mental powers? Who is Esther?* I wondered. She walked into another modest building that looked vaguely familiar. *The main house?* I wasn't sure. I followed her into a bedroom. Aunt Carly was sitting on the bed tending to a boy who I could only assume was one of her sons.

Aunt Cara was standing over her when Mother walked in dressed differently from when she was in my aunt's impoverished home. I could tell that it was a later period than before. Aunt

Carly was dressed more like I was used to seeing her with every hair in place.

"Is he dead yet?" Mother asked casually. Her demeanor reminded me of Aunt Carly.

"Celeste!" Aunt Cara was appalled.

"What? I don't see what all the fuss is about. She knew he was going to die sooner or later," Mother snapped.

Aunt Cara was disappointed in Mother. "You know how sensitive she is. She feels deeply."

Mother barked, "She is a demon. We don't feel."

"No, you don't feel. We do. We don't have your parents. We still can connect with our human side," Aunt Cara added.

"All the more reason I can't relate." Mother rolled her eyes. "Feelings are weaknesses."

Aunt Carly cried out, "Are you talking about me? I can still hear, you know, thoughts and all."

"No, but if you are curious about how I feel, we can clear the air now," Mother said. "I think you are pathetic, and I don't understand why you are Esther's favorite pet. You're not worth me talking about. You're not even worth my thoughts."

"Celeste!" Aunt Cara said, aghast.

Mother walked over to the dying boy, who was screaming and crying. "I can take away this pain, Caine, if you trust me," she purred.

"Don't you dare!" Aunt Carly shouted. Her eyes turned black.

"Fine," Mother huffed. "I thought maybe you would want this to be over. He's been dying for two weeks. It is starting to get bo-o-ring," she sang.

"You heartless bitch!" Aunt Carly stood up ready to fight.

"Exactly. That's what I am, and what you should be. I can't see why Esther thinks you are so fucking awesome." Mother laughed. "You are a joke."

"You have always been jealous of my relationship with Esther!" Aunt Carly retorted.

"Let's calm down." Aunt Cara broke up the confrontation. "Caine needs a relaxing environment right now."

Mother snorted. "A relaxing environment, to die? Funny. You two need to go on the road with your comedy act. I need a drink in order to handle this death environment." Mother turned away, then added, "I haven't had one in a hundred years. I guess I am a bit bitchy."

Aunt Carly said, "I'll bury my son. I don't need anyone's help, especially yours, Celeste. So don't worry, I'll do it myself."

"Awww, I'm so …" Mother started to laugh. "I can't even lie." She giggled again. "Good. You and your human sister have fun with that," Mother called as she walked out of the room.

I woke up.

"Demon!" I jumped up. I tried to focus my eyes; everything was fuzzy. I realized I was sitting on my bed. So that meant I was in my room. My eyesight hadn't fully recovered, but I knew I was in my room. I recognized the color scheme. I was surrounded by blurs of purples, lavenders and blues. I rubbed my temples.

"I'm home," I said. My throat was scratchy. I guess I hadn't talked in a while. I cleared it. I rubbed my eyes. I needed them to work. I needed to see. *What was that smell?* "Flowers?" I smelled flowers. Why? "C'mon eyes! Work, damn it!" I shook my head.

Then as though someone flicked on the light switch, I was able to see my room.

I surveyed it. Nobody was in the room with me, that I could tell.

There were flowers in every possible place in my room, in the corners, on my desk, in my window, on my night stand. There were numerous cards displayed on my nightstand as well. One huge card taped to my wall proudly stated HAPPY 18th BIRTHDAY!

"It's my birthday?"

I needed to think.

135

Think!

What was the last thing I remembered?

I noticed I was wearing pink silk pajamas. I didn't recall putting on PJs. "This is something that Aunt Carly would want me to wear to bed."

My vain aunt must have dressed me for bed. I normally wore tee shirts and shorts, articles of clothing that she dreaded.

Wait...

Why did Aunt Carly dress me for bed? What happened to me that I couldn't get myself ready for bed? *Did I get drunk on my birthday?* That would explain the monster of a headache I was experiencing.

I grabbed my head and placed it in between my knees. I hated being disorientated.

My vision was still a little blurry but, I could make out the shape of the blood tree outside the window.

"That tree is one of a kind, the only one in existence. It has a story, and maybe you should try to figure out what it is before you condemn it."

I knew the story of the blood tree now. I knew why it bled. *It had a lot of blood on its hands.* The tree was where my cousins were buried, where Caleb was buried. They were dead. *Why wasn't I?*

I saw myself die. The tree showed me my death. Why am I not dead?

I was almost sure I was alive, well, about eighty-five percent sure. That was a good percentage of aliveness, so I wasn't too worried.

I still felt my body wasn't mine. My head was still pounding, and I had difficulty moving my own limbs. Thinking was nearly impossible.

"I hate you," Frances mouthed through her chalk-white lips, but I heard her.

"I know. But now at least now you have a reason."

"I remember!" My thoughts were becoming more cohesive. Frances's father was a horrible man who did horrible things to her. It was becoming clear. Wait… the library incident…was that the last thing that happened to me?

More memories came pouring in.

"You will be perfect," she said as she stood back to admire her work.

"I don't look anything like you, or Aunt Cara or Aunt Chris, so I'm not perfect."

"Not yet, but soon."

The party…I went to Tonya's party.

I actually went to a party? The thought of me going to a party, or even being invited to a party was a foreign concept.

Aunt Carly helped me get dressed?

Of course, that was the only logical choice due to the fact she was the only one of my aunts who was truly and utterly vain.

I got sick at the party. "That's right! I totally got sick." My throat was still sore. My voice was about three octaves lower than usual. I still had a tickle in my throat. "Noah came to get me from the party. OMG! He kissed me!" I grabbed my mouth, which was also sore. "He kissed me." I plunged backward on my bed. I remembered Noah's lips touching my forehead, the sweetest thing anyone has ever done to me.

My memory was still fuzzy. I was missing some things, however, I still felt great about remembering what I could.

Why couldn't I remember?

I looked around my room. I had get-well cards as well as birthday cards. I picked up a random card from the night stand. It was from Toby and Kathy. It read GET WELL on the front. On the inside Toby wrote, "Please get better and call to let everyone know you're okay." Kathy wrote, "Dude, you totally rock for a demon!"

"Demon?" Was she serious or joking? I still couldn't remember.

Then my eyesight sharpened, instantly.

It was as if I was seeing in black and white before, now I was seeing in high definition. I saw all three hundred and seventy-eight imperfections in the paint job done to my room. I was able to see every brush stroke, every time the roller was placed on the wall, and every time it rolled off. I was also able to conclude that Aunt Carly did not paint my room. It was a hack job.

I looked at my desk and saw that the wood was from a very old tree from on the farm land near the stables.

It smelled the same and… how on earth could I see and know those things? I jumped off the bed to, I don't know, find my aunts, get Noah, something. I felt the need to tell someone, about my new gift of sight. However, I found myself in the most peculiar position. I was on the ceiling.

"Holy shit! Am I still dreaming?"

This had to be a dream. I looked down; and there was my bed, shoes, and the wooden floor.

"This is so fucking weird!"

How do I get down? How did I get up here in the first place? I wondered what would happen if I let go? I would fall on the bed, right?

My feet and hands were touching the ceiling in an attempt to grab it. I slowly removed one foot from the ceiling.

Nothing. I was still in the air.

Okay…

I removed my other foot from the ceiling. So now my feet were hanging. My hands and my head were still touching the ceiling. I took one hand down and placed it by my side and then I slowly did the same thing with the other.

I was flying?

No. Not really flying, but levitating. So now I was really in a pickle. How do I stop floating?

"This is one wicked ass dream."

I was standing in midair, just floating.

I was still disoriented. My mind couldn't complete the picture. I needed to get a grip on what was going on. Was I still dreaming? I didn't have a clue.

"Maybe I should swim down to the bed?" My voice was now sexy and husky and my throat didn't tickle anymore. Okay… so I literally attempted to swim downward to my bed because I didn't know what else to do.

It was the weirdest experience ever. Well, swimming to my bed was no weirder than floating, but pretty high up there on the weird shit list. Amazingly, it worked! When I was within grabbing distance, I yanked fiercely at my sheets. I pulled myself onto the bed and hugged my mattress.

"What the hell?" I needed to gather my thoughts, which were scattered everywhere. My memory still wasn't functioning at a hundred percent. I thought about calling my aunts, but I didn't want them to think I was crazy because every second of this…*dream*, I was feeling more insane by the minute.

It is true, there is a crazy gene, and I am going crazy, just like Mother.

I eyed the door. There was about three feet between my door and my bed. From a strategic standpoint it might as well been a thousand feet, now that the possibility existed that I could get sucked up into the air by some invisible foe.

I had to pump myself up. "I'm going to make a run for it on the count of three." My adrenaline started pulsing through veins so fast that my skin tingled. I anchored my body on the edge of the bed. I had no idea where I was going, but I needed to get out of my room. "One…two… Aaaaaahhhhhhh!" I screamed as I jumped up and came face to face with myself in the mirror.

I stopped dead in my tracks. Well, dead in my floating tracks, because once again my feet never touched the floor.

I floated toward the mirror to inspect myself more thoroughly. I was sure that the young lady staring back at me in the mirror was me because she mimicked my movements exactly. My face was *my* face, but at the same time, it wasn't. My skin was no longer pale and dull. It was now vibrant and golden, like my aunts', the color of honey. My pimples and other imperfections, such as my scars and blemishes were gone. My skin was now flawless, taking on an instant glow.

My eyes, once hollow and blank, were now green as emeralds, like my aunts' and Mother's. My lips were no longer thin they were now full and pink. And my thinning, shedding hair was longer than it had ever been in my life. My full, wavy, jet-black hair now fell to the middle of my back.

I was beautiful.

I was perfect.

"You will be perfect."

"I don't look anything like you, or Aunt Cara or Aunt Chris, so I'm not perfect."

"Not yet, but soon."

"Oh, wow!" I studied my new self in the mirror. Aunt Carly, how did you see that coming?

"This physical change happens when the demon takes over."

"No." I remembered what Mother said to me in my original crazy dream. "I'm dreaming, right?"

I had to be. My cell phone materialized in my hand. I remembered seeing it on the nightstand, but I didn't remember picking it up. There was only one person I wanted to call, that needed to call.

"Care Bear?"

"Noah?"

"Carrie, are you all right? Thank God, I was so worried. You haven't called and you just left the party without telling anyone. It's been weeks and I came by, I left messages--"

"Weeks?" *Weeks, it felt like I've been sleep for only hours.*

"Yeah, Carrie, how are you? You sound different. Are you okay?"

"What day is this?" I asked.

"Carrie, where are you? Why are you so confused? What do you mean what day is it?" Concern was pouring out of Noah. *Why was he so concerned? This was just a dream, right?*

I was still looking at my new beautiful self, floating in the mirror. "Noah, just tell me, what's today?" I asked, a little annoyed.

"I'm coming over. Your aunts can't keep me away forever."

"My aunts?" What in the hell was he talking about?

"Don't do anything and don't go anywhere," Noah ordered. "I'm on my way."

"Right." Still not knowing if I was dreaming or not, I floated downstairs. I was hungry all of a sudden. As I floated down the long staircase, my mind wondered.

Weeks? Had I really been out of it for weeks? When I entered the kitchen, I noticed that everything still looked the same; nothing felt out of place. I looked out of the window and saw that the leaves had changed colors and fallen off the trees near the main road. The blood tree, surprisingly, wasn't so creepy as it had been in the past.

I looked at the Hottest Hunk calendar that belonged to Aunt Carly. It was flipped to October Hunk, Baltimore Ravens football legend, Ray Lewis.

"October?" I whispered as I opened the stainless steel refrigerator and retrieved the gallon of milk. I went in search of a glass, but I dropped that idea because my throat was extremely dry. I drank straight from the gallon jug.

"Man, Aunt Carly is going to kill me." But once that ice cold milk touched my lips, there was no going back on my decision. I couldn't stop drinking it. It was as if I never drank anything before. Ever! The flavor of the two-percent milk danced on my tongue like never before; it made me desire more.

I urgently tilted my head to make sure I received every ounce of the delicious milk. Before I knew it, I drank an entire gallon of milk in mere seconds. My throat was still dry and my stomach was still growling. I was so hungry. I dropped the empty jug on the spotless ceramic tiled floor and flung open the refrigerator door in search of new treasures to consume.

Macaroni. There was an entire pan of macaroni. I didn't even think about it, I dug my hand deep into the pan. It was cold, but there was no time to heat it up. I clawed even deeper into the pan the second time.

I placed the container straight to my face and didn't even come up for air as I inhaled the starchy food. It was almost gone with the exception of the bits of macaroni that clung to the side of the bowl for mercy...no need to fight with them. I threw the canister on the floor. Pork chops, apple juice, apple sauce, peanut butter, vegetable soup, bread, cake—I ate everything that was in the fridge.

Butter. I downed three sticks of it. It was so good. I was still hungry, so hungry that I didn't think twice when I ate the ketchup, mustard, and hot peppers.

"Care Bear! Care Bear! Did someone break into your house?" Noah called from the door. I looked up from the fresh dill and pickle juice I was drinking. "What the hell!" Noah said as he slowly entered my house. He looked at the waste left I on the floor. I was hunched over eating raw shrimp I found in the back of the ice box. "Carrie, what the hell?" He circled around me and leaned in front of my face. "Carrie, is that...you?"

"Of course it is." I managed to say as I cracked open four raw eggs and drank them. *Oooh, ice, yum!* I munched on the ice as if it were potato chips. I could feel Noah's stares boring holes into my head, but I was too concerned with downing the frozen soft pretzels to care. Nothing satisfied my hunger.

"I know this is weird, but I am so hungry." That was the only explanation I could offer as I leaned into the freezer.

Noah looked at me as if he was in some trance. "Carrie," he whispered, "you are beautiful." He pulled my hair gently. "I mean really, really beautiful, not like before. Your hair feels like silk." He was amazed. "But you are scaring the shit out of me."

I was annoyed. "What now?" I asked as I ate the bag of frozen mixed vegetables. My emotions were just as scattered as my thoughts.

He had a dreamy look in his eyes that he quickly shook off. "Carrie, what the hell is going on? You disappear from the party then no one hears from you for weeks, damn near two months, and now look at you; you're eating frozen veal. Don't eat that! Explain!"

"What's today?" I asked as I swallowed the veal whole before he could protest again.

"Carrie—"

"No, honestly Noah, I don't remember. My memory is messed up. I don't really remember the party or leaving—"

"Wait, you don't remember the party, at all?" That caught him off guard.

"No. Not really. Weird, right? And then today I woke up looking like...my aunts! I don't know what's going on. I just know that I am starving." After eating everything in the freezer, I moved on to the pantry.

"Oh, peaches." I didn't feel like floating to get the can opener out of the drawer by the sink, so I just crushed the can open with my bare hands and drank the peaches down.

"Holy shit! Carrie, how did you do that? Are you on steroids? This is unbe-fucking-lievable." He stumbled backward into the kitchen door. His face was pale.

I cracked another can open using only my bare hands. "What?" My hunger wasn't allowing me to actively engage in our conversation.

"Carrie, you are really scaring me." He grabbed the counter close to the door. His breathing became more deliberate. I lightly lifted up off the floor and floated. Noah gagged.

"Well, Carrie, I see you're up." Aunt Chris walked in on the chaos in the kitchen. She looked unsurprised by my new state of being or by the mess I made.

"Aunt Chris." I was having difficulty getting my feet planted on the floor.

"Concentrate really hard on making contact with the floor," she instructed me as she walked over to Noah, who by this time, regained his composure and was ready to bolt out of the door. She stared at him, and after a few seconds he passed out. He hit the floor with a loud thud.

"Noah!" I floated at his side.

"He's fine. I just convinced him this is a dream, that's all. We don't need him telling people that you are the devil."

He lay in my arms, lifeless. "Close enough," I growled.

"Not even close." She looked around the kitchen to survey the damage. "I see you ate everything except the corn flour."

"There's flour?" I placed Noah back on the floor, went to the pantry, and dumped the five-pound bag of flour into my mouth. "Why am I so hungry? I feel like I have never eaten anything in my life."

"In a way, you haven't." Aunt Chris put down her bags, walked over to Noah, and picked him up.

"Where are you taking him?" I growled. Anger and rage exploded out of me. At that moment I could have killed my aunt if she was about to hurt Noah.

"Upstairs. We are going to clean up this mess, and we need to talk about what has happened to you and what it all means." She was calm as if she were explaining plans for dinner.

"I'll take him," I barked.

She waved me off. "Fine."

I flew, literally, upstairs to my room and laid Noah on my bed. He looked like an angel. He was indeed beautiful. I smelled him. He smelled like heaven. I was in love with my best friend. I almost locked him in my room. I wanted to protect him but, I also needed to know what happened to me, so I reluctantly left him sleeping in my room.

As I shut the door, I peeked at myself in the mirror. Something was off; I looked different, again.

How many times was I going to change today?

I examined my face and noticed that my eyes were no longer green, but black. As I scrutinized my facial features and my newly acquired pitch black eyes, they started to lighten back up. The more I focused on my eyes, the more they went from black to dark green, to a lighter green, and finally to the emerald green color of my aunts' eyes. I could now do the spooky changing eye color trick just as my crazy mother did.

I gathered my thoughts and floated back downstairs to find all three of my aunts sitting at the kitchen table in a remarkably clean kitchen.

"Okay, talk." I ordered.

"Perfect," Aunt Carly sang as I sat down at the table beside her.

Aunt Cara smiled. "What your mother told you was true. We are the descendants of angels and humans procreating, but there is more history than just that."

"Excuse me?" I asked. I couldn't believe she knew that. *How did she know that?*

"Let's be honest from now on, shall we?" Aunt Carly cut in. "We know she came to you in a dreamlike state and you saw us come and take her away, it was an illusion of her, at least. She is a little crafty devil." Aunt Carly chuckled at her joke.

Everyone ignored her inappropriate anecdote. I responded, "Right. That is just insane. I can't believe that was real." My dream was a dream, but real at the same time. "So, tell me what I need to know." I was officially one of them now, whether I wanted to be or not, I might as well know all of the truths.

Aunt Chris started. "Not all demons are created equal. When Lucifer and the others fell from the heavens, most of them followed him to hell. Some stayed on Earth, and those who stayed on Earth bore half-human offspring are known as The Originals. There are six original demons. They are Ezekiel, Raphael, Uriel, Azrael, Malik, and Esther."

"Are they still around?" I asked.

"Yes. Lucifer placed a curse on all of them for not following him," Aunt Cara answered. "They openly seek vengeance against him and vice versa."

Aunt Chris continued. "We are descendants of Esther, who is the only Original to take a female form."

"Is that why all the males in our family die?" I asked.

"Human genes are so funny and fickle," Aunt Cara said. "One slip here, an added chromosome there, but we really don't know if Esther's choosing to be a female had anything to do with it. It could simply be a genetic mutation that just passed down through the bloodline."

"Be truthful, Cara; no need to sugarcoat anything now," Aunt Carly interrupted. "Esther was beautiful, *is* beautiful. She is the most awesome creature anyone has seen ever, including Lucifer. He wanted her; he coveted her, but she refused him. Of course, being who he was, he wouldn't stand for that, so he came to her in the form of an incubus and poisoned her womb. Esther didn't find out that it was Lucifer until afterward. He still wanted her, and he confessed to her what he did. He offered to lift the curse if she would belong to him. She again refused. He captured her anyway and now she sits on the throne beside him, unwillingly.

"And here we all are, her children with poisoned wombs. I don't think it's so bad anymore, though. You get used to the pain." Aunt Carly smiled. "That wasn't hard, was it, Cara?"

Aunt Cara smiled, but I could tell there was a real threat behind it. I tried that mind reading trick with Aunt Cara. A mental wall instantly went up, I felt as if I had been hit by a boulder. She examined me closely, but then she quickly focused her attention back on Aunt Carly.

"In due time, Carly, everything will be over. Your number will be up," Aunt Cara warned. Aunt Carly could rub a pillow the wrong way. She was the equivalent of emotional sandpaper.

"Oh, Cara, I love it when you talk so lovingly to me," Aunt Carly taunted.

I refocused the conversation back to me. "Is it true? About Esther and the Originals?" I inquired.

"Yes," Aunt Chris said. "I'll give you The Book and you can see for yourself."

"The Book?" I questioned.

"It's a real account of what happened," Aunt Carly answered.

There was a lot to ingest, and there was still more that I needed to know. I sat there, trying to take all of it in. Suddenly I thought about Mother.

"And my mother?" *Where is she?* I wondered.

"What about her?" Aunt Chris asked as if they hadn't placed her in a mental hospital.

"I need to see her," I demanded.

"We would like to see her, too," Aunt Carly said. "Wouldn't we, Cara?"

Aunt Cara shot Aunt Carly a look that would make Medusa blush. "We don't know where she is," Aunt Cara responded.

"You said you took her away!" Anger coursed through my veins.

"Yes, we did, but then again, we didn't. It was an illusion. She created the dream we were in. She is more powerful than the three of us put together. She let us make it appear that we took her away. She never wanted you to see her like that, fighting with us.

"We knew that, so we took advantage of the situation," Aunt Cara explained.

Aunt Chris noticed me growing angrier and she admonished me, "Easy, Carrie. Breathe."

"Did her demon make her crazy?" I managed to get out once I calmed down. All of my aunts just looked at each other. I guess they wondered if they should tell me the truth or not. "Just tell me. I demanded.

"To be honest, your mother did struggle the most with what we are, but that came later," Aunt Chris finally answered.

"Yes," Aunt Carly chimed in, "because, to be quite honest, your mother was a bitch to me in my beginning."

Aunt Cara cut in before Aunt Carly could continue. "She agreed to the hospitalization to protect you. She could have left at any time."

"So why didn't she? Why didn't she try to get me?" I asked like a pathetic lost little girl looking for a mother who didn't want her.

Aunt Cara soothed me. "It's complicated. I'm sure she's fine and will return when she is ready."

I decided to accept that answer for now.

I glanced out the window and noticed the blood tree. "So tell me the story of the tree."

All three of them looked out the window then back at me, and finally at each other. I knew they were having a conversation that they didn't want me to hear. Aunt Chris spoke, "I think you know at least part of the story."

Part of the story? So there was more.

I still wanted them to tell me.

I wanted them to tell me that their dead sons were buried out there. I wanted them to tell me the reason why the tree bled. I wanted them to tell me that the tree was born of evil. I wanted them to tell me that it was a part of them, and a part of me. But I knew my aunts, and they weren't going to tell me anything.

"So what do we do, exactly? Do we eat humans or something?" Those stupid classmates of mine weren't so stupid after all. I should have just believed the rumors and asked my peers about my family; they obviously knew more than I did.

"Oh, no!" Aunt Carly laughed. "That's Malik's descendants' claim. They are Blood Drinkers."

"Vampires?" I asked.

So vampires were real. That wasn't so unbelievable, given my situation. I was a demon, so anything at this point was possible. I looked at Aunt Chris and asked, "So what do we do?"

"We are demons and do demonic things," Aunt Chris said. "Our purpose is to make mankind sin, tear them away from God, and attain power in the process. That is why we are. "

"And the other demon descendants? Do all demons serve the same purpose?" I asked.

Aunt Carly weighed in. "They want the same thing. We all want the same thing. We, meaning us, go about our evil in a different way. We have strong mental capabilities."

"We are the influencers," Aunt Cara stated. "And we are telepathic. It's our most effective and powerful weapon." *I can talk to you just by using my mind.* She stared blankly into my face without moving her lips.

I heard you before when I was just a human. I could hear you sometimes talking to each other. I thought I was crazy, I answered back using my new gift.

"Yes, we know," Aunt Chris said. "And no, you weren't going crazy."

"We don't know how you were able to hear us. Humans can't hear us unless we want them to," Aunt Carly added.

"It's unheard of for our telepathic ability to manifest when we are still just human and the demon hasn't awakened," Aunt Cara offered.

"It's unique," Aunt Carly concluded. "You are unique, Carrie." That was a sincere compliment I received from Aunt Carly and I welcomed it.

Aunt Chris smiled. "It might have something to do with your mother's abilities that she must have passed down. As I said, she is a very strong demon, one of the strongest of our kind, possibly the strongest on earth."

As I sat there, all three of my aunts looked at me as though I was some sort of science experiment.

I asked, "So, Aunt Chris, you can knock people out?"

She twisted her lips wryly. "Yes and no. I gave Noah a blast of mental energy that knocked him out. I can do what your mother does only she is much stronger. I tried to convince Noah he was asleep and dreaming when he saw you flying. I'm not sure how much he will believe. When he wakes up, you have to make sure that he believes it was all a dream, Carrie. Only you can make him believe."

"Noah is upstairs?" Aunt Cara asked.

Aunt Chris nodded her head. "When I came home, Carrie had emptied the fridge and was floating around the house. Noah was about to have a heart attack —"

"Noah is upstairs and I didn't have time to PAINT!" Aunt Carly screamed as she floated upstairs. "Great! Just great!" In Aunt Carly's mind, if one thing in the house was not up to her standards, the whole house was a mess.

"Yeah, about the buoyancy?" I asked.

"It's only natural for us to fly. So if you want to walk, you have to really concentrate on placing your feet on the ground and keeping them there. After a while, it becomes a habit," Aunt Cara explained.

"So, do we do spells?" I asked.

"There is no such thing as magic," Aunt Chris explained. "When we encounter a sinful human, we can't resist them or them us. It's as if we become their conscience. We speak to them in their thoughts and we can hear their thoughts, at least their evil ones."

I wondered, since Noah was human, why hadn't I heard him? "Well, I've been around Noah all day and—"

"Unlike most humans, Noah has a genuinely true heart. Christine has been trying to influence him for years," Aunt Cara said, but soon regretted after she saw my reaction.

"Calm down, Carrie," Aunt Chris calmly cooed. "Rage is easy for us to feel, isn't it? Look at your reflection in the fridge."

"How dare you?" I roared. I was ready to rip Aunt Chris's head off. I floated in the air and caught a glimpse of myself. My eyes were black as onyx. "How?"

"When our demon takes over, our eyes are empty because we are soulless. Be very careful when you are around humans, and make sure you don't allow yourself to get excited—whether it's a sin, Noah, or whatever gets you worked up—because there is no way to disguise or explain that reaction," Aunt Chris explained.

I eased back down in the chair and sat very still. I thought long and hard about not killing my aunt.

"Better?" Aunt Cara asked.

"Just barely," I breathed.

"Why don't you get dressed before Noah wakes up? You have a lot of explaining to do," Aunt Chris encouraged. "We have an eternity to talk about this."

"Eternity?" I questioned.

"Yes, we are immortals." Aunt Cara smiled as she opened the kitchen drapes to let some sunlight in.

At eighteen, most teens really don't think about death unless they are very depressed or they have seen a lot of it. I never thought about dying, but to live forever never crossed my mind, either.

Immortality…was that something to want, to never die? Was that natural? It was understood that we lived to die. Everyone else that I knew would eventually die, except me, my mother, and my aunts. Did I want that? *Probably not.*

"How old are you?" I wasn't really asking anyone in particular.

Aunt Cara answered, "I'm not sure. I was born to a poor family, before Jesus but after the flood."

"Jesus? As in Jesus Christ?" I quizzed.

"Yes, do you know another one?" she asked earnestly. "He was a rather decent man."

Sickness washed over me. Naturally I was taken aback by this. I knew that they were old, but I wasn't expecting centuries old, or even millennia old. "So being immortal stops the aging process? I will always look like this?" I asked.

"Part of our power is in our beauty and youth, well, at least looking youthful," Aunt Cara said. "But this is the face you will have for the rest of your existence."

I was not sure how I felt about that. To never change, was that something to want?

"And you, Aunt Chris, how old are you?"

She got up from her seat and stood above me. "I'm the baby in the family. I was born to a second generation freed family."

"You mean slavery?"

"I was born around the time of Reconstruction." Aunt Chris gently pushed me toward the staircase.

"Do we work for…?" I wasn't quite sure how to ask, but I needed to know if I came downstairs one day would I find Satan sitting at the table, eating popcorn. I wanted to be a little prepared.

She laughed. "We answer to no one, Carrie. We are here and *he* is down there. He never leaves his throne; he's very vain. Though I think Carly may have him beat in that department." She giggled, "There is a governing body of demons, if you will."

My eyes asked for her to continue. "Master Demons, very powerful demons that tend to stick together because they are children of the Originals, second generation demons. They feel very entitled, much in the way spoiled, wealthy children feel because they are born into privilege."

"What do they do?" I asked.

"What all rulers do, exercise their will, using their power over everyone."

"So you don't cross them?"

"You can, if you like trouble." She smiled.

"So how many generations are we removed from Esther?"

"Go tend to Noah. We can talk later. We have many lifetimes to talk." She floated back into the kitchen. I imagined the only reason they bothered to walk around the farmland was for my benefit. There was no need to continue that façade anymore.

I flew upstairs to my bedroom. Noah was still sleeping. I sat on my small bed and watched him. It was the most peace I felt all day. I looked outside my bedroom door into the hallway. Aunt Carly painted the hallway an apple green color.

"I love it, don't you?" Aunt Carly asked as she stepped into my doorway, talking about her paint job, of course. She painted the entire hallway while wearing a black satin dress and somehow managed to not get a single drop of paint on her. She looked amazing, not a hair out of place.

"Yes, it's beautiful," I answered.

"You should wear the blue and black short sleeve baby doll dress with the black tights and platforms that I picked out. Noah will love it."

"Thanks."

"Oh, and Carrie, as a courtesy, no more fishing around in our heads and we will do the same."

I wanted to say something in my defense, but I agreed, "Okay."

"Good, because if you continue to think the way that you are thinking, I might just have to kill you. I don't want to, but I will. It would be more fun just to torture for an eternity instead. Now that I think about it, killing you sounds equally as fun. So it's a tie, totally up to you how we proceed. I'm good either way." She threatened me, but she sounded so sweet. She was creepy when she talked like that.

"What?" What was I thinking about that had my aunt upset? I had so many things on my mind, and yet I managed to stay focused on all of it without being overwhelmed: demons, immortality, good and bad, God, my soul, Mother, Caleb, sickness, Noah, death, beauty, sin, school, anger…

I was angry. It was a minute rage that was building in the very back of mind. I focused on it, as if it was calling my name. I was mad that this happened to me, mad at my aunts for taking Mother away from me, mad because I wanted Mother. I was enraged. I looked at Aunt Carly as she stood in my doorway. I could actually kill her. My eyes must have been giving me away because Aunt Carly growled, and her eyes blackened.

"Careful, now, young demon. You need me. More than you realize. I saved your pathetic life once before. I might not be so nice this time around."

I slowed my breathing in order to calm down. Aunt Chris was right; rage was easy to feel. I closed my eyes and counted to a thousand, which was about the equivalent of counting to ten.

She continued. "I know you better than you know yourself." She came into my room and was in front of me before I could blink. She smelled me. "Tasty. Sin is the sweetest smell in the world, isn't it?" Her eyes were beginning to turn back to green. "You could never kill me, even if you wanted to."

"How can you kill a demon?" I dared to ask.

"Like I would tell you. Oh, Carrie, this is going to be so fun." She smiled devilishly. "Once you go into someone's mind and play with it...their memories that is... like Christine just did to your Noah, they have problems remembering other stuff, too."

I tried to look as though this conversation didn't bother me. I tried to think of peaceful things, calming things, like Noah kissing me, Noah doing other things with me. She continued, "There is no exact science to it. You try to focus your energy on the one thing you want the person to forget and then, oops! You hit another memory, a kiss, a party..." Her eyes grew dark again. I sat on the edge of my bed, gripping the hell out of it. "How is your memory, Carrie?"

"Fine." I strained.

"Really?" She chuckled. "I'm glad to hear it. You know, in the past you had a memory problem. You were five, and you just simply forgot, a lot. I suggested to Celeste that she take you to the doctor, but she refused. Mother knows best. Do you remember? Of course you don't." She continued to rant. "Maybe you should talk to the tree outside. It has a lot to say, I hear." She smiled and glided back to my doorway. "Noah will be up in twenty minutes, so you might want to bathe and get dressed. We wouldn't want him to see you in your night clothes. My, what the neighbors would think!" she called over her shoulder as she exited.

Why did she hate me so much? I looked out the window at the blood tree. I remembered that she hated Mother. I could literally see my Aunt Carly and Mother arguing over Caine.

I got dressed in one of the many rooms that the main house had to offer. I did put on the ensemble that Aunt Carly suggested, and I did look great in it. Along with my face, my body also received an upgrade too. I went from a 34 B to a 34 D. My waist was always small, but now I had a perfectly firm behind, something I always wanted. I went from being an emaciated size two to a curvy size six. Though my dress wasn't clingy, it did show off my new body. I let my hair hang loose, remembering how Noah ran his fingers through it, hoping he would do it again. I sat on the very end of my bed. Actually, my backside was off the bed with my new flying capabilities. I floated and watched Noah as he slept. It was very easy to float. It was second nature.

I wondered what I should say to him when he woke up. I took a deep breath and inhaled the paint smell from the hall. I flew to the hallway and retrieved a paint brush and lightly dabbed paint on his clothes. He came to help me paint. *Noah, we had a great day together painting. All day, we painted.* I focused really hard on that thought.

Will he believe me? I asked my aunts.

Make him. You have a very strong demon; you can do it. Aunt Cara encouraged.

You can always just make him jump out of the window, Aunt Carly said quite matter-of-factly.

Why would you say that? Aunt Cara asked.

Yes, why would you say that? I wondered. *Never mind, he is waking up now.*

"Hey," I cooed as Noah lifted his head off the pillow. I positioned myself so that I was fully sitting on the bed. "How was your nap?" I leaned toward him. He smelled so good.

"Damn, I don't even remember going to sleep." His eyes still hadn't focused yet. "How long was I out?"

"A couple of hours," I said without thinking.

"What time is it?" he asked. His voice was still groggy.

"Like five. Don't worry, my Aunt Chris called your mother and told her we were painting and you got sleepy and took a nap. I must admit, she wasn't too keen about you sleeping here, but she wants you home before ten. School tomorrow," I informed him.

"Yeah," he croaked. "Man, I must have really been tired; I don't even remember painting." Then he looked at me, I mean really looked at me, as if he were seeing me for the first time. "Carrie?"

"Yes?" I said very slowly.

"You look…" He was at a loss for words. I could hear his thoughts. He lusted for me, and I was very pleased.

Easy, Carrie, Aunt Cara warned.

Why are you in my head? I asked Aunt Cara.

She responded, *Not yours, his; you shouldn't get excited,* she cautioned.

"Look weird? I know. Aunt Carly made me put on this dumb dress. I feel so stupid, especially after we've been painting all day." I ignored my aunt's warning.

"You don't look weird, Care Bear. You look different, but not weird." He swung his feet to the floor and fully sat up.

"Different, is that much better than weird?" I asked.

He struggled to find the right words, he wanted me to know that he thought I was beautiful without crossing any lines of our friendship, and I wanted him to just come out and tell me. "You look different in a good way, Care Bear, like Halle Berry different.

166

It's funny because in my dream, you kind of looked like this, too. Your eyes were black, though. It was creepy as shit! That was one crazy dream. You were like a demon or something." He scratched his head trying to remember. Yes, I heard the demon remark but I chose to ignore it. He called me beautiful and that trumped all other comments.

I couldn't stop the smile from creeping across my face. "You think I look like Halle Berry?" That was the ultimate compliment.

"Hey, Noah, are you hungry?" Aunt Cara came charging in.

"No, not really, Ms. Cara."

"I ordered some pizza for you kids, why don't you go and eat a slice, Noah. I'm sure you need the calories after painting all day. Carrie, can you help me in the hallway bath? I seem to have made a mess." Noah was about to wait for me, but Aunt Cara escorted him out of my room. "Noah, she'll be down in a few," she assured him.

Aunt Cara waited for Noah to leave the room. "Carrie," she admonished in a hushed voice, "you cannot get excited in front of Noah or any human for that matter. You don't know how to control yourself yet. Maybe this is too much temptation for you."

"Why does it matter if he or anyone else knows what we are?"

"It doesn't, at least not to me or the rest of your aunts. I just don't want to see you get hurt, Carrie. You're young, too young to understand now, but if you tell him or show something he is not ready to see, he will leave you. If he knows, he will tell the whole State of Maryland, not that I care, but I know you do. So you just need to calm down," she instructed. "You will have your time soon enough."

"What's wrong with my thoughts? Why can't I think of him like that, in a boyfriend type way?" I must admit, sex was something that I was afraid of as a human girl, but as this creature, it was something that I was all of a sudden greatly interested in.

"Our demons are very sexual. You haven't even scratched the surface of our sexuality," she mused as she sat on the bed with me. "If we have sex with humans, most of them don't survive the encounter."

I had a hard time processing what my aunt was saying. "He will…die, if we…"

"Almost certainly that will happen. It's too much for humans to handle. The ones that survive go mad. They are never the same afterward; trust me, I know. Everyone knows that you love Noah. Do you want to take that kind of risk with him?"

The person that I wanted the most I could never have because of what I was. I was heartbroken.

"Go, sit with Noah while he eats," she politely ordered.

I got up slowly and made a conscience effort to walk. "Aunt Cara is that what happened to your husband, Clark?" Clark died from an illness. Was he crazed from sleeping with my aunt?

My aunt was unprepared for my question. She almost turned white when I mentioned the name of her dead husband. She didn't know I was that informed. She just smiled and led me out of my room, and without responding. I guess I had my answer.

I Have a Choice

I stood at my bedroom window for a week. I looked at everything and nothing at the same time. I even managed to avoid looking at the blood tree. The visions that the blood tree shared with me still visited me from time to time and I was still haunted by them. Aunt Cara thought I was depressed. She was right.

I didn't eat, drink, or sleep. I didn't need to. Apparently because I was half human, I didn't need to eat as frequently as a normal human did. I remembered that fateful hospital visit with Mother.

"Ma, when was the last time you ate?"

"Thanksgiving."

"Ma, stop playing. That was almost nine months ago. You need to eat. And sleep… When was the last time you slept? You look tired."

"Can't really remember. I think it was almost a year ago."

At the time, I thought I was listening to the ramblings of a crazy woman. It turned out that Mother was perfectly sane. I wondered where she was and hoped she was safe and healthy. I still missed her.

"Knock, knock," Aunt Chris called from my opened bedroom door. I turned to acknowledge her. Then I immediately went back to watching the world outside my window.

"I got you something, The Book." She tossed The Book on my bed.

The Book explained our history and had all the answers to my questions about my new life. I wasn't sure if I wanted to know.

"Thanks." I said blankly.

"And a birthday present." Aunt Chris announced. That was unexpected. I never received a birthday present before at least that was not what my aunts called them. I would receive gifts and presents around my birthday and Christmas, but the gifts were never called birthday presents or Christmas presents. "Happy birthday, in more ways than one."

She tossed me a little gold box wrapped with a bow. I opened it. It was my second piece of jewelry, my first piece being Mother's Caleb locket. This was a very old, very expensive necklace that

171

looked appeared to be from another time. It was a very heavy silver necklace with a huge diamond hanging from it. My human neck would not have been able to support the weight, but my new neck held the necklace as if it was a feather.

"Thanks, Aunt Chris, this is absolutely beautiful," I said as I held the giant stone in my hand.

"It's from all of us, actually. Carly used to know a man who owned diamond mines in Africa. She has many of these flawless diamonds—" She stopped short of telling me her story. "I'll let her tell it. You know she loves the sound of her own voice," she said, smiling.

Does she even want me to have this? I asked mentally, too afraid to ask aloud. Things had been tense between Aunt Carly and me.

"Yes, of course. If nothing else, Carly wants everyone to be envious of us. Vanity is her favorite sin."

"Are you sure? She seems quite upset with me these days."

"Oh, yes," Aunt Chris agreed, "she is. She has been dreading the day your demon would wake ever since your birth."

"Why?"

"Simple. She is resentful. She has always been emulous of Celeste. Caleb lived the longest out of all our sons. We all thought he would actually survive the change. Carly was literally praying that he wouldn't. And then, of course, Celeste got pregnant with a girl, which meant that she would have you forever.

172

"Carly feels motherhood was robbed from her in more ways than one. She's not as superficial as you think. Actually she is, but she's also the most sensitive of all of us."

"She does hate me. I've seen it. The rivalry between her and my mother——"

"Has nothing to do with you," Aunt Chris interrupted. "I mean, it does, but you are not the root of it. Carly is just having a hard time right now, Carrie. That's all, and it will pass. Cara wants to know what kind of car you want."

"I'm getting a car?"

"Well, unless you want to walk everywhere. I'm sure it's lame to have your aunts drive you; quite honestly, I truly loathe doing it. And what was the point of taking driver's education as an elective in school if you didn't plan to drive?" she asked.

"I definitely want a car! Any will do!" I couldn't hide my excitement. Surely my eyes were giving me away.

She replied, "Great. I'm glad your spirits have been lifted, even if it only temporarily. Carly also got you a new wardrobe. She's hoping you will be more fashionable now because demons can be very vain. Carly, however, is the exception, not the rule."

"That sounds about right." I said thinking about Aunt Carly. She hated the way I dressed as a human.

"I'll leave you to your thoughts, Carrie."

She was about to leave, but there was something I wanted to ask her. "Aunt Chris,"—she stopped at the door—"were you married?" I was very curious how all my aunts were able to have offspring.

"Yes, once."

"What was his name?" I asked her.

"Samuel Quincy Davis." She sounded as if she were reading a grocery list, not saying the name of her husband. She turned around to face me.

"Did he die?"

"Yes," she replied, "all humans die eventually, Carrie. It's only natural," she answered, still with no emotion.

"No, I meant after you guys had children."

"Oh, that. My story is a little different, Carrie. Samuel didn't father any of my sons. Times were different back then. You didn't engage in sexual activity unless you were married."

"When I started seeing Samuel, he was a widower. His wife had died years before from some awful illness, and he was quite lonely. He was twice my age and was looking for a young wife to take care of him, and my family was looking for someone wealthy to take care of me.

"When I had Cole, my eldest son, I was working on my family's land that they received during Reconstruction. Samuel asked my father for my hand in marriage. Of course, my father agreed. One night an angel flew into my bedroom window, days before Samuel and I was to be married. He was beautiful in a way that I can't properly describe. He was bronze—more like golden—he emanated so much light that I thought someone would come to investigate, but no one came to inspect. His eyes were like fire and his hair was the color of snow. He wore only a loin cloth. He had a wing span of twenty feet.

"'Jesus?' I asked, because no worldly creature could possibly be so beautiful."

"'He wished. No, you may call me... whatever you like,' he responded.

"His voice was like music but there was something in his tone that made me afraid of him. There was a winged man in my bedroom, of course I was apprehensive. I was cowering under my covers. 'I do not wish to harm you; if that were so, I would have done it already. Please tell me your name.' I was staring into his orange eyes. There was a real sense of evil in them. I closed my eyes and prayed, silently. He must have noticed my horror, and he quickly adjusted his eye color to an orange-brown, but this action only frightened me even more."

"'Christa. Christa Mary Freeman, ever...everyone calls me Mar...Mary, sir,' I stammered.

"'Mary, what a lovely name, and it suits you. You remind of someone I knew a long time ago by that name. She was really something herself. She had an amazing son, too. I'm sure you have heard of him. He is quite famous.' He tucked his wings behind his back. "

"'May I call you Mary, too? I wish us to be friends.' He asked me. I just nodded yes. He leaned toward me. I leaned away from him. 'Mary, please, I do wish to be your friend. We can be friends, can't we?' he asked as he sat on my bed. I nodded yes again very slowly. 'Good. Mary, as your friend, I wish to greet you properly, may I?'"

"I looked at him with dismay. He held my head in his hands. 'You have the most beautiful skin, and your eyes, such a lovely hazel. It is as if I could see straight through them to your soul; and my, what a beautiful soul I see.' I started to weep. I felt like I was in a noose with no escape. I could literally feel a tightening around my throat. 'No, no sobbing,' he ordered. 'I promise you, you will enjoy this…'"

"And then he raped me." She paused and took a breath. "It was unlike anything I have ever experienced. Every part of me, every inch of me was on fire. It was a fire that consumed me. I drowned in it. I was in so much physical pain and when I thought it was over, he raped me again." My aunt's face looked pained. She clenched her fist, she was still angry about her encounter. "Afterward I thought I was dead; I couldn't see anything for two days; my hearing was all but gone, not to mention the scars. My family thought I had gone mad; and not really knowing what to do, they covered it up. They told everyone that some sickness of the mind."

Aunt Chris played with the outlines of The Book as she told me her story.

"I'm so sorry, Aunt Chris." That was all I could offer her.

"That's why when Matthew Shaw tried to rape you, I was so angry. All I wanted was rip his heart out of his chest, something I didn't get to do when it happened to me," she snarled. This was the first time I'd seen my aunt get excited; it frightened me. Her wrath was something to be feared before I knew what she was and even more so now.

"I wasn't supposed to survive," she added. "He infiltrated my mind. Unlike a possession, he didn't have control of me, but was just in my head."

"Wait! So I wasn't dreaming? You actually came and got me from the party?"

"We heard you screaming at us. How could we not hear you is the more fitting question. You were possibly the strongest human I have ever encountered. You saw us, that night, didn't you?"

I nodded my head in agreement. "You were talking to a man, Aunt Cara was playing her violin, and Aunt Carly was in the mirror," I said in awe. It was as if I was home.

"As usual," she chuckled. "Yes, you saw us and we saw you. We flew there and brought you home. You were turning."

"So what happened? After you discovered you were pregnant?"

"I got married, consummated the marriage, and passed Cole off as Samuel's. It was easy to do at first, but then Cole started to physically change. He grew very pale and his hair lost its color and started to change from black to white; he looked a lot like his biological father."

She paused and looked out window. I peeped as well. I was sure she was looking at the blood tree. She continued. "My family disowned me when they saw my fair skinned child with white hair. Samuel vowed to leave me. I was labeled a whore by the community. I was alone. It was just me and my beautiful son. Then I changed. I remember being in so much pain that it was unbearable. I was hospitalized and Samuel said it was the demon trying to get out of me." She smiled as if she was remembering some intimate detail. "He was wrong. After a week of fevers and pain, I was a new creature, born again. I had never felt so alive. Then I heard my husband's thoughts for the first time—about how he was going to beat me, rape me, and hurt me as I had him."

Her eyes grew black from the memory. "He thought I cheated on him. I couldn't explain being rape by a creature that many believed didn't exist. I was experimenting with new power when I convinced Samuel to drink himself to death. It was actually rather easy. My first official act as a demon."

She smiled. "I was bored with the idea the instant he put the whiskey to his lips." She spoke so casually. I wondered, in time would I regard someone's demise with no compassion.

"I knew he would be dead within a month's time," she purred. "Before he died of alcohol poisoning and kidney failure, he did convince the people of the little southern neighborhood we lived in that my baby was a demon who needed to be killed because he had possessed me."

She took an exaggerated sniff of the air and laughed. "An angry mob came to take my son and burn him at the stake. I could hear their thoughts. Half of them hadn't even met Cole. He was two years old then, and yet they wanted to kill him, a child, an innocent! No matter, I got rid of them just as I did Samuel, by making them expose their dirty little shameful secrets in front of each other.

"It was beautiful, simply beautiful. In the mob was my future family: Cara, though she was Claudia in those days. Carly was Jane, and your mother was Sara.

"They heard me in the minds of the hapless humans and asked me to join them. Cole and I left with them. We traveled all over the world. Cara met Clark Coolidge and fell in love with him. She went with him to Maryland to start their family. Cole died when he turned fourteen. I came to Maryland to bury him on the farm.

"Carly's son Charles died soon after. I settled in and conceived Corey. Celeste left. She had enough of our lifestyle by then. No one knows where she was or what she was doing when she went off by herself all those years. Carly was vexed after the death of Charles, so she went off by herself soon after. It was just Corey and I with Cara and Clark. Clark grew ill. He was rejecting Cara's blood."

"Rejecting her what?" I was stunned.

"That's how Clark was able to survive having sex with Cara. She fed him her blood. He was still batshit crazy, however. Cara was just good at disguising it, but that's what she wanted; she wanted him. They both paid dearly for it. Clark hadn't been the same since Chase was conceived, and having Carl made him even more insane."

So there is a way to be physically intimate with a human male without killing him.

"What about the angel that raped you? Did you find out who he was or what he wanted?"

"He's a descendent of Raphael, a second generation demon. His name is Simon. He was able to see what I was going to become; that's why he chose me. I hear he is still around raping woman before they turn into their demons."

"Why?"

"Because that's what he does. It's his purpose. I heard he's trying to create his own race of super demons."

"There is a lot of chaos as far as domination over earth and human souls are concerned. If you're not on the other team, you're pretty much on your own. The creature that had his way with me is on his own personal quest to rule. So his plan is to create a new race of demons and lead them to overtake the world."

"Wow. That's deep."

"For many demons, that is their personal mission and all they live for. There are no loyalties, one way or the other."

"What about you and your sisters? You all are loyal to each other."

"I can't speak for the others, but when I joined our family, it was out of mere convenience. I came to be loyal years and years later. Cara has other plans for us and that's part of my reasoning for staying."

"What plans?"

"Too many to list."

"What about my mother?" I wanted to know about her more now than ever. "Tell me everything!"

"Well, I can't tell you everything. I didn't know her in her beginning."

"Please, Aunt Chris. Tell me what you do know," I begged.

"She struggled the most with our purpose. She was unlike Cara and Carly." She paused.

My eyes begged her to go on with her story.

"Celeste is very humane. She has connected with her human self a great deal more than any of us."

I jumped in. "She wasn't always like that." The blood tree showed me.

"No, she wasn't. But none of us are who we used to be. In the end, she wouldn't have chosen this life for herself or for you. She tried to find ways to cleanse herself."

"Cleanse herself? How?"

She hesitated. "Your mother didn't like the monster she had become, so she tried to deny herself. It's a very hard thing to do. I tried it once just to see how strong I was, but I didn't last a second. She had this peculiar notion that she could get rid of her demon, or at least deny it.

"She found a group of very powerful demons that had been able to refrain from or control that side of our nature, so after Caleb's death she went off on her own to find what she was in search of. She once shared that not being around us made it easier for her to cater to her human self. Then she met your father—"

"My father!" Up to this point, none of them, including my mother, had ever mentioned my father. I couldn't hide my excitement.

"I don't know much about him. She kept him away from us. Cara didn't approve of the relationship at all."

"Why?"

"Your mother was very successful fitting in with human society, and her ties to your father made it even easier for her to all but absolve herself."

"Was he…"

"I really didn't know much about him. All I knew was his name."

"What was it?"

"William Carrey."

"William what?"

"No, his name was William Carrey. His first name was William and his last name was Carrey. You are named for him."

I was speechless. "Is he dead?" I finally managed to ask.

She shrugged.

"And her hospitalization?"

"An arrangement, her life for yours." She lowered her eyes. "There were plans in motion, and your mother simply did not want to follow them. I do envy her resolve."

I remembered the whole scene when Mother was taken and shipped to the psych ward. I recalled Aunt Chris being openly hostile toward Mother, more so than any of my other aunts. "You were upset with her."

She nodded her head slowly. "I was, but then later I became bitter and angry with myself. I was originally angry with your mother. She had left us. We all had lives outside of our sisterhood, but none of us tried to just walk away. Even when Cara married Clark, she was very much a demon and very much an involved sister. Your mother was just about able to completely leave. I couldn't understand her decision, so because of my lack of understanding or not wanting to understand, I felt it was easier just to hate her. She had been so caring when I joined our family, I simply couldn't see why she would want to leave it.

"Then when it was time to punish her for choosing William and you over us, I was all too willing to help. But after you came here and started living with us, I got to know you" —she pointed to her head— "intimately. And I must say, for a human child, you were unique in your thinking."

She smiled a happier smile than before; her sparkling teeth never seemed more beautiful. "I could see why she would want to preserve your humanity. Then I wondered if I were her, if the roles were reversed, would I want the same thing for my daughter. I couldn't truly answer the question, but I did begin to sympathize, which, I might add, is rather hard for a demon to do, we being naturally selfish and all. Then, as you were beginning to change, as you were evolving, I could see much of her in you.

"I was feeling …"

"Shameful?"

She winced. "Please, it is taboo, to feel so human. Nonetheless, I was feeling an emotion that I didn't desire to feel." She made a gagging noise. "I was feeling a heap of emotions. It was a horrible experience, it felt so…"

"Human?"

"Please." She did appear to look as if she were getting sick just from the thought. "It was a lot, trust me" she added.

I went back to our original conversation. "And Corey, your son, what became of him?"

"I know that you know about Corey, Carrie. You read about him in that Baltimore publication."

"You are not supposed to be in my head as a courtesy, remember?" I chastised.

"Yes, and maybe if you spent more time with Sprinkles, you would know when I clean the stables."

Point one for Aunt Chris. "He's buried outside, isn't he? With all the others?"

She nodded her head yes. "What did you call it? A blood tree?" she asked.

"Yes. What is it?"

"A tree." she answered.

"A bleeding tree," I countered.

"It has a lot of blood on its hands," she answered.

"So I have heard."

Stalemate. No more information about the blood tree was to be given. I was going to find out; I was determined.

There was something else that I was curious about. "Aunt Chris, you were in pain when you changed?"

She nodded. "It was ten times worse than childbirth, though not so bad as my night with the angel."

I thought about what she said, why I didn't remember the pain. I simply had been passed out for weeks. "So why don't I remember the pain? Did one of you take away my memory of the transformation?"

"You have holes in your memory?" She seemed genuinely surprised.

I nodded yes. "And this is not the first time, is it? That I couldn't remember things?"

She thought about her answer, "Carrie, the experience is different for everyone. Not every transformation is exactly the same."

"And how long was I out?"

"Weeks. Three, to be exact. I have never seen anyone just go to sleep. Watching you turn was both very peaceful and scary at the same time."

"Why would it be scary?"

"Seeing my nephews and my sons go through it and recalling my own personal experience, changing is a horrible thing. I was scared because I thought that you died. A female has never died from her demon; and if it weren't for your chest movements, I think I would have called the EMTs, not that they could do much."

The blood tree showed me lying in bed with my aunts standing over me. I thought it meant that I was going to die, but it showed me my change. The tree showed me that I was going to be just like them, I misunderstood what the tree was trying to tell me. All this time I was scared of that creepy tree, but now I realized that it had been trying to show me things I needed to know. "Thank you, Aunt Chris, for sharing your story with me," I said.

"It's great for me to tell you everything and not need to keep secrets." Her face softened. "Carrie, we are what we are. I want you to be happy and do well."

"Happy and well as a demon?" Of course, they wanted me to be like them. When Mother refused, they punished her by sending her away and making everyone believe she was crazy.

"Happy and well, period. It doesn't matter to me what you choose, as long as you choose."

"I have a choice?" I asked. I thought this was my fate, that nothing could change my situation. My aunt was now telling me I did not have to choose this life.

"Don't we all?" she asked.

Time moved differently. A week felt more like a day, a month felt more like a week, and so on. Aunt Cara and Aunt Chris gave me my space because they thought I needed it; Aunt Carly gave me space because of my attire.

"Why are you walking around here in those gaudy rags?" Aunt Carly asked me.

"I'm not going anywhere, but if I do, I promise I will change." I wore a tank top and a pair of sweatpants.

I saw no need to prance around the main house in designer clothes like my aunts. Aunt Carly had on a skintight black long sleeved tea length dress.

"Your diamond pendant would look better accompanied by a dress."

I made a face that displayed my disgust.

"Fine then, jeans, a suitable t-shirt with a cardigan and those Chanel boots." She was disappointed.

"Aunt Carly, thanks for my diamond; it's the most beautiful thing I have ever owned."

She beamed. "Isn't it, though? Well, I simply couldn't have you walk around without any jewelry. You looked destitute." She was pleased that I loved my necklace. She floated away with a partial victory.

Our relationship was still shaky, but with the praise I just given her, we were on the road back to our normal banter.

It was November. I was only aware of that fact by hearing the thoughts of the humans outside. They were thinking terrible things about Thanksgiving dinner, what awful deeds their dad did, what size clothing some random aunt should wear, not the size she bought, obviously.

"People's minds are filthy," I concluded in my solitude. No Mother, no Noah, no one. I hadn't talked to Noah since my change because I was afraid that I would hurt him. I loved Noah and wanted to be with him, but I loved him enough to isolate myself from him.

I felt less threatened by the blood tree and wanted to ask it what happened between Mother and Aunt Carly that caused the rivalry—other than Mother being a bitch. The tree wanted to share insights with me, and I wanted to know everything.

I floated downstairs; no one was there. I heard Aunt Carly in her mirror; Aunt Chris was in the stables, and Aunt Cara was flipping pages of a book. Everyone was here, but they were giving me my space. *Good.*

Someone's thoughts were becoming more and more pronounced in my head. It was a human close to the farm.

She can help me. He needs to go! She knows all about him! The human thought.

I opened the door, I couldn't see anyone, but I could tell these thoughts were coming from of a female. Her thoughts were becoming increasingly vile as she became clearer in my mind.

I decided to ignore the human girl's thoughts.

HE MUST BE STOPPED! Her mind screamed about some awful man.

"Who is that?" Where was it coming from? This female voice was sounded vaguely familiar, but who was she? And why was I hearing her? Maybe the voice I was hearing was a memory I had forgotten.

Aunt Carly came crashing downstairs with the outfit she told me to wear. She threw the clothes at me. "You are about to have a visitor; the least you can do is look presentable," she chastised.

"Who?"

"Where is the fun in that if I tell you?" she joked as she flashed her teeth at me.

190

Aunt Cara spoke to me using telepathy. *She needs you. Maybe you can help her. I think you should.*

"Who is it?" I demanded as I put on my clothes and Aunt Carly flew out of the kitchen with my sweats.

I will burn these, Aunt Carly thought.

Hey, you will not, those are my favorite sweatpants.

Exactly! Aunt Carly purred.

DING DONG! I didn't know we had a door bell because we never had a visitor before.

It's for you, Aunt Cara informed me.

I pulled my long silky hair into a quick braid and headed for the door. Aunt Carly approved.

Very nice, you look like a chic preppy girl, she cooed in my head.

Our relationship was definitely getting back on track.

"Gee, thanks," I responded as I opened the door. It was Frances. Frances from BCHS; Frances, MJ's best friend was at my house.

What in the hell did she want?

"Frances? I wasn't even aware that she knew where I lived. She looked like she had been crying for days. The last time I had seen her was in the library when I told Noah about Matthew and MJ. Frances was on the other team.

This had to be good if she was here, and all I wanted to know more than anything was what her purpose was. "Come in." I opened the door wider to allow her access. She breezed right in; as she passed me, I smelled her sinfulness. It was so sweet and alluring. I almost reached out and grabbed her.

No, this is a test, isn't it, to see if I would get excited, to see if I was in control? I convinced myself.

You can do this, Carrie. This is just a pitiful human. She has no power over you. I assured myself.

Frances had some explaining to do. She was thinking horrible things. I closed my eyes and tried to imagine the worst smell possible…the horse stable, a sewer, anything that wouldn't alarm Frances by my new state of being.

She lowered her head and looked up. She must have lost about ten pounds. She was bald in some spots as though she were purposely pulling her hair out. Her face was drained of all color and her eyes had no life in them. "It's true, you are beautiful," she said in admiration.

What did I look like before? If she wanted my help, she was going about it the wrong way. "Frances—"

"I need to speak with you, please. Noah has been telling everyone how beautiful his best friend is, inside and out. I didn't mean to offend you, Carrie. It was a compliment. You just never looked quite this amazing at school," she offered.

"Okay." Noah was telling people I was beautiful. *Get a grip; don't lose it. Calm down.* I ordered myself.

"Can we be alone, to talk?" she asked.

Not that it mattered if we were alone in this house, alone in the state of Maryland, or alone on Mars, my aunts, all of them, could hear her thoughts. Hell, Mother, who was God knows where, could hear her thoughts. They could tell her what she wanted before she could even speak it to me. "Sure, in my room we will have privacy." She smelled so sinful, so delicious. She made me want to do bad things.

Did I want to do bad things? I smelled Frances again. The answer to my question was yes.

As we entered my room, I closed the door so Frances could have a false sense of privacy. "What's going on, Frances? What do you want to talk about?"

She walked over to my bed. "May I?"

I motioned that she could. I hadn't slept in a month, so I had no objections to her sitting on my bed, but I had the nagging suspicion that as soon as Frances left, my bed would get redressed and my room would probably get a total makeover. I knew Aunt Carly was probably dying inside because I invited Frances up to my room that she hadn't had a chance to renovate.

"You have such a lovely home," she whispered. She was really annoying me. Why couldn't she just come out and say what

193

she wanted? I was about to knock her out with some metal energy; at least that would be something interesting.

"Frances, I know you didn't come here to talk about how pretty I am and how nice my home is, so what do you want?" I had to admit she was right about both. Then I looked into her mind. It was easy enough to read. I got excited. I closed my eyes again and counted to five hundred so I could slow down my pulse. I knew what she wanted, but I still wanted her to say it, aloud. I wondered if that was the demon in me that needed to hear her proposition. My demon wanted to feel that power.

"I'm sorry. It's just that I need your help with something, something no one else can do," she began.

"You need me." I repeated. I don't know why, but her choice of the word *need* made me feel even more powerful.

"Yes. I need your help and I know I have been a bitch to you in the past."

"Oh, yeah, you are a total bitch." I used the present tense because she still was a bitch as far as I was concerned.

She frowned. I didn't really care for Frances when I was human, and I damn sure cared even less now. "I want to apologize about that, Carrie."

"No need. Go on. Tell me what you want, Frances," I urged.

"You know MJ is still mad at you. She wants you dead." She was absolutely getting on my nerves now. I would deal with Melissa later. She was on my to-do list.

"So, is that why you are here, to warn me about that whore Melissa?" I knew Frances's true intention, and to tell me about Melissa was not it. "I think I can handle anything her elementary mind can cook up, but thanks—"

"No, I just thought you should know that. She's not normal. She can be very evil. And Noah won't even speak to her now."

"Noah?" My face lit up.

"They were never a good match to begin with. She just liked him because everyone else did, and she wanted everyone to be jealous of her." She shook her head. "She does the most horrible things only because she can get away with them."

"Like most people who get away with stuff; that's why they do it." I created an opening so she could ask what she wanted of me. "Is someone else getting away with horrible deeds that you know of, Frances?"

She looked down at her disheveled clothes. "You know. You already know."

"Yes, I do."

"I never told anyone," her voice strained. "Not even MJ. How you did know? Who told you? How did you find out?"

I was in better control of myself; I wasn't overly excited but I closed my eyes to be sure. "You did. You told me."

"Impossible," she countered. "I never—" She looked down at the floor. I stood in front of my door, posing as if I were making sure no one would disturb us.

"I would like to make a request," she breathed.

"I will not promise you anything, but I will see what I can do," I answered. I understood what Aunt Chris meant about having the advantage of knowing something before someone could say it. This conversation became irrelevant and boring.

She closed her eyes. "I would like it if you could… would…kill my father?"

There it was. I felt like a dentist pulling teeth. Frances was firm in her belief that her father needed to die as she walked up to the main house. Once she got here, however, she realized that I could actually give her what she wanted, she wasn't as sure as she originally thought.

"Kill him?"

She nodded yes.

"Frances, I don't know if—"

She looked up at me. "Carrie, I know you have a special gift."

I twisted my face. "You think I have a gift?"

She nodded again.

"It's not a gift, Frances."

She shook her head to disagree. "I know you can see things. I know you can make things happen—"

"How do you know this?"

"I just do!" She spoke so emphatically that I was about to question her sanity. Was she attracted to my demon as much as my demon was attracted to her? "You knew about my dad and MJ and Matt. And what happened at the party—"

"What happened at the party?" I asked.

She covered her face with her hands. "I," she spoke very slowly and deliberately, "heard that…Matt tried to hurt you." She covered her face to hide her shame. "Like the way my father hurts me and my sisters."

I started to fish around in her mind. "Who told you that?" I demanded.

"It was all over school. Everyone who was at the party was talking about it the first day back."

"Look at me," I ordered. She did as she was told. "And what else did you hear?"

"Everyone said Noah came just before Matt actually got what he wanted from you. Then they said you disappeared into thin air. No one saw you leave, and yet you were gone. It was a great mystery. And then no one heard from you after that. They believed that the reason we were having so many eclipses was that you and your aunts were planning something major, really big."

I stood there and listened intently, hanging onto her every word.

"And then Matt committed suicide—" she said.

"HE WHAT?" I roared. My reaction scared her because she literally jumped up.

Everything poured out of her in a rush.

"Matthew Shaw?" She questioned.

She looked perplexed. She thought I knew he was dead, but I didn't. "He's dead. He was an asshole, but he would never kill himself, not in a million years. He was like that guy in that Greek myth that was in love with himself."

I helped, "Narcissus."

"Yeah, him. It was so strange. One day he's bragging about how great he is, then the next he's jumped off the ledge of his bedroom window." My eyes definitely grew darker. She studied my face, not afraid but intrigued. "Everyone was talking about Matt's suicide. It was a big deal. People just couldn't understand why he would do that. Then everyone started whispering about you and your aunts, saying that you killed him or something like that because he tried to hurt you. Then one by one everyone who was at the party starting talking differently."

"Talking differently? What do you mean?"

"They said that Matt had been depressed and was talking about killing himself for a long time—Toby, Tonya, all of them. They said that they didn't remember Matt and you being alone or seeing you at the party at all. It was like they were under a spell. Do you do spells?"

I shook my head no. I was deep in thought. Matthew Shaw was dead, and people's memories were being fooled with. This was indeed the work of my aunts. The excitement left and my eyes and they were turning back to green even though I was enraged.

"Don't make my dad jump off a building or anything like that. My mother would literally die if she saw him ripped to pieces like that."

"Frances," I said, "I didn't agree to do anything. That's if I can do anything at all. Furthermore, I didn't kill Matthew Shaw. I didn't even know he was dead until you told me."

"No, you made him kill himself. Is that how it works? I would appreciate it if it wasn't suspicious, more like an accident."

Kill her father? Did he deserve to die? Truly he did some horrible acts, but did that justify a sentence of death? "Frances—"

"Frankie," she corrected me. "And I need you to do this, not just for me, but for my whole family," she pleaded. "He has tormented us all. I will do anything you ask of me if you grant me this request."

"Do not make promises you cannot keep, Frances," I admonished.

"Carrie, please!"

"You need to go home, Frances. Your father will be home soon, and Liz is home by herself."

At the sound of her sister's name, she jumped off the bed and gathered herself. "Thank you for speaking to me, Carrie, and I hope you come back to school. I want us to be friends."

I just nodded. "My Aunt Cara will escort you to the front door."

She looked puzzled.

"She's downstairs, and she didn't hear anything." She left my room, solemn and somber.

I waited until I heard the front door close. "Matthew Shaw!" I barked at my aunts, who were all over the house, but I knew they heard me.

Aunt Carly was the first up to my room, "Congratulations, Carrie, your first cult member!"

"Huh?" I was blindsided. I was ready to argue about Matthew Shaw, not receive accolades for Frances's sick request.

"She totally adores you," Aunt Carly continued. "She will be worshiping you in no time, especially after you take care of her father." She grinned as she reflected. "Personally, I have enjoyed him for years."

"Wait, is that something to be proud of, being a cult leader?"

"Not leader, deity, and yes!" Aunt Carly answered.

"We are not gods."

"Honey, speak for yourself," she quipped.

I wasn't going to be distracted any further. "Matthew Shaw—he killed himself?"

"Sad, but true." Aunt Carly didn't seem sad at all.

"You didn't…" I started to ask Aunt Carly.

"Please," she laughed, "I have better things to do than to play with high school children."

"Aunt Chris?" I could smell the sinfulness coming off her skin. She was upstairs in my room before I had time to finish asking my question. "Matthew Shaw…did you…were you the one who…" I attempted to ask her if she had done the deed.

"No, I would want you to have made that decision," Aunt Chris said, then left.

I looked at Aunt Carly, bewildered.

"What?" Aunt Carly began. "I know you like to put Cara on this pedestal, but guess what, honey, she is a demon just like the rest of us. And you can't even imagine the evil she has done. The evil she is planning to do." Aunt Carly was really insulted now.

Aunt Cara appeared in my room, "Carrie—"

"How could you?" I inquired. "Why would you?" Not that I cared for Matthew Shaw, especially after what he tried to do to me, but it was still wrong.

Aunt Cara peeked at Aunt Carly. "Do you mind, Carly?"

She started to protest, but decided to leave the room. "I need to rearrange the furniture in the living room anyway," she said to justify leaving. Then she looked around my room. "And I need to give this room a breath of life. Honestly, Carrie, this is ridiculous."

"Carrie," Aunt Cara began, sitting on my bed, "there are things that you don't understand…"

"Well, I want to, so tell me," I demanded. All this secrecy crap was irritating me. I thought we were clearly past the evasiveness.

"Carly is right," Aunt Carly squealed with excitement from downstairs at my aunt's statement. In Aunt Carly's mind, she was always right. "I am a demon, you are a demon, and nothing can change that fact. And it is a fact, Carrie, and as much as you may wish it weren't true doesn't make it any less true. We are what we are, Carrie, and it's as simple as that. I do not apologize for Matthew's plight. He had it coming, trust me. In fact, the highlight of his tragic little life would have been high school anyway, so technically I did him a favor. He would have died young, from anything: a motorcycle accident, drinking—"

"But that would have been his choice!" I argued.

"And so was jumping. I can't make anyone do anything that they don't want to," she rationalized.

"No, but you can poison his mind, make him think that jumping off the roof was his own thought."

"I can only suggest. *We* can only suggest. It's called free will. I can't take that from him. I can only give him another option. It's up to him, or any human for that matter, to listen and then to act or not," Aunt Cara reasoned.

"You had no right."

"I HAD EVERY RIGHT!" she thundered. "In fact, it is my purpose, your purpose, and even your mother's purpose. For you to try to deny the very reason that we even exist is insanity."

"Will you have me committed like my mother if I don't do what you want?"

"No, because you will come around and see things my way, the right way." She was so sure. She almost had me convinced.

Almost.

"I would rather die." I said with conviction.

I could tell that my favorite aunt was losing her patience with me. "Carrie, don't be so dramatic. You cannot deny who you are or what you are any more than you can deny that the sky is blue. You may not have wanted this, but this is the hand dealt to you, so deal with it," she admonished.

"I don't want to talk about this anymore." I was done. She wasn't budging on her position, and neither was I, so there was no point to our conversation.

"You may not want to talk about it, but it will not go away. Your desire for sin will not go away. It will only grow stronger. It's a part of you; that's it and that's all." She left my room.

This whole new lifestyle was one that I didn't ask for and didn't want. Why couldn't my aunts see that? I was already pretty lonely, and now I felt more isolated than ever. I went back downstairs to find something to do. I was in the process of going to the blood tree before Frances made her outrageous request, but I didn't feel the need to go to the blood tree anymore.

I went to the kitchen in search of food even though I wasn't hungry. "May I have a word?" That was Aunt Chris. I nodded for her to proceed.

"I know that this change has been hard on you. I've been there. We all have been there. Some of us have taken to this life better than others. Initially the transition can be tricky. You are depressed, you miss your mother, you miss Noah, and you miss the life you had before, right?"

I didn't answer her but I listened. Aunt Chris continued. "No one is saying that you can't have it both ways. Our life may be the only circumstance when you can have all you want and all the things you never thought you could get. How does the saying go? You can't have your cake and eat it too? Well, in *our* life, you can!

"You don't like being a demon, okay? Then don't think of yourself that way. You are special, you are powerful, and that should be an idea you can live with. You don't want your new life, but think about it; you didn't really love your old one, did you?"

I could not argue with her on that point because she was right. I didn't love my old life but, I kept silent.

"And you haven't even tried to live your new one. You weren't happy before you changed; maybe you can have a chance at happiness now."

I kept a poker face even though my resolve was wavering. I continued to listen. Aunt Chris made valid points. "Carrie, Frances wants you to kill her father. You know how awful he is, and how awful he has been to those girls, so maybe you will do some justice if you create a situation where he no longer exists. We don't kill anyone to begin with, do we? You can live with that, right?"

Her eyes probed however, I wasn't giving away anything in my face to let her know she was winning. She continued with another approach. "I'm not saying I haven't made any bad decisions. As old as I am, I've made plenty of bad decisions; but I made the decision, I decided. I tried this life out and you know what? It really wasn't that bad. There are times when I wish that things were different, but I accept it, all of it. Carrie, do what's right for you, but be happy with what you choose. You have to choose because to choose nothing is far more criminal than living the demon lifestyle."

Aunt Chris's gambit worked. I was already under her spell. I was a demon and she had full control over me. Humans didn't stand a chance with Aunt Chris. I had never heard her speak so passionately before, not even when she shared her story about her life, nor even when she talked about her sons. "Are you happy?" I asked her.

"On the days that I am not, I persuade humans to do things that will make me happy." She grinned. Aunt Chris was quickly replacing Aunt Cara as my favorite aunt. Of the three of them, she seemed the most reasonable, even with her anger issues. "Would you like for me to cook for you?" she asked.

I shook my head. "No, that's okay, Aunt Chris. I'm not that hungry, but thanks anyway." She smiled again and went on her way.

Was being a demon really that bad?

I floated to my room and laid down on my bed. I was able to hear only sinful thoughts. I could probably stop a despicable human from doing harm to his fellow men, and because of his intentions I could possibly do away with him altogether.

That didn't sound so harsh. I could get rid of only the truly worst of the worst. Right? Like a superhero, or maybe I was more like an angel who been born into the wrong family. Mother was able to leave and live a pretty normal life. Maybe I could do the same?

I could try.

Nothing was wrong with trying this life out. *Yes, I would try.*
As I made my decision to at least try to be a good demon, I looked
out the kitchen window. It was pouring down raining.

The ground that surrounded the blood tree was stained with
more blood than before.

After wrestling with my aunt's proposal, I made my decision. I got dressed for school.

I was going to try to be happy.

Aunt Carly heard me struggling with my new wardrobe in my newly renovated room.

"Going somewhere?" She peeped in my door. It was seven in the morning, and my aunt was flawless in a backless dress with her hair in loose natural curls.

"Yes, and I need your help." She slid right in. "I'm going to school—"

"You're going to school?" she asked before I could finish.

"Yes, and I would like to know what I should wear."

She quickly gathered herself. "You are actually trying to be fashionable?"

"Yes," I answered with a grin.

"GREAT!" she sang. "Wear your gray cashmere dress with a black belt, black tights, and booties. Your hair should be pressed straight."

"Can you help me?" I asked her.

"Of course, and wear your diamond necklace."

"Isn't that a little pretentious?" I asked.

"Exactly," she replied.

Aunt Carly did my hair and made sure that I was absolutely fabulous.

"Thanks Aunt Carly," I said.

"Sure, now with you out of this room, I can get it right."

"You already fixed it. It's perfect." I defended my new room. I loved what she done. My room wasn't the same juvenile room it had been. My aunt truly gave me a bedroom that would make anyone envious. She actually knocked down a wall so that I had more space. She gave me a balcony so that I could sit outside my window and pout because she claimed I was making her depressed.

She repainted over the purple and made my room the color of the ocean, a very pale, beautiful blue. I had a huge sixty-five-inch flat screen mounted to the wall. She got rid of my little bed and put a king size bed in its place. She gave me a sleeker, smaller desk to replace the bulky wooden one. My room could have easily been on featured on television. What more could she do?

"I got work to do, so get out!" she ordered. I picked up my book bag that was lying in the hallway, something I hadn't done in months. It felt foreign as I placed it on my shoulder.

"Will you take me to school?" I asked.

Aunt Carly looked at me like I was crazy. "Why would I do that, when you have a car sitting in the carport?"

I'd forgotten that I was gifted a car for my birthday. YES! So far, making my decision rendered great results.

"Aren't you a vision?" Aunt Chris complimented me as I passed her on my way out.

"Aunt Chris, I decided."

She smiled. "Good, I'm glad."

"Thank you for…everything."

She nodded and glided out of my way.

The wind howled when I walked outside. It was December and Mother Nature herself announced it. However, I couldn't feel a thing. I walked slowly past the blood tree. I wanted to ignore it, and yet I still wanted to touch it. I quickened my pace. I wasn't going to be distracted by the blood tree today. I was hesitant once in the carport because I didn't know which car I owned. My aunts all had many cars. However, they kept only a few on the property. There was Aunt Carly's Range Rover, Aunt Chris's Bentley, and Aunt Cara's Pontiac, but which one was mine? I walked over to where the keys were stationed, and I saw a laser cut key for a Lexus.

I have a Lexus?

Yes, is that not to your liking? Aunt Cara asked exhausted. *You said any…*

I know, but I wasn't expecting a Lexus. Who gets a Lexus as their first car? The excitement poured out of my eyes.

You! All three of my aunts said in harmony.

"YES!" I screamed.

I eased into the vehicle; it was a perfect fit. The lambskin covered leather seat hugged me as I sat down. The tan interior felt so familiar. The steering wheel even seemed to greet me. The new car fragrance was heavenly.

The ride to BCHS was peaceful. I felt completely alone in my thoughts, and it felt great. I looked in the rear view mirror and smiled. I felt free. It was the best feeling in the world.

Maybe all I needed to do was leave the main house?

As I drove into the student parking lot, all eyes were on me; they should have been. The boys looked at me and lusted over me, and the girls looked at me and instantly begrudged me. Some of them even thought I was a new student. I laughed on the inside.

This is great! I'm glad I decided to live this life.

"Care Bear?" Noah looked handsome bundled up in his blue parka. The contrast of the light blue of his eyes and the dark blue of his coat made his eyes sparkle like some precious stone. "Wow!" he breathed.

I was able to control myself, just barely.

"Too much? You know my Aunt Carly, once she gets started—"

He helped me out of the car and grabbed my black leather bag from the back seat. "No, you look amazing. Tell your aunt to keep it up." He ran his fingers through my hair. "Your hair is so silky and smells like honey and vanilla." he commented.

He wasn't thinking anything lustful at the time so I was uncertain if he liked my new natural scent. "So I smell, ok?" I asked.

"You smell great. Not that you never did before, I just never noticed how nice you smelled till now. Please stop me before I put my foot farther into my mouth." He awkwardly smiled.

"Thanks, Noah. I know what you mean." He stood very close to me in the parking lot. The wind blew, and he shuddered; I, on the other hand, didn't even flinch.

"We better go in; it's freezing out here. Where's your coat, Care Bear?"

"Left it home. I was in such a hurry this morning." I saw the look of concern on his face. "No worries, Noah, I'm fine. I have this nice car to keep me warm." I smiled.

"This is yours?" he asked.

"It's a birthday gift from my aunts. They are something."

"Yeah, 'something' is right. C'mon, we'd better get inside." He reached for my hand as we walked, and I gladly placed my hand in his.

Why didn't I decide months ago?

Being back in school was the best. Everyone wanted to talk to me or sit with me. I was popular, I was wanted, and I had the power. This was best decision of my life.

I did hear some whispers about my aunts and Matthew Shaw, nothing too disturbing or anything I hadn't heard before. But mostly people were attracted to me.

Everyone loved and adored me, everyone except Melissa. I felt her stares when I walked past her or entered a classroom she was already in. She hated me. It excited me to hear her thoughts. She was jealous of me. I had Noah by my side, and she was just the slut who had sex with the young man who committed suicide. One of the rumors was that Matt committed suicide because Melissa was awful in bed.

I laughed. *Humans are ridiculous.*

When I entered the cafeteria, I spied Frances sitting by herself looking utterly dejected, even worse than she had when she came to my house. She was no longer a beautiful one, no longer a desirable. She was who I used to be, an outcast.

"Hey, Carrie, you coming to sit with us, right?" That was Tonya. I was now accepted by the Witches of Eastwick. Melissa and Frances were out and I was in. More points for me, but who was counting?

"Yeah, in a sec," I called as I sat beside Frances. "Frances," I began, already knowing the answer to the question I was about to ask. Things had gotten worse since she made her request to me. She needed a lifeline. She was dying, literally.

"I decided."

She looked up at me. She looked relieved. I had come to save her. This was what she had waited for.

"I will do what you asked," I continued, "but you have to do something for me."

She looked at me incredulously. "What could you possibly want? You have everything."

Melissa walked past us and rolled her eyes at me. My eyes started to creep to a darker hue. *Calm down, Carrie, get a hold on yourself.* I admonished myself. I closed my eyes and counted to a thousand.

"I want Melissa's hair."

"What?" Frances drank her water.

"Melissa's crown, I want it."

"You want me to dye your hair like MJ's?" Frances was bewildered. My hair was way more fabulous than Melissa's.

I explained, "No. I want the hair that is on Melissa's head in my hands."

"So, wait, how am I supposed to get her hair? Shave her head bald?" she asked.

"If that will make your task easier, then yes." I pulled her smelly black hair back off her face and spoke very slowly. "I want her hair, Frances, all of it. I want her bald." My eyes grew dark at the anticipation of MJ's hair in my hands. I knew Frances would agree to anything I asked.

I didn't need Melissa's hair for anything satanic. I could have dealt with her myself just as easily, but I needed to see Frances's devotion to me. I needed to see how far Frances was willing to go if I was to commit the ultimate crime against man.

Frances deliberated for a few seconds. I wasn't asking for much. She could cut MJ's hair. I wasn't asking her what she was asking of me. She agreed. Obviously her father's death was worth more than MJ's natural blonde locks. "I'll do it," she whispered.

"Frances, you have one day. And in twenty four hours, your dad will be…well…you know." I got up. "And Frances, please take a bath and do something about your clothes; you look like shit."

She bowed her head and continued to do what she had been doing before I sat down, and that was looking pathetic and going unnoticed.

"What did you say to her?" Noah asked as he handed me a lunch tray. He had gotten my lunch for me. That was so sweet.

"I invited her to sit with us," I lied.

"Why?" Tonya asked.

"Yeah, why?" Toby echoed. "She's really weird now, like creepy weird." She took a bite of her pizza. "I never really liked her before. She always thought she was better than everyone else. Who cares who her father is?"

"I just wanted to be nice," I answered. "I remember what it was like to be an outcast." I eyed Tonya and Toby, and of course this was a conversation they didn't want to have. I lied to them, but what else was I going to say? *"I just promised to off her father, who by the way is raping her"?* The lie sounded better than the truth.

"That was very thoughtful of you." Noah lightly touched my nose with his. He whispered to me, "You are truly beautiful inside and out. After everything Melissa and Frances put you through, you are still nice to them. Amazing." He winked at me.

I restrained myself from jumping on top of him at the lunch table. "Please, that's not necessary." I blushed. I wasn't paying any attention to what the annoying teenage girls were talking about. I was focused on Noah; and, though we weren't alone, the moment was so intimate, so loving and tender, we might as well been.

Best day ever!

After school, I sat at the kitchen table and did my homework. Aunt Cara glided in, fishing around with the bowls. She was about to eat for the first time since... since… I have no idea.

"Homework?" she asked as she continued to make busy in the kitchen.

"Yes."

"Very good." Aunt Cara seemed to be in a better mood.

"Are you going to eat?" I asked. I realized that the only person who used the kitchen was me; now I knew why.

"Why yes, for the first time in two years. I am quite hungry," she said.

"Wow!" It was still hard to wrap my head around the whole concept of a demon not needing to eat or sleep as much.

"When was the last time you slept?" I asked.

"The eighties. I'm grateful. Have you seen the eighties? They were dreadful."

"You slept a whole decade?" The idea seemed impossible.

"Well, not quite, almost about a good solid six years."

"How long can we go without sleeping?" I asked.

"Carly went for almost fifteen years once. Christine went about eleven years and Celeste---" She stopped midsentence. "We do need sleep. You may become less affective as a demon if you don't have at least some rest. Heaven forbid that at some point you have to fight. I personally wouldn't recommend going longer than five years." She changed the subject. "How was school, today?" she asked. She emptied what seemed like everything out of the fridge.

"It was good." I tried to hide my excitement, but I knew my eyes were betraying me.

"Good. Are you going to help Frances?"

"I told her I would. She looked worse than she did the last time I saw her. I feel sorry for her."

"Why ?" she asked.

"Why?" I was puzzled. "Because she is having a rough time right now."

"And?" Aunt Cara questioned. I realized that Aunt Cara wasn't as compassionate as I had originally thought.

"And?" I was still puzzled.

"She's a human, Carrie. You shouldn't be so attached to them. Plain and simple, humans have rough patches, and they don't need our sympathy. I'm surprised you still have some sympathy left in you, but that will change."

"I'm still very attached to my humanity. I'm doing a public service. Orion Lee is a bad apple that needs to be thrown out."

"Okay, whatever you need to tell yourself to get you through the day, Carrie, you go right ahead." She laughed. "It will be more beneficial for you to lose the human emotions. They are playing tricks on your mind." She laughed again. She sounded like Aunt Carly, and I didn't like it.

"My mother thought it was important for me to hold on to my humanity," I snapped.

"And where is she now? If she cared so much about us, about you, where in the hell is she?" she quizzed me. "I took you in when your mother gave up. We have cared for you. Your mother abandoned us all, in more ways than one. How can you still be loyal to her?"

Her eyes were as black as a moonless sky. She frightened me. I pushed away from the table, still seated in my chair.

She calmed herself down before she continued. "All your mother had to do was accept us— hell, accept you—but she chose solitude.

"She loved William and Caleb more than she loved anyone, even more than you, and you still defend her?" She glided out of the kitchen.

Had my aunts been right all along? Did my aunts have my best interest at heart and my mother was the one who was poisoning my mind? If my mother wanted the two of us to be together, then all she had to do was submit, right?

Mother didn't have to fight with them. She could have just conceded and we could all be together. She could protect me if she were here. She wasn't crazy. She was selfish. She wanted nothing to do with me. If she did, then she could have taken me with her if my aunts were really all that bad.

My thoughts and feelings were conflicted. I didn't want to be angry with my mother, but this creature inside of me made it very easy to feel pain and belligerence. The rage I felt was overwhelming. I wanted to do something about it.

Aunt Carly pranced into the kitchen. She seemed to be sympathetic, if that is possible for a demon. Correction, as if that was possible for her. "Your mother is your mother. No one can change that, but can you please stop pissing Cara off every day? You are taking all the pleasure out of my day... well, not all the pleasure." She rolled her eyes. "You know it does my heart good to upset her." She handed me something that looked like a very expensive robe.

"What is this?" I asked.

"It's a cloak. One of my favorites. It was given to me by a monarch in the early sixteenth century. He pledged his allegiance to me if I helped him win an unwinnable war. It was a Pyrrhic victory with many lives lost. Anyway, whenever I feel like doing something naughty, I put this on and go out. Go on, put it on," she ordered.

"Why do I need this?" *It wasn't going to give me super powers or anything,* I thought.

"You don't. But it makes you feel more mysterious. I like it when I go flying. I have many. It is yours, if you want it."

I took off my dress and tights and put on the black short sleeved tee shirt and jeans my aunt handed me. Then I put on the lightweight, burgundy colored, velvet cloak. It felt like feathers on my skin and it smelled sweet. It had the scent of death, blood, and war. It was as if I were there. I could see the battles in my mind, the endless fields of dead bodies, and my aunt smiling at her masterpiece. It felt so familiar and normal to me. I put on the over-sized hood and went out the door. I ran to the blood tree. I grabbed one of the bleeding branches.

"Show me what I need to know," I ordered the tree. The tree didn't show me anything. I touched the trunk; it still felt like skin.

"Please show me."

Nothing.

I kicked the tree.

I waited for images to flood my mind, still nothing.

"Fine!" I ran and leaped off the ground into the air.

I'd never gone flying before. I just assumed it was forbidden, but it was a relief to be in the air, free of all inhibitions. I could smell the sinful humans down below. I felt more like a demon, more like my new self, in the sky.

I felt as if I was a kid on Christmas with a new shiny toy. This freedom was amazing. When I took to the skies, they grew dark as if I were painting them black, just as my aunts had in my dreams.

I flew around aimlessly, watching frantic humans observe the eclipse—*an eclipse caused by me*— when I came across a familiar scent.

Frances.

Her mind was so sinful these days, she was easy to find. I zeroed in on her essence. I could hear her mind clearly as if she were talking directly to me.

I was intrigued as I perched myself on an oak tree that stood directly in front of her stately house. It was much like I imagined her house would look with a four-bedroom, three-and-a-half-bath structure with an attic and a basement in a suburban neighborhood. I observed her family. Frances's father, Orion Lee, was forty-five years old, obese, and balding, not from stress like Frances, but naturally. He was of mixed heritage, his father Irish and Black, his mother was Black and Indian. Frances's mother, who had the misfortune of being his wife, was Asian and Black. No wonder Frances was such a beauty, before she started pulling her hair out and losing weight. She was an exotic beauty and more beautiful than Melissa's all-American looks. Frances had almond shaped light brown eyes, olive skin, a wide nose that fit her face, full lips, and long beautiful black hair. She shared these same features with her sisters. They were a beautiful family, on the outside, at least.

I remained perched in the tree as I observed the dysfunction. Liz, the youngest, was as frail as Frances. Their oldest sister, Rochelle, was obese. She found her escape in food. She reasoned that if she was fat, then her father wouldn't want her. Sadly, her logic was flawed.

Orion was up in the master bedroom, getting ready to call Frances to join him.

Frances, take Liz and get out of there! I ordered.

"What the hell?" she mouthed as she heard my voice in her head for the first time.

You heard me! Your father is getting ready to call you for some alone time. GET YOUR ASS OUT OF THERE! I screamed in her mind.

"What is it?" Liz asked as she saw the confusion plastered over Frances's face.

"Not sure." Frances looked around to see if she could see me.

Frances, if you want my help, do as I say. Now get the hell out of there.

Frances asked aloud, "Is this how you killed Matt Shaw?"

I didn't kill Matthew. Now do as I say.

"What?" Liz asked as she got off the floor and stood front of the television. Liz was concerned about her sister's odd behavior. "What is it?" She asked Frances again.

"Liz, come with me to the basement—" Frances started to say.

NO! OUT OF THE HOUSE!

"Store," she corrected herself.

"Why?" Liz asked.

"Because I want your company, now come on!" Frances instructed.

Liz wasn't moving. My mind screamed at Frances, more frantic this time.

Frances, get your little sister to go with you, or it will be her he chooses if you are not there.

Frances grabbed their coats, shoved Liz toward the front door; they both left the house.

Look up.

Frances saw me in the tree. When her sister looked up to see what Frances was looking at, I danced around a huge branch so she wouldn't see me. A sinister smiled crept onto Frances's face.

"Frances, what on earth is going on?" Liz asked as her older sister asFrances led her away from the house. They quickly put on their coats. It was freezing out.

"Not sure," she said, "not really sure." But Frances knew the time had come. The hell they lived in was about to come to an end.

What about Rochelle? She thought in a panic when she realized her sister was still in the house, alone with her monster of a father.

She will be just fine, I promised. *Your father was only interested in you two. He is no longer attracted to Rochelle.*

I leaped from the front of the house to the back so I could be closer to Rochelle. She was in her room, sneaking Bonbons and other various treats. In two months' time, Rochelle gained over fifty pounds. She was still pretty, just bigger, and sadly, the weight didn't look good on her. It aged her.

Rochelle, I sang, *why so sad?*

She looked around her room to see where my voice was coming from, but to no avail.

Rochelle, don't be afraid. I'm here to help you, to take care of you, something that your mother has not done.

She still looked around. "Have I gone completely crazy?" She asked as she stuffed more chocolates in her mouth.

No, for the first time in a long time, you are thinking clearly. Your father has damaged you and your sisters, hasn't he?

"Who is this?" she hissed. She sat on her bed, still in search of the body that owned the voice she heard.

Your guardian angel and I came to help you with your situation. I can make it all go away, I purred.

"Frankie? Liz?" She opened her bedroom door to see if her sisters were there.

No, Frances and Elizabeth went to the store; it's just you, me, and your father.

She sat back down on her bed. "Okay, say that I'm not completely psycho and I really have a guardian angel, what can you help me with?"

Your father. We have to make him stop. We can end this now.

"What?" She grabbed a chunk of cake from beside her bed and ate it. Her voice broke. "What should I do?" She ate another huge piece of the sugary treat.

What has to be done! Your father will never stop. You must make him.

"I can't," she cried. "I can't do it."

Yes, you can, and you must. Look at yourself, Rochelle.

She stopped eating her chocolate cake long enough to walk to a mirror. She stood there and stared at what she had become after binge eating. She frowned in disgust.

Look at what he has done to you. You have gained over fifty pounds to stop him from taking advantage of you. And now you repulse him. You repulse him? Very pitiful, Rochelle.

Rochelle continued to stare into the mirror, looking at herself. "You're right. I am pathetic," she admitted, then walked to her bed and sat down.

He thinks you are hideous because you gained so much weight. That's why it's been so long since he has called upon you.

You're not even attractive to him. He has made you gain all this weight, and now he thinks you are disgusting because of it. He made you go to extreme measures to make him leave you alone, and now it hurts that he rejects you.

"I hate how he makes me feel. I just want it to stop!"

You can make it stop. You can fix this, Rochelle.

"I can end this. I can stop him," she cried.

Yes, you can. You have to.

"But he is my father," she reasoned.

And what type of father does this to his own children? Rochelle, be the strong one; do what everyone else is afraid to do. Do it now!

She got up off her bed and tiptoed to the door, opening it with exaggerated slowness. She crept to the stairs past the closed door of the master bedroom.

This was the perfect time to make Frances's wishes come true.   Rochelle ran down the stairs and went straight into the kitchen.

She got a butcher knife from the counter and crept back upstairs to the master bedroom where her father was.

I knew what was about to happen, and I was downright giddy with anticipation. My eyes were black as soot. Excitement raced through my veins like electricity.

I enjoyed every minute of it. My aunts were right. I never felt this good in my life.

I was sitting on my balcony when my Aunt Cara came into my room.

"Your hair," she announced. She tossed a plastic bag onto my bed.

The bag was filled with blonde hair. Frances kept her word. She was three days late, but she kept her word.

"Thanks." I went back to looking at the beautiful scenery. The landscape of my family's property was absolutely breathtaking with the small pond, the rose garden, the stables and the houses. I never really appreciated it before. The farmland reminded me of a painting minus the ugly bleeding tree.

"That was an amazing job you did," Aunt Cara added.

"Excuse me?" I came inside so I could give my aunt my undivided attention.

"The whole Frances and Melissa Project. I'm really proud." She grinned. "Very cunning of you."

It was weird being praised for making one person shave someone's head and then convincing another person to kill someone, and even though I was conflicted, I still very much enjoyed the accolades. "Thanks."

"It's all over the news, you know. Rochelle is the only suspect, of course. She was taken into police custody for questioning tonight. Carly and Christine are impressed as well. One hundred and six stab wounds. He was unrecognizable." She walked toward my bedroom door. "Oh, you know to expect a visitor tonight."

"Frances, I know. She is not pleased about her sister committing the murder. I could have made him commit suicide, but where would have been the fun in that?" I wasn't sure if I really meant what I said or if I was just being facetious.

"Where, indeed? No, I meant another one."

"Oh, really?"

"Have fun. One of the benefits of this life is there are no consequences," she closed my door behind her.

I went back to staring into the endless sky on my balcony. I could see a figure making its way up to the main house. It was Frances. I was really a popular demon. My aunts never had any visitors return. Hell, who was I kidding? They never had any visitors.

I flew downstairs to greet Frances before she could ring the doorbell. She looked better. It was amazing what a murder could do for your overall beauty. She was dressed like a skier with her heavy down coat and winter boots.

"Hey, Frances," I greeted her.

"Hey, can we talk?" she asked as she took her coat off. She seemed quite comfortable in a house full of demons. I commended her.

"What's going on, Frances?" I asked casually.

"You!" she started. She then remembered whom she was talking to and where she was. She was in a house full of supernatural creatures. Killing her would be as easy as ordering take-out. She was fully aware of this. She knew to change her tone. "I can't believe that you would do that to Rochelle. That's not what I wanted." She sat on the couch.

I remained standing, "I did what you asked of me Frances. I got rid of your father," I said confidently.

"Yes, but," she whispered, "you got Rochelle to do it. I thought he would commit suicide like Matt or get mugged or something."

"First of all, I had nothing to do with Matthew's death. If Matthew committed suicide, then that's exactly what was— a suicide. That was his choice. Secondly, your father wasn't suicidal to begin with. He was too much of a narcissist. No one would have bought that story. And thirdly, how else was I going to get rid of your dad? Would you have preferred I used Little Liz to do it? I did what you asked; you should be thanking me." My eyes grew dark.

"Thanking you for what? Making my sister into some psycho killer? And after I burned MJ's head for you?" she accused.

"You burned Melissa's head for YOU!" I began to float. My rage was growing and I could not control it. Frances balled up on the sofa, afraid of me. She needed to be.

"Frances,"—my voice became dark—"you asked me to get rid of your father; I did just that! You burned Melissa's hair off because what you wanted was far more important than your friendship with Melissa. I didn't make you do anything. You did what you wanted to do!"

"You asked me to—"

"And you could have refused me, but you didn't. Don't blame me for your remorse."

She whimpered, "But why Rochelle?"

"Why not?" I sneered. "Your father is dead and your sisters are safe; you should be happy. You got what you wanted."

"Rochelle stabbed him over a hundred times. She is going to jail for the rest of her life."

"Well, that's what happens when you kill someone, Frances. There are consequences for everything we do." I started to calm down. "Your sister sacrificed her freedom for you. That is love," I insisted.

"It's all over the news. Everyone knows about the abuse, Rochelle's life is over, and my family will be dragged in the mud."

"Is that my problem?"

"I don't wish for Rochelle to go to jail for something I asked for," she said full of guilt.

"Is that a request, Frances?" I probed.

She nodded yes. "Just save her from my mess, please," she pleaded.

I gave her the same guarantee as before: "I won't make any promises, but I will see what I can do."

She eyed me suspiciously. "No funny business."

I grimaced. There was nothing funny about my business.

She gathered her things. "I guess I will have to do something for you in return?" she questioned.

"Nothing in life is free, but we will cross that bridge when we get there. See ya soon, Frances," I cooed seductively.

She didn't utter a word as she let herself out. I continued to smile. Frances was in pretty deep, and it felt wonderful. I loved Frances's desperation. She would do anything I asked of her if that meant her dreams would come true.

"Damn." That was Aunt Carly. "I must say you are pretty wicked to be so young, demon."

"You say it like that's a bad thing." I was almost convinced my demon was not the monster I originally thought.

Aunt Carly was rebuilding the basement or something that she thought was out of date. She had tools in her hands. However, she was dressed as if she could walk any red carpet at a Hollywood premiere. "And Melissa's hair—I was impressed."

"Thanks," I responded.

"Did you just say 'thanks'? You're not going to go and mope around on your balcony about being evil and how you didn't ask for this? No 'woe is me' crap?" she asked.

"Not tonight. I'm feeling better about things. I think I will go out."

She stood very still. She was listening to something I couldn't hear. Since she was a trillion years older than me, I was sure she had that ability.

"Quickly," she ordered me as she dropped everything in her hands and pushed me up the stairs.

"Aunt Carly?" I had never seen her drop anything. What was so important?

"Noah will be here in six minutes, and we only have five minutes to get you ready."

He was *that* important.

Once we were up in my room, I allowed her to dress me the way she saw fit, with no complaints. She was rather easy on me tonight, dressing me in a pink collared polo tee, dark blue skinny jeans, and pink and brown loafers. She grabbed my long, beautiful hair into a ponytail. Aunt Chris opened the door for Noah and led him to my new room. Aunt Carly flew out the window.

"WOW!" Noah said as he entered my room. I wasn't sure if that was directed at me or my room. The last time he saw my room, it belonged to a human teenager; now it was the room of a young demon. "This is awesome. Your room."

"I know. Aunt Carly, again." I laughed. "She is great at this kind of stuff."

"Yeah." he agreed as he sat on my newly acquired bed. "What do your aunts do for a living? It's just that I never hear you talk about your aunts' jobs."

Yikes!

"They don't work," I said nervously. "My aunts are independently wealthy. Aunt Cara married a wealthy man, and when he passed away, he left her his fortune. My Aunt Carly owns diamond mines; somehow she inherited them. And my Aunt Chris owns stocks that have done really, really well."

All true but when you live forever, your money has a tendency to be endless. Who would want to be a broke immortal?

"Oh." That seemed to have appeased him. He changed the subject. "Have you noticed that some weird stuff has been going on around here lately?" he asked.

"Weird? How?" I wondered if he knew I was the cause. I couldn't hear his thoughts. Aunt Chris was right; he had one of the purest minds.

"Have you seen MJ?" he asked as he searched my face. Melissa was still a soft spot for me. I didn't want him to even think about her anymore.

"What?" I asked.

"I'm not seeing Melissa anymore. I haven't been with her since the whole Matt thing in the library. Please stop me from putting my foot farther into my mouth. I'm dying over here."

I smiled. He stopped seeing Melissa. *Good.* "Continue with your story, Noah."

"I wanted to know if you have seen MJ, around? She hasn't been in school the last couple of days, and Mr. Anderson sent me to her house to check on her and to give her the assignments she missed... Carrie, the girl is bald!"

"Bald?" I asked as if I didn't already know. "Is she okay?"

"The girl is bald, Carrie! She said that Frances did that to her."

"Frances made her bald, on purpose?"

232

"I don't know. I think they were doing her hair and let the perm burn her hair off."

"A perm? What? So it wasn't on purpose then?"

"I don't know. She made it sound like Frances was trying to take her hair out. I'm not sure. Melissa is kind of a drama queen. She has bruises and scars on her head. She was crying. I felt really bad for her. She said that her hair will never grow back."

"That sucks." I felt a little pang of jealously because of the sympathy Noah was showing this insignificant human girl. Why did he care about her anyway? She was a nobody.

"Something is in the air, and it's making everyone crazy." He concluded.

"Yeah, I know what you mean. It's a lot." I tried to sound like I cared because in reality, I didn't.

"That is not the reason I came over. I wanted to ask you something."

"I'm listening." I sat down beside him. He was so close and smelled so good--- not in the way that sin smelled to me but in the way that a man smelled to a woman. I had to keep my thoughts under control.

"What are your plans for Christmas?" he asked.

Christmas wasn't a holiday that we celebrated. I did get gifts around Christmas time, but they were never disclosed as Christmas gifts. "We really don't celebrate holidays."

"That's what I thought. You guys are like Jehovah's Witnesses right?"

"Something like that." I couldn't say, "*No, we're hell spawns.*"

"Would your aunts mind if you spend Christmas with me?"

NO! They all said at once, in my head.

I should have known they were listening to our conversation. "No, I don't think they will mind." I smiled. I felt like a different person with Noah, as if everything in the world was the way it was supposed to be and I was not a demon but a young woman in love.

"Good." He paused. He was struggling with telling me something else. His indecisiveness was written all over his face. "I have been talking to my parents about you."

Shit! "And?"

"My mother has always liked you, Carrie. She said that finding someone like you is very rare. She told me you were special, but then again she always liked everyone better than MJ."

"Yeah, well, I can see why she would feel that way." I looked into his deep baby blue eyes. I was spellbound by them. He was the most beautiful human I had ever seen.

He smiled that perfect smile then gently pulled at my hair. "I like your hair down. It smells so good and it feels like silk."

I yanked out my ponytail. I wanted him to run his fingers through it.

"That wasn't an invitation for you to take down your hair. I mean, I like your hair in the ponytail too. Never mind." He laughed. "Care Bear, you make me nervous sometimes. You are not like other girls. You are smart and caring and fun…"

"And pretty?" I added.

"You were always pretty, but your beauty is more than skin deep. I'm attracted to you, Carrie. All of you." He reached for my hand and I gladly placed mines in his. The perfect fit.

"Noah, what if I told you I wasn't who you thought I was?" I started but then stopped. There was a long pause as we stared deeply into each other's eyes.

"You are exactly who I think you are and more, Care Bear."

"What if all the rumors about my family were true? That my aunts were cult leaders or witches? Would I still be the same person to you?"

"You are not your aunts."

"If I were a cult leader or a witch, would it matter?" I pressed. I needed to know his true feelings for me. Could he love the horrible creature I was? Did it matter that I did bad things? Would he still want me? Could he still love me?

"But you're not." He played with my hair; I instinctively leaned into him and closed my eyes.

"I could be," I whispered with my eyes still closed.

He stopped playing with my hair to rest his head on my shoulder.

"Anybody could be those things, Carrie. It's called a decision." I laid my head on top of his. "Carrie, if you were a junkie or an alcoholic, I would still be there for you, to love you through it," he promised.

Why did he have to be so perfect? "You love me?" I asked. I couldn't believe it. Did I hear him right?

"When you love someone, you try to be there for them."

He did love me.

He lifted his head up. "Carrie, look at me please." How could I resist? He was in my bedroom, telling me everything I wanted to hear; somehow I kept my eyes closed. "Look at me." My skin was

235

tingling all over. My heart was beating out of my chest. I opened my eyes very slowly.

"I love you, Carrie Colleen Carter."

I shook my head no.

"Yes, I do. I was afraid to tell you before, but not now. I don't want to lose you, especially since everything else is going crazy. I needed for you to know how I feel about you."

I countered, "But we are friends, Noah; I don't want to lose our friendship."

I closed my eyes really tight. Was this really happening?

"We are still friends. Nothing can change that, but we can also be boyfriend and girlfriend." He laughed.

I opened my eyes. "Noah," I whispered. He kissed my forehead, then my eyes; he kissed my nose. I wanted to cry tears of joy. Then he kissed me so passionately I wanted to die. This was great. This felt so much better than getting Frances to skin Melissa or getting Rochelle to kill her father. And then my excitement rose to a new level. I was about to pounce on Noah. I abruptly stop kissing him and ran to my desk. I closed my eyes tight and I counted to three thousand.

"I'm sorry for that, Care Bear. I didn't mean—" He was embarrassed. He thought he done something wrong. He thought I was rejecting him. How foolish of him! I wanted him now more than ever. I needed to calm down.

"Noah, I love you. I always have and always will."

He chuckled, "Yes, I knew that. I think everybody knew that!" he teased.

"Us, like this, was all I ever wanted. Ever since we were in the first grade and you pulled my hair out."

"No, I didn't. I remember that differently, it got caught in my jacket's zipper." he countered.

"Please let me finish. I'll let you think that today but, in reality, you pulled my hair out. I have the bald spot to prove it." He and I both chuckled. "Noah," I smiled, "I don't want to rush." I made hand movements to express the physical attraction. "I want our first time to be special."

A vision came to me in the middle of my speech. I saw my mother, pregnant, in the living room downstairs, only the furniture was different. Everything was different. My mother was talking to Aunt Carly. I couldn't hear them. Their voices were like static. I tried to focus, but the harder I tried to focus, the more static I heard.

"Care Bear? Are you all right?" Noah walked over to me. He placed his hand on my shoulder. "Do you want me to leave?" he asked. He was still embarrassed about my retreat.

"NO!" I came back to reality.

"No." I said again as I rubbed my head. "Do you remember Tonya's party?" I changed the subject.

"Very little of it," he said.

"Don't you think that's strange?" I questioned. "That no one really remembers the party?"

"No, Tonya's parties are normally lame, anyway. That's why everyone who goes and gets wasted, so they can't remember it. Are you okay? Tell me what you are thinking."

237

"Yes. I'm good." My aunts had the perfect cover. No one would question that night because everyone was drunk. "I'm sorry. I'm all over the place, aren't I?" I smiled. "I didn't mean…I really…" I gathered my thoughts. "I want to make this—" I grabbed his hand. "I just want it to be special, to mean something."

He smiled, too, and hugged me. "It does. It already does mean something… more, but I understand how you feel. I want what you want."

How could he? He didn't know the real me, the true me. The me that wanted to hurt people, the me that craved to hurt people. No matter how understanding Noah was, no one could overcome my type of evil.

"I'd better get going. It's late. If I don't leave soon, I can't guarantee that I won't try you again," he admitted. His mind was clear to me now. I saw what he was thinking. He wanted to take my clothes off and I wanted him to.

"Okay." I gathered myself. I walked Noah downstairs. He put on his coat. "Hey, Noah, where's your car?"

It wasn't parked on the pad, where he usually parked, near the entrance with the blood tree.

"Oh, I parked on the main road. That tree scares the shit out of me."

"Yeah." I looked at it. "I know what you mean."

"One day, you'll have to tell me the story with that thing."

I smiled. "Of course."

We kissed and said our goodbyes. I watched him walk to his 1983 Crown Victoria. It looked like a dinosaur compared to the cars on the property. Before he drove off, he texted me an "I love you." I never before felt so much joy.

Hours after Noah left, the doorbell rang again. "Who the hell is it now?" I changed my clothes and was quite comfortable, and the last thing I wanted was to be disturbed. I just wanted to be left alone with my thoughts of my new boyfriend. The doorbell kept ringing.

Why hadn't one of my aunts gotten the door or at least crucified the bastard that was ringing the bell?

I jumped off the bed and flew downstairs. Whoever it was, that person was about to get the scare of their lifetime. My eyes were already black in anticipation of this individual's pending fear.

"Who is it?" I barked as I flung the door open. No one. I went out on the porch to investigate. I didn't see anyone. Where were my aunts? I glided back upstairs to my room and slammed my bedroom door shut.

Carrie! Carrie!

I looked out of my balcony and saw my mother at the blood tree. One of the tree's arm-like branches wrapped itself around her arm. She looked back at me with white eyes. She mentally brought me her.

"Mother?"

She was absolutely stunning as if all the years being in the hospital never happened. She was more striking than Aunt Carly. Her eyes glowed, her skin gleamed, and her hair was long and flowing again. She looked healthy. Her skintight white dress hugged every inch of her body. Models would be invidious.

We stood about a foot apart. What should I say? I felt so many things at once. "Is this a dream?" That was the best I could do; but, to be honest, I did want to know what I was I seeing and how I was seeing it.

"An illusion. You are in your bed, lying down watching television. At least, that's what your aunts will see and think."

"You can create illusions?" I asked.

She offered, "You can create illusions. I see Cara hasn't shared with you the full extent of your power."

"No," I answered. "She hasn't told me anything."

"Nor will she. She needs to keep you under her control."

"For what?"

"So she can control you."

The tree uncoiled itself from Mother.

"So Caleb and the others are buried here?" I pulled out Caleb's locket and threw it her.

"Yes." She caught the locket and kissed it. Then she placed the locket on one of the tree's branches. The tree grabbed it and stained it with blood. Then the tree dropped the bloodstained locket on the bloodstained soil. The roots grabbed ahold of it and then consumed it.

"Rest now, Caleb," Mother said as she bent down to kiss the red earth.

"Is that why the tree bleeds? It's their blood on its hands?"

"No. The tree bleeds because it is dying, and it's been dying for a long time. It used to bear fruit a long time ago."

"So what happened to it?"

Mother stood up. "Mankind sinned and it started to die instantly. And every time a sin is committed, it bleeds and continues to die a slow death."

"So are you saying that this is the tree—"

She answered. "It is the Knowledge tree, the oldest tree in existence."

I looked at the tree. It definitely wasn't so creepy now. It was dying. It was more than just some burial ground for demon boys. It was something much more. I actually felt sorry for it.

"The tree shows you what you need to know," she continued. A strong wind blew past us. Mother reached for a branch and grabbed it again. "I see it has already talked to you."

I guessed the tree told her it showed me things. "It still hasn't showed me what I asked of it."

Mother reached out for me. "Come, Carrie. We will show you, together." With her other hand still connected to the tree, I grabbed her free one. Then instantly we were in my house. My home, the home I was taken from when I was in middle school, but this was a different time, different furniture. I didn't know this house.

We were in the living room. I let go of her hand, but she quickly grabbed me. "Stay connected to me; I'm connected to the tree," she ordered.

I obeyed her.

Another version of my mother materialized; she was pregnant. My pregnant mother walked toward the door and opened it. All of my aunts glided in.

"You saw us coming. No surprising you," Aunt Cara taunted.

"So then you know our duty," Aunt Chris added.

Aunt Carly was quiet and looked uncomfortable. My pregnant mother let my aunts in as she grabbed her stomach. Mother grabbed her flat stomach, as if she was reliving the whole scene again.

"You don't have to do this," my pregnant mother insisted. "This doesn't have to be."

"Christine, would you mind?" Aunt Cara asked.

My pregnant mother reasoned. "Chris, you don't have to. I'm not fighting. You're only going to hurt yourself."

That statement seemed to infuriate Aunt Chris. Her eyes went instantly black, and then she closed them. When she opened them again, her eyes started to lose color, but they were not completely white. Aunt Chris tried to move my pregnant mother with mental energy. Aunt Chris started shaking; my pregnant mother was too powerful for her to control.

"Carly, make her stop. Christine is going to kill herself. I'm not fighting," My pregnant mother again tried to reason with her sisters.

Aunt Carly did nothing. She just stood there and looked at Mother's stomach.

Aunt Cara looked at Aunt Chris, who was now on the floor at this point shaking violently.

"Help me, Carly," Aunt Cara instructed. They both placed Aunt Chris in the nearest chair. "Will she live?" Aunt Cara asked Aunt Carly.

Aunt Carly still didn't say a word.

"Chris will be fine," my pregnant mother answered. "She needs time to heal." She was still holding her stomach. She was protecting her unborn baby from them. But why?

"Fine," Aunt Cara answered. "You know why we are here. We need the fetus." Aunt Cara walked toward my pregnant mother. A knife from the kitchen flew into her hands.

"Cara, I do not wish to fight you, but I will kill you if you try to take my baby," my pregnant mother answered as she sat on the sofa, still holding her stomach.

"So be it." Aunt Cara charged toward my mother with the knife in her hand. Aunt Carly moved fast, like the wind. She shielded my pregnant mother from my aunt.

"Cara, wait." Aunt Carly finally spoke. She looked over to Aunt Chris, who still hadn't quite recovered. She then stared down at my pregnant mother and then back at Aunt Cara. Aunt Carly bent over my mother and placed her hand over my mother's hand.

"It's a girl." Aunt Carly smiled. "She's having a girl."

"Good. Now get out of my way. We need the fetus's blood for Esther's return. This is the reason we are here," Aunt Cara scolded.

Aunt Carly lovingly rubbed my mother's stomach, and my pregnant mother allowed her. It was such a tender moment. I was confused, considering how I witnessed them fight in the past. I thought they never like each other.

"Why would we kill an immortal? We need that baby to live," Aunt Carly faced Aunt Cara. "A dead fetus is no good to us, but a live child will be of great use to us and can help us free Esther from Hell. I see no need to kill the baby," Aunt Carly concluded.

My pregnant mother was still sitting on the sofa. She said nothing. My pregnant mother permitted Aunt Carly defend her.

"And what about Celeste's betrayal of leaving the sisterhood? What do you recommend for that, all great and wise Carly?" Aunt Cara asked.

Aunt Carly started, "We—" I could hear keys from outside. Someone was about to open the front door. I noticed Mother's attention shifted from the confrontation to the door. Mother looked on with expecting eyes. My pregnant mother's eyes turned white as she simultaneously snatched the knife from Aunt Cara's hand and propped Aunt Chris up in the chair. All three of my aunts froze. They were not expecting an interruption.

"William! How are you, Honey," my pregnant mother called as the door opened. There he was, my father.

I got excited. I never even heard my mother mention him, and here he was, in this memory, not only did I get to finally see him but I got to see my parents interact. "I thought you wouldn't be home for another hour." My pregnant mother got up and walked over to my father and kissed him on the lips. She stood slightly in front of him as if she was protecting him from my aunts.

"Yes, but I have great news." My father was pale like I used to be when I was human with rich black hair. He was of medium build and height. He was very attractive. I was pleased that he wasn't an ogre. "Hello," he said with a warm smile, acknowledging my aunts. "Celeste, why didn't you tell me, we were having company? I would have come home sooner, Sweetie." He rubbed my pregnant mother's stomach.

My pregnant mother's face lit up as my father lovingly stroked her stomach, "William, these are my sisters, Cara, Carly, and Christine." My pregnant mother said as if this was a pleasant visit and my aunts weren't trying to cut her unborn child out of her.

"I finally get to meet your sisters. Celeste talks about you guys all the time. I feel like I already know you. Are you lovely ladies staying for dinner?" he asked. He playful brushed my pregnant mother's long black hair out of her face. They were in love. Even I could see that. They reminded me of Noah and me.

"No, but thank you. We must be off," Aunt Cara said. She was the first one out of the door. Aunt Chris, who was still weak, stumbled out next, and finally Aunt Carly, who glanced backward at my mother.

As she watched her sisters leave, my pregnant mother mouthed "thank you" to Aunt Carly, who said nothing, she didn't even acknowledge her. Aunt Carly closed the door behind them.

"She saved me." I said to Mother, talking about Aunt Carly.

"Come," Mother said as she led me to the kitchen of the main house.

My pregnant mother was sitting at the kitchen table, and Aunt Carly was standing over her.

"Thank you for the other day," my pregnant mother said. Mother and I watched as we stood off to the side.

"I don't know what you are talking about." Aunt Carly snapped.

"Yes, you do, Carly. You could have let Cara kill my baby, but you didn't." My pregnant mother admitted.

"Oh, yeah...that," my aunt responded. "I saw no need for Cara to ruin your tacky furniture. We all know how hard blood stains are to remove. You can never fully cleanse yourself."

"No, it was more than that," my pregnant mother recognized, rubbing her stomach.

Aunt Carly expressed, "Did you know I mourned for Caleb? Even when you did not, I did. I mourned for all of them." My pregnant mother froze. My pregnant mother listened very intently to my aunt. "I would have never chosen this life for me. You of all people know that. I had a family, a hardworking, loving husband, children... I had a life, a meaningful life and now I have you so I have nothing." Aunt Carly paused. She tried to rid her voice of emotion. "I want your baby, Celestial. I want your girl."

My pregnant mother grabbed her stomach. "Oh, I get it now. You saved her so you can keep her for yourself."

Aunt Carly went to rub my pregnant mother's stomach and Mother grabbed her own stomach with anger in her eyes. I could see that this still bothered her to this very day.

"Cara wants to kill you and the baby. Christine is willing to go along with whatever Cara wants. I just want your baby and you can keep your little horrible life."

"I almost believed you were a decent person." My pregnant mother said as she batted Aunt Carly's hand away. "No way am I giving her up! So you, Cara, and Chris can all go to hell." My pregnant mother tried to stand up, but my aunt pushed her down.

"Sorry, Celestial. It's already been arranged. It's either that or it's killing time; and, trust me, I'll make sure you live long enough

246

to see it done. Oh, and don't forget about your precious human. I wanted to kill him the moment he walked in the door."

"You bitch!" My pregnant mother's eyes grew black. "I'll kill—"

"You'll do nothing of the sort. Now eat something for the baby. I want her to be healthy."

Mother pulled me into the living room and let go of my hand. We were instantly outside in front of the blood tree.

"Ma," I began, but what could I say to her? "I had no idea…"

"They need your blood to bring Esther back. That's why they wanted you, why they still want you. Carrie, all those years I was in the hospital were to protect you. I wanted nothing more than for the three of us to be together."

"Do you mean you, me and my father?"

She nodded. "I'm sorry about what happened to him. I loved William." My mother collapsed beside the blood tree.

"So what now?" I asked.

"Make a choice," Mother demanded. "Being a demon is very seductive...the power, the bliss of it all. I know it's hard to resist. But now you know more of the story than you did before. They need you, Carrie. They are just using you. Now it's up to you to decide for yourself what to do."

"And you? What will you do?" I asked.

She got up. "I'm leaving. I have something I must do."

"Take me with you." I said without thinking.

She shook her head no. "I can't. It's dangerous and you would be safer here than you would if you were with me. I promise to come back for you." She hugged me.

247

I didn't even see her leave. I stood there looking at the blood tree, reached to touch its trunk. No magic, no visions. I guess I knew all I needed to know for tonight. I floated back into my room and closed my balcony doors.

I learned so much tonight. So I could have something else? I could be with Noah? I wanted to be with Noah, I wanted to be a normal human, but my demon... would it let me? The monster inside of me needed to be satisfied. So I was faced with the most important question of my life.

To sin or not to sin, that was the question...

Frances wanted me to save her sister from the death penalty. In exchange for her sister's life, Frances gave me her mother's most expensive jewelry: onyxes, opals, pearls, diamonds; every stone, every expensive metal you could think of, I now owned. Even Aunt Carly was astonished with my newly acquired jewelry collection. Of course, my crowning achievement was still the diamond she gave me for my birthday. I taunted Frances by wearing her mother's jewelry to school, and in the process I made Noah even more curious about my new lifestyle.

The Friday before Christmas break, I wrote Frances a note and passed it to her as I left the cafeteria.

It simply read: *Today*

Frances knew exactly what I meant. Her nightmare was about to be over thanks to me.

Truthfully I hated the fact that I loved the way my demon made me feel. I wanted desperately to be normal. I didn't want to do bad things, but my demon did. I recognized that the monster was a part of me.

I tried to resist. I really did. But once I saw Frances and smelled her aroma, I could no longer deny my demon. I had to do something.

I told Noah that I was leaving early and I wanted him to meet me at my house after school. He walked me to my car and kissed me on the cheek. He didn't ask about the business I needed to handle. I was grateful.

I dropped my car off at my house because I wanted to fly. I knew it was broad daylight, but I felt comfortable flying. None of my aunts questioned why I was home in the middle of the day, and none of them seem to care. Nor did it interest them that I was dressed like a sexy Harry Potter movie extra with my cloak on.

Flying during the day was a much different experience from flying at night. The darkness was my cover. I could fly low. But in the daytime I had to fly high in the sky. I wasn't exactly eager to incite hysteria amongst the masses. An eclipse blanketed the sky as I flew, just as it had done before when I flew at night. The skies grew dark. They seemed to know my intentions.

You know you don't physically have to be there in order to influence someone, Carrie. Aunt Cara's voice came ringing in my head. In the high altitude it wasn't appealing.

I know. I want to be there, I told her.

I wanted to watch the havoc I was about to unleash. Actually, it was more like mercy. I was being all too kind to Rochelle.

I landed on the top of the prison that housed Rochelle. I could smell her. She smelled stale. When she hacked up dear old dad, she had the most amazing fragrance coming off her skin. Her redolence was so appealing like freshly baked cookies. Now she was not as alluring, as she once was.

Since killing her father, Rochelle lost almost half of the weight she gained. She looked like herself again.

What a waste.

Orion had torn his family apart. He needed to die. He was a waste of space. Rochelle did a good job, too. The coroner had to identify him by dental records. He deserved to be butchered. Poor Rochelle was in prison, damaged and scared. Rochelle was about to give her father even more of her. No one deserved to serve time or be put to death for his murder, and I was going to see to it that no one was.

Not another waste.

I concentrated really hard. I almost burst a blood vessel in my head as I projected the illusion of me in the cell with Rochelle. I could see clearly in my mind.

"Rochelle," I called. She was the only person who could see me.

"Oh, shit!" Rochelle yelled. "How in the hell did you —" She stopped. "I know you."

We never met before, but she recognized my voice.

"Yes, you do," I cooed. I walked closer to her and pulled down my hood so she could get a better look at me. "Rochelle, how did it ever come to this?"

She was not afraid of me. She sat up and pulled out a cigarette from under her mattress. She actually looked a little cute in her state issued orange jumpsuit. Prison agreed with her.

"Rochelle, those things will kill you," I admonished her.

"So what now? Kill the guard, get out of here?" she asked sarcastically.

"No, Rochelle, how would that help you?"

"Oh, so you are helping me now?" She took a long drag. "You are the reason I am in here. I know what you are." She indicted me. She was angry and I could smell her hatred. I became intoxicated by her smell. I became excited.

"I know what you are and what you are trying to get me to do. GO AWAY!" she demanded. She started to shake uncontrollably. She took another drag in an attempt to calm her nerves.

"Rochelle, wasn't your father the one who was hurting you? He hurt you, Frankie, and Liz. He made you gain unwanted weight. You didn't want to gain all that weight, but it was the only way to stop him from messing with you. Then he rejected you. HOW DARE HE?" My eyes grew dark. Excitement raced through me. I was about to burst from the high I felt. I began to float.

"He deserved what he got," I continued, "every little bit of it." Rochelle nodded in agreement then she retreated to the corner of the cot farthest away from me. I felt so powerful, Superman himself couldn't stop me. "Your sisters are safe now, too. You didn't do this just for you; you did it for them," I reassured her.

252

"I saved them," she whispered.

I was winning. Her will was weakening.

"Yes, you did. You were so brave and strong. They needed you. And you didn't disappoint them," I added.

She smiled weakly. "I did it for them, for all of us." She sat upright with her feet on the concrete floor. "But now, I'm in here," she sobbed.

"Yes, and you are going to the gas chamber."

She jumped up. I placed my bare feet on the concrete floor and sat down beside her.

"What?" she asked.

"You haven't been following your case? Tsk, tsk, tsk, Rochelle. The prosecution is seeking the death penalty. It's all over the news."

She had no idea. "How? They know what he did to us!" she screamed.

A guard walked past, seeing only what looked like Rochelle talking to herself and the guard laughed. "Pipe down, Lee. Pretending to be crazy now isn't going to help you out much," the guard mumbled and she walked away.

Rochelle whispered to me, "How can this be?"

"Rochelle, you killed your father. You stabbed him over a hundred times. They could hardly identify him. He wasn't attacking when you killed him. You can't even claim self-defense. That's premeditation. It was clearly something you thought about. Not to mention how rich and powerful your father was. You had to expect some form of retribution, right?"

I placed my arm around her to make her believe I was comforting her.

"What can I do to save myself?" she asked.

"There is one thing, but I don't know if you are strong enough." I got up from beside her. "Only a strong and brave person can do what I am about to suggest."

"I'll do anything to stop them from taking my life."

"What life, Rochelle? If they don't kill you, you will be in prison for the rest of your life. That's not living. You're already dead. What did you think? That they were going to let you waltz out of here? This is it for you, unless you can make a case for insanity, but not too many people have successfully won an insanity defense. And let's say you do win, you will be doped up in the psych ward for the rest of your life. It's over, Rochelle. It's going to be this cell or a padded room." I spread my arms out to illustrate her possibilities were limited.

"No! I… I …" She struggled with her words, but I knew what she was thinking without having to see her thoughts. She killed her father for what she thought was the greater good. I agreed with her, but unfortunately the State of Maryland didn't share our opinion.

"Shh, it's okay," I soothed her.

"I don't know what to do. I don't want them to kill me. And I don't want to stay in prison for the rest of my life."

"I'm so sorry, Rochelle, but that is the way it has to be. Unless…." I stopped short of finishing my sentence, so she would take the bait.

"Unless what?" she asked.

I began to pace around the room. "I can't ask that of you. You have already done too much."

"Please, please help me!" she cried.

Music to my ears. "I don't know if I can. You're in way too deep."

"There has to be something else."

"What if there was something else, another choice...would you be willing?"

"Anything!"

"Rochelle, life has failed you tremendously. It's no one's fault. Well, for argument sake, let's blame your father. He was a dick. There is nothing left for you here, in this world." I sat beside her again. "Maybe you should leave it all behind."

She looked confused. I had to spell it out for her. "It's time to leave this life and go on to the next one."

"What are you saying?" She stopped crying. She knew exactly what I meant. She thought about it once before, right after she killed her father, but she was afraid then. Now she had nothing to lose.

"I've seen you happy, Rochelle. I've seen you going to college, getting married, having children, but not in this life. I saw it all in your next one," I explained.

"Is there such a place for me?"

"Yes. Unlike these stupid people, I knew how disgusting your father was. He needed to die. You did this world a service. And this is how they repay you, by penalizing you for your noble deed. But in your next life, you shall be rewarded with the life you deserve."

"So there is another life? An afterlife for me?" she asked. She so desperately wanted to believe what I was saying.

"Rochelle, you know this already. It's all true. How else you can see me and talk to me? I'm your guide there."

"But I have to—"

"Yes. That is one of the setbacks. You can't continue on in this life if you want to live in the next one."

She thought for a moment. "Would you tell my sisters I will see them again? That I loved them?"

"Of course, I will. Rochelle, you are the best sister anyone can have. Now do I need to tell you how to tie that rope so it won't give under the pressure from the weight of your body?"

She shook her head no. "Will it hurt?" she asked as she started to loop and tie the sheets together to make a sturdy rope.

"I won't lie to you, Rochelle; that's another setback. In order to receive the joy that awaits you, you need to experience some pain, but it won't last. You won't even remember it once you have crossed over," I assured her. "Are you ready?"

"Yes." She placed a chair under the pipe to help her wrap the sheet around it to assist her in her death.

"Good girl." I almost passed out, I felt so good.

Noah came charging into my room.

"Noah?" I was reading a book and not even a good one.

Funny how I didn't even hear the door, nor did my aunts warn me.

This must have been the work of Aunt Carly.

She wanted this encounter to be as eventful as possible.

"Turn on your TV!" he ordered.

"What is going on?" I jumped up from my relaxed position and searched for the remote to turn the television on.

It was all over the news; Rochelle Coco Lee was found in her cell dead. She committed suicide by hanging herself. "WOW!" What else could I say? That was me.

"Can you believe this?" Noah asked.

I actually could. I was there. I saw it. "This is something else," I answered. I wanted to say it was amazing, but I knew that would not go over well. My handiwork kept making the news, and I was feeling pretty pleased with myself.

"Yeah, 'something else' is right. Something wicked is really going on here." He paced around the room. I thought he was going to wear out my floor.

"Noah, calm down." I went to rub his shoulders, but he pulled away.

"Did your aunts have anything to do with this?" he whispered.

"Noah?" Ever since my change, we haven't really discussed my aunts. It just never came up again. But here we were having the one conversation I hated having when I was a human. I guess I would have to address it one day, and he was making today the day.

I wish I could take the credit for this one. It was a thing of beauty. Aunt Carly laughed.

Before I could answer, he added, "Never mind. I just hope you didn't. I don't care about your aunts, Carrie. I care about you.

257

You know, ever since you came back to school, some real ill shit has been going down."

"Noah, please—" What was I going to say? What was I going to tell him?

He stopped pacing and kissed my forehead. "Good night, Carrie."

"Noah, wait..."

He stormed out of my room, down the stairs and out of the door. I could have stopped him, but honestly, what was I going to say? I couldn't explain to him what was going on. I mean I could, but why would I do that?

Thanks a lot, Aunt Carly, you could have warned me, I said coldly.

She was still laughing. *Anytime. I don't care whose misery it is, as long as it isn't mine.*

She enjoyed that too much.

I tried calling Noah, but he didn't answer his cell phone. Of course, that was to be expected.

Give him space. He adores you. Aunt Chris added.

"He thinks we're monsters," I said, defeated. I sat back down on my bed.

My cell phone rang. It was needy Frances. She was starting to behave like an ex trying to win me back, so naturally she was getting on my nerves.

"Rochelle is DEAD!" she screamed.

"Sorry to hear that," I said.

"Why couldn't you save her? Help her like I asked?" she sobbed.

"I did help her. I did *exactly* what you asked."

She stopped sobbing, "What? You did that to her?" she asked in disbelief.

"She is safe. No more harm can come to her, and she can't do any more harm. That is what you wanted, is it not?"

"I didn't want her to die!" More sobs followed.

"How else could she be safe?" I asked earnestly. Frances was silent, so silent, in fact, that I thought she had hung up on me. "Frances?"

"Thank you, Carrie." she said dryly through her tears. "I have to go."

"We will be in touch." I was not sure that we would be. It just sounded like the appropriate way to end our conversation. We had unfinished business. No way was I going to allow her to dismiss me. I was the demon and she was the pathetic human, not the other way around.

After my conversations with Frances and Noah, I felt drained. For the rest of the day and the days that followed, I was like a zombie. I wasn't really there. I felt empty. I hadn't really talked to Noah. Sure we were with each other at school and we hung out, but it wasn't the same as before our disagreement. I didn't feel the overwhelming sense of joy when I was with him; instead, I felt ashamed and isolated, as though he was aware of my unbecoming behavior.

Had I been fooling myself? Was I ever really happy when I decided to give this demon life a try?

The closer time inched toward Christmas, the more disgusted I became with myself. My aunts didn't say anything about my sudden mood change, either. None of them tried to convince me of the demon life. They appeared not to care anymore.

I noticed when I was around sin and when I was influencing people, it felt good in an addictive kind of way. The more evil I did, the more I needed to do. I began to feed off that feeling; I wanted it more and more, like a drug addict or an alcoholic. With Frances, I felt a need to be around her. We both wanted the same things. It felt like the high you get when you did something you truly loved, an indescribable rush.

But when I was with Noah, I felt good in a different way. It wasn't obsessive or consuming, just natural. I wasn't trying to fill a void that couldn't be filled, but more like my life taking its natural course. I did conclude I couldn't have both. I was two people living in one space, both competing for supremacy. Also I hated hiding my true self from Noah. I wanted him to love me through my imperfections.

You're perfect. Never mind what your human says, Aunt Carly insisted.

Please leave me to my thoughts.

Fine, stop screaming them at us.

It had been rough after Frances's sister committed suicide, but I was trying to rebound. The doorbell rang. Again I was startled because that wasn't a sound I heard often.

It's for you, Aunt Cara said. She was practicing her cello. She was laughing, and so were my other two aunts.

Really? Who is it and what do they want on a Saturday morning?

To my surprise, it was Noah. *What's so funny?* I probed.

"Noah?" More laughter poured into my head from all three of my aunts. I did my best to ignore them.

He was dressed like he was going on a job interview or a funeral. Was Rochelle's service today? I never seen Noah in a suit and tie before; he looked really good.

"Good morning." He smiled. "And Merry Christmas." He had a beautifully wrapped box in his hand.

I was completely caught off guard. For one, I didn't know it was Christmas, and secondly, why was he dressed like that?

"May I come in?" he asked.

I escorted him through the foyer. "Are you going to get dressed first, or do you want your present first?" he asked.

"What?" I thought he was mad at me. I thought we weren't speaking to each other. I was completely blindsided by this.

"It's Christmas," he responded. "And you said you would spend the day with me and my family—unless you've changed your mind."

"People get dressed up for Christmas?" I asked aloud not really meaning to. Aunt Cara stopped her practice and walked over to us with her cello still in hand.

"Good morning, Mrs. Carter, and Merry Christmas," Noah said to my aunt.

She smiled. "Same to you, Noah. Will you be staying for breakfast?"

"No, thank you, ma'am. Carrie and I have to be on our way." He looked at me to see if I was still going on our Christmas date as I promised what felt like years ago.

"Of course," Aunt Cara said as she walked past us, grinning.

Is there a private joke going on? I asked my aunts, perturbed.

"Well, I guess you should get ready first," Noah said as he examined my outfit. I had on tee shirt and gym shorts. "You can't wear what you have on."

"Your family gets ready for Christmas dinner rather early." I started to walk slowly up the stairs.

"Dinner is at four. We are going to church for Christmas service."

My aunts were all laughing in my head. I shut my bedroom door.

Gee, thanks for the heads up.

Still laughing.

Am I going to…you know…burst into flames if I go in a church?

More hysterics from the peanut gallery, it was getting on my nerves.

Why? Is that what normally happens when you got to church? Aunt Chris managed to ask in between laughs.

"Okay, fine, joke all you want," I said. My aunts laughed even more.

The biggest devils are in church, Carrie, Aunt Carly finally said after laughing.

What to wear? I never been to church before; as I previously stated, my family was never very pious, for obvious reasons. In a flash, Aunt Carly was in my room with an appropriate black dress with cap sleeves that hit me right above my calves. She handed me two wrapped gifts. She pulled my long silky black hair into a bun and handed me some super red high heels.

"Thanks." I smiled.

The gifts are Noah's of course. The small one is watch, Omega, and the big one has swimming gear in it. He'll love it, she told me after she finished getting me ready.

Thanks again, Aunt Carly.

Well, it gave me a reason to shop. She left my room.

I put on my diamond necklace. Surely that would make her just about die with satisfaction. When I came down the stairs with his gifts, Noah looked surprised.

Oh, no, was I dressed wrong? Was this not Christmas attire? I was growing mad at my aunt for setting me up for failure. "I can change," I said.

"Why would you do that?" he questioned. "You look...wow. I can't describe how beautiful you are." He smiled. He was about to hand me my gift.

"I'll wait till dinner. Let's go to church."

My first church experience as a demon just wasn't what I expected. My aunts were right. The biggest devils were in church. I heard what was on the minds of humans in church, and it was unnerving. All the sin that was on the minds of Christians was unbelievable. I had the hardest time trying to stay calm and not getting excited. The choir, however, was amazing. I was almost brought to tears by the harmony, along with the message. The sermon was what really got me. Was I to believe that God, no matter how badly I messed up, no matter how poorly I behaved, would still love me? Even if I didn't choose him? Why would He do that? Then He sent His Son on Christmas to die for me? Really? I had a hard time with that one. Why would He bother in the first place?

Something about unconditional love, Noah said.

As we drove to Noah's house after service, he asked, "So what did you think?"

"About what?"

"Church? Did you like it?"

"It was cool." That was about all I could say. The jury was still out about how I felt. My feelings were mixed. As a demon, church would be entertaining. I could only imagine the anarchy I would create. People in church were the same as the people who were not. The only difference between the two, one group dressed better. They all sinned, every last human. There were no exceptions. That was the rule. The thought of making a Christian sin, only turned me on even more. However, I would follow Noah anywhere including church. I loved him that much. I would try to be good and pretend to understand God's love and why it was so sought after. I would put on a fake smile and sit there torturing myself if I thought it would make Noah happy. Surprisingly, I did enjoy the choir but the choir couldn't change me…maybe Noah could. Maybe Noah could with God's help. I was sure that didn't want to risk Noah seeing my demon side. I was not sure if God was powerful enough to cure someone as wretched as me.

"Cool, huh? Well, I was wondering, how would you feel about going back?" Noah asked.

"I wouldn't mind." I smiled at him. That was the truth. I would go anywhere with Noah.

"How about every Sunday? Would you go every Sunday, with me?"

Wow, I didn't see that coming. I wondered if my aunts had. Maybe that was what all the laughter was about: the demon and the angel going to church, being the ultimate odd couple, now that was kind of funny.

"Can I think about it?" I asked.

"Sure." He smiled and leaned over to smell my hair. "I won't make you do anything you don't want to do."

If only it were that easy. I was born of sin. And most times, that was all I wanted to do.

Christmas Sucks

Noah's family was great, with the exception of Mr. Greene, Noah's father. He wasn't particularly fond of me. I couldn't figure out why. Everyone else loved me. *I hope it's not a race thing. Interracial dating is so accepted these days,* I thought.

"Carrie, let me get your coat," Mrs. Greene offered as she literally ripped my coat off of me. I didn't need it but Aunt Chris reminded me as I was leaving out, *It's December and twenty degrees out, people will notice.*

Personally, I felt stupid wearing a coat.

Noah's sisters were very welcoming. "I hated that Melissa chick," the oldest whispered to me as we sat in the living room. "She thought she was so much better than us or anyone for that matter."

"Yeah, that sounds a lot like MJ," I agreed. I did a public service by knocking her down a peg or two.

"Oh, you know her? I heard she shaved off all her hair. I knew she was crazy underneath that perfect facade."

"Yeah." I laughed on the inside.

I loved to watch The Greene family interact with each other. They were the definition of a real functional family, key word being functional. Noah and his sisters played and teased each other while Mrs. Greene prepared dinner and Mr. Greene was stoic as he sat in his Lazy Boy, watching sports. There were gifts were under the Christmas tree. It was like a Hallmark card, too perfect and so unreal, yet here I was in the middle of it. It felt different in a good way, as if the universe was showing me what I could have if I was normal.

Noah led me to his bedroom.

"Can you even have company upstairs, in your room?" I asked him. I knew things were a little relaxed at my house so I was unsure about the average human household.

"Can you?" he asked as he kissed me on my lips and closed the door. He led me to his bed, still kissing me. "My family loves you."

"Why, because I'm not MJ?" Noah could have been dating a dog and his family would approve as long as it wasn't MJ.

He stopped kissing me. He leaned over me as I was laid on his full size bed. "Yes." He smiled. "But they *like* you, Carrie."

"Not your dad, though. Is it because I'm… you know, a Democrat?" I joked. We both laughed.

He sat beside me, and I rested my head on his shoulder. He changed from his three piece suit into a gray Polo sweater and charcoal jeans, even Aunt Carly would approve. "No. It's not that."

"Then what is it?" I probed.

"It's your family. He's worried that I'll get hurt. Just like Pop, he is worried too."

"My aunts?" It was always my aunts.

Noah nodded to confirm.

"Noah-"

"Don't worry. I am where I want to be. So far your aunts haven't come to eat my brains," he replied.

It wasn't like that was not so farfetched. "No, not yet. They usually wait till News Year's for brain eating," I teased. We both laughed again.

"I kind of wanted them to see for themselves that you were not them, whatever they may think your aunts are," he said. Then he kissed my cheek.

I asked, "And what does your family think my aunts are?" He looked at me with pleading eyes, letting me know that he didn't want to ruin Christmas with talk about my evil bloodline. "I want to know."

"Carrie..."

"Just answer the question."

"Pop thinks they are witches or something and he has my dad believing it too. It's nothing."

"Witches?" I wished.

"I told you, it's no biggie. I know better than that. Your aunts are just different. They are beautiful and a little odd. "

268

I asked, "Why does Pop feel that way?"

Noah reluctantly answered, "Something about your aunts. Well, it can't be your aunts because your aunts aren't that old, but maybe their mothers or grandmothers. It's probably not your family at all. He thinks your family killed some of people of Howard Town with witchcraft or something like that. I told you it was silly."

"Impossible!" My aunts couldn't kill anyone literally, at least I hoped.

"Yeah, and then we read that article in the library and all that crazy stuff started happening. He had me believing it there for a while, but it's all a load of crap."

"What?"

"I know. Just let it go. It's over."

"Noah, why didn't you tell me this?" I felt betrayed. I read his facial expression. He was wondering why he said anything at all.

"Carrie—"

"Hey, Dog Breath!" That was Noah's oldest sister bursting into the room. "Ma-Ma, Pop, and Gramps are here." She darted out the room as quickly as she came.

"C'mon. Now we exchange gifts and eat." He smiled as he ran out of the room and down the stairs. He was relieved that our conversation had been interrupted.

Interrupted, yes; forgotten, no. We would discuss this later.

I put on the best fake smile and followed behind the Greene siblings. I wasn't as eager as Noah and his sister were, but I was glad to see Noah happy.

As I walked down the stairs, Noah ran into two members of his family as they walked in the front door. An older gentleman stood next to a woman that must have been his wife. The two older people were Noah's great grandfather and his great grandmother, which meant that the slightly younger looking gentleman must have been his grandfather. Everyone crowded around the three as if they were celebrities, with the exception of Noah's father, who seemed to be perfectly comfortable in his Lazy Boy. He was the only one who noticed me as I came downstairs. I eased into the confusion. Noah quickly grabbed my arm.

"You ready?"

I nodded yes.

"Okay." He smiled and turned to his grandfather. "Gramps, you remember Carrie?"

"Hello, Carrie." Gramps had to be in his sixties. He was still in good shape. Noah told me that his grandfather ran a mile almost every day. He had salt-and-pepper hair and the same pretty blue eyes that almost everyone in Noah's family had, except for Noah's dad and his youngest sister.

"Noah, you didn't tell me you were dating a movie star," he joked. Then he whispered to Noah, "She sure did cute out."

I pretended that I didn't hear the comment about "cute-ing" out. "It's a pleasure to see you again, sir." I commented. He smiled at me as he released me.

"Noah, you did pretty good." He winked at Noah. "I might have to steal her from you."

"Gramps, you need to hang out with my Ma-Ma. She was able to remarry and did a good job with picking out Pop," Noah responded.

His great-grandmother remarried? At her age? I guess love can happen to anyone at any time, so there was still hope for me and Noah. I smiled to myself. I was ready to meet the love birds who found each other each at such an old age. Noah led me to his great grandmother and step great-grandfather. I stopped dead in my tracks. My heart literally stopped beating. I stopped breathing. My eyes were deceiving me; they had to be. "Pop, Ma-Ma, this my Carrie. The one I told you guys about."

"Greene." Pop said with recognition. "Carrie Greene?"

Noah blushed. "Well, not yet, but I am hoping one day, maybe." He shrugged.

It was Pastor Cross from the Archangel Michael Lutheran Church. The same pastor who gave me the articles on my aunts, was here, with me and Noah, on Christmas? *What the hell?*

It is him.

Ingrid didn't recognize me, I guess due to my demon. I changed physically since the last time she saw me. I would look different to her. "Oh, Noah," she crooned, "she's beautiful!" She reached for me. Pop, or Pastor Cross, fought against his urge to slap her hand down. He turned beet red as she hugged me.

"How would you know, Ingrid? You can't see." Pastor Cross snapped.

Everyone ignored his comment. "So, Pop, what do you think?" Noah asked.

He grabbed me and hugged as tightly as his frail arms could. He pulled me close and whispered into my ear, "You are one of them? Aren't you?"

We both smiled as he abruptly let me go. I looked at Noah. "I see why Ma-Ma remarried. Pop is charming," I said with as much love as I could muster.

"Pop, what did you say to Carrie?" Noah asked as his mother led everyone into the dining room for dinner.

"Ancient Chinese secret," he embraced Noah from the back as though he protecting Noah from me as I followed behind them.

This must have been what was so funny to my aunts.

"Noah," I whispered, "your family has been in Maryland for a long time, right?"

Noah replied, "My family was instrumental in the development of Howard County. Carrie, you knew that already." That would explain why Noah's father thought my aunts were witches; his family knew the history of Howard County.

"And Ma-Ma is now a Cross?" I asked

"No, she didn't marry Pop until a couple of years ago. But they have known each other since they were little. She kept her name from her first marriage, Peterson. You all right?" he asked me.

"You should have told me he was the pastor mentioned in the article we read in the library?"

"What article?" He questioned as if he didn't know.

"The one about the Coolidge Carters." I answered.

He replied, "I asked him about that. It was one of his great-grandfathers or something. That's when he told me the stories that are more like fables about your aunts. The man went crazy and burned down the whole town. I did my own research."

"That's why you were distant with me? Why we kind of chilled out for a minute there?"

"Yes. Carrie, please, don't worry about it." He grabbed my hand as we all stood in the dining area. There was assigned seating complete with name tags. "I decided that I wanted you, not your aunts. I know you are not like them. Or maybe you are, and then that makes them great human beings because, well, you are."

I could feel my face tremor from the anger that was building up inside of me.

"Are you all right?" Noah asked again as he sat beside me at the dinner table. He smiled and rubbed my face.

"Tell me why didn't you say something at the library about your great-grandmother's husband?" Everyone else sat down at their seats and started to talk amongst themselves.

"A lot happened at the library, remember?" Noah paused. "Besides, I didn't find out till later." He whispered.

"How much later?" I wanted to continue the inquisition; this was vital information that he hadn't told me. I was sure he could tell was bothered.

Noah kissed my check in an effort to diffuse the situation. "Care Bear, let's just enjoy the rest of today and figure the rest out tomorrow." I could feel the stares coming from across the table from the Pastor, he was watching us.

"Noah—" I started. I was too focused on finding out all the facts to care that Pastor Cross was gazing at us.

"Drop it," Noah ordered. "It's over." When my face fell, he asked again, "Are you all right, Carrie?"

"Yes, just ready to eat." I played along. I fixed my mouth to smile, a little. I wanted to fly out of the window and go home. This must had been what was what was so funny to my aunts. They knew and didn't warn me about Noah's lineage. I never felt so stupid in my life.

They would pay.

I didn't let my thoughts grow any darker. This was not the place or the time.

We sat at the dining room table, waiting on Christmas dinner. I had seen this scene in many movies and on television before. I never thought that I would be having Christmas dinner with my boyfriend's family or a Christmas. Hell, I never thought I would have a boyfriend.

The food didn't look all that appetizing. I turned down the collard greens, the corn on the cob, the mashed potatoes, and some other foods I couldn't identify.

"Not very hungry, are you?" Pastor Cross asked.

"Just trying to make sure there was room for the ham," I lied, as I tried to sound excited about dinner. I took two slices of the dry looking ham and a scoop of macaroni.

I want to die.

"Are you okay?" Noah asked as he ate his dinner. "You haven't quite been yourself."

If he asks me that question one more time, I swear… "I'm fine. I'm just a little nervous, this being my first Christmas." I didn't know whether or not Pastor Cross wanted to go to war at dinner. That was the real reason for my anxiety. Noah grabbed my hand under the table and held it. He looked me in the eye and gave me a reassuring smile. I wasn't so sure.

"So, Carrie, tell me about your parents. Are they native Baltimoreans?" Pastor Cross asked. So he wanted to go to war at Noah's expense. Fine, the battle lines had been drawn. I had no choice.

I ate a piece of ham. It tasted like paper. Great, not only did I have to eat when I didn't want to or need to, the food wasn't even good.

"My mother is from here. I don't know much about my father." That was the truth.

"Your mother's name?" Pastor Cross continued.

"Celeste Carter." I ate a scoop of macaroni. It scraped the inside of my mouth. It tasted like paste.

"I wonder if she is any kin to the Carter family from Howard County?" Pastor Cross asked.

"Carter is a common last name," Noah's grandfather interjected as he ate his sweet potatoes.

I declined those. They didn't look sweet at all.

"I doubt it, Pop." Noah's grandfather added.

"Harry, don't get worked up." Ingrid rubbed the back of the pastor's hand as she ate with the other hand.

Noah's younger sister, who was sitting on the other side of me, said, "Pop thinks that this Carter family is like witches or something. He thinks they are responsible for killing his mother. Ma-Ma says his mother committed suicide. But he will swear to you up and down that the Carter family killed her." She paused. "His

275

grandfather went crazy and burned down the whole town trying to kill those women."

She ate her food as if it was good, then continued. "So be careful, Carrie, all the men in our family are crazy," she joked.

Noah was annoyed with his sister, "Pam, go to hell."

"See, what I mean, Noah likes fire, too." She continued to eat.

Noah's other sister chimed in, "We are supposed to be related to the saviors of the town," she said, making a face as though she didn't believe it, "who got rid of the evil Carter demons."

"Really?" I asked.

"Yeah, if you get Pop worked up, he'll tell you all about it. Ma-Ma saved Pop from killing himself. He said he heard voices in his head telling him kill himself. She prayed with him, and that stopped the voices. He will swear you up and down that demon women possessed him. Ma-Ma, Pop, and some other guy are the last living members of Howard Town. The story is better than any Stephen King novel. I told Ma-Ma that we should publish it."

My stomach ran to the back of my throat.

"Enough of the crazy talk! You guys will have Carrie thinking we are all loony." Noah's mother demanded. She cleared her throat and spoke in her normal tone. "Well, you have her thinking we are crazier than we really are." She smiled and I smiled, too.

She was on my side. I was glad somebody was. Everyone went back to eating. There was no more talking after that.

"Dinner was great," Noah's younger sister said.

Really? Did I eat the same meal?

276

After dinner we exchanged gifts in the living room. Aunt Carly was right; Noah loved the swim gear and the watch I gave him.

"You brought Noah an Omega?" his mother asked.

"Yes, ma'am," I replied.

"Wow." Mrs. Greene mouthed, "An Omega," to her husband, who went back to sitting in his Lazy Boy, watching TV. I got the feeling that Mr. Greene wasn't into Christmas, dinner, or me.

Noah stood by the Christmas tree, handing out gifts and taking pictures. Once he was finished, he came over to me. Everyone was too wrapped up in their gifts to notice Noah and me. "Come with me upstairs," he requested as he took my hand. We went to in his room. He shut the door behind us.

"I thought we were participating in the gift exchange?" I asked.

"We did." He led me to his bed. "I wanted to give you your gift alone, just the two of us. I want you all to myself."

I smiled. "Really?" I melted. That comment almost made up for dinner. Almost.

He went over to his closet and pulled out the same box from earlier this morning. "Yes, this being your first Christmas and all, I wanted to give it to you as soon as you opened the door this morning, and it was killing me in the car and all during church service but…" He handed the box to me. "I hope this is an acceptable gift. Merry Christmas, my Care Bear."

I rubbed my hands against the pretty box. "I don't even want to open it." I smelled the box. It smelled old, not stale, but aged. "I'm sure that whatever it is, it is perfect."

He stood in front of me. "Well, open it," he demanded. I slowly took off the wrapping paper. "Care Bear, just rip the damn thing open."

I smiled. I did as I was told. It was a wooden keepsake box like from Things Remembered. It had the name of Ingrid Jones engraved on it. "Ingrid Jones?" I asked.

"Open it."

I opened the wooden box. Inside was an antique sterling silver jewelry box with onyx and opal accents. It was the most beautiful jewelry box I had ever seen. "Oh, no, Noah, you didn't."

He explained, "It belonged to Ma-Ma. She has several of these. There is a lot of history associated with this jewelry box. It is as old as Howard Town, when it was still Howard Town. Anyway, my mother has one and my sisters each have one, and you have one. You are one of us now, Carrie Carter. I love you."

"Noah, I can't." If I could cry, I would have. Here it was, my aunts were most likely responsible for the death of some of his family members, and he was giving me one of Ma-Ma's prized possessions. "Please, Noah, I can't accept this." I tried to give the jewelry box back, but he wouldn't take it.

"What's wrong? You don't like it?" He panicked.

"No, that's not it. I love it, but I can't accept this."

"What is it, then? I thought it would be a great place to keep your beautiful jewelry collection."

"It is, but it belonged to your great-grandmother. Keep it in your family." I placed the box on the bed.

"That's what I'm hoping for. That we could give it to—"

"STOP IT!" I didn't need to hear the rest. He was making a future with me. All this time, all I ever wanted was for him to look at me the same way he looked at MJ, and now that he did, now that he wanted me, I couldn't have that future. I was a demon. I was a monster.

"Stop what, Carrie? What's really going on here?" He crossed his arms. I was pissing him off. Here he was giving me the very best part of him, and I was rejecting it. What was wrong with me? I just couldn't take his gift, I felt unworthy.

I stood up. "I have to go." I went for the door, but he blocked it.

"Not until you tell me what's going on."

"Noah!" I closed my eyes. I didn't know what they would look like. My human side knew this was wrong and knew that there was no way I could accept the jewelry box, but my demon side wanted the gift the more I tried to deny it. My will was growing weak. My demon was slowly taking over. I spoke as slowly as I could. "I...will...not...accept...your...gift." I peeked out of the corner of my eye, too scared to fully open them. He moved from the front of the door and retreated to a corner in his room.

He looked heartbroken. I wanted to die right then and there. He walked over to me. "Then I cannot accept your gifts, either."

"What?" Was this really happening?

He went to the corner of his bedroom and retrieved the box of swimwear and handed me the watch.

"Noah, don't be ridiculous. They're yours. You can't give them back. I won't accept them." I shoved the gifts back at him.

"It's not your choice; it's mine." He tried to hand me the items, but I walked away.

"No. I won't accept your gift because it was your great grandmother's. I don't deserve it," I admitted.

Noah stood in front of me with the presents I had given him.

I shook my head. "I can't take those back home." I couldn't take them back even if I wanted to. Aunt Carly would kill me and Noah. No one gave back a gift from her. "I'm sorry." I swiftly left Noah's room before he could say or do anything and made a beeline for the front door.

Before I could make my escape, Pastor Cross stopped me. "Don't you need a coat, young lady? It's freezing out."

I kept walking toward the door.

"So you knew who I was, didn't you? When you came to see me at my church? You conned me and my great grandson."

"No! That's not true!" I growled. What did he know? He didn't know me.

"Stay away from him," he ordered through gritted teeth.

"Old man, get over it." I huffed. "I do not want to hurt Noah. I love him!" I wanted to fly, but then I remembered that I drove my car. So I walked over to my vehicle.

"What do you know about love?" he asked.

"It hurts," I answered, then got into my car and peeled off.

I hated Christmas. It sucked.

Something To Think About

I was so irate that driving was difficult. I couldn't focus. I was consumed with one thought one thought only: how I was going to kill my aunts?

My eyes were pitch black. I was ready to fight. I left my car on the pathway I didn't bother to park it in the car port. I slammed the door shut and flew up to my balcony.

My aunts were already in my room waiting for me.

Of course, I should have known to expect this scene, I thought.

Aunt Carly looked very pleased with herself, Aunt Chris looked a little upset, and Aunt Cara looked indifferent. Even though I was angry at them, they still were the most beautiful creatures I had ever laid eyes. They looked like they were doing a photo shoot.

"How was your Christmas?" Aunt Carly asked. She was laughing so hard, I hardly heard her. I was so mad I was about to leap the five feet that separated us and pounce on Aunt Carly first, then hopefully neutralize Aunt Chris, then Aunt Cara. But instead I concentrated really hard and focused all my energy, all my rage, on a beach a calming place. I could see an incredible ocean with a marvelously decorated ocean floor. I saw awesome and exotic creatures through the crystal clear water. The unbelievable colors danced on the ocean bed. The sky was clear—no clouds in sight, just a perfect endless blue.

The sun wasn't visible, but heat from it was present. The warmth wrapped my body like the warmest embrace. The light brown sand was warm and soft, like slippers on my feet. My nose was seduced by the pleasant smell of honey and salt. Small waves whispered hello as they greeted my feet. I was in a happy place.

"You do very powerful illusions." Aunt Chris interrupted my thought process with her observation. Everything I saw in my mind was all around me. Apparently my aunts could see my vision as well. Aunt Carly looked around; she was impressed. It was written on her face.

Breathtaking. Aunt Carly playfully kicked the sand with her bare feet.

Aunt Cara held her cards close. She didn't want me to know what she was thinking.

"Why wasn't I informed about what you all did to Noah's family?" I asked in my calmest voice. The skies grew dark, as did my eyes. A storm was brewing in my paradise.

"Would it have made a difference? You made your choice, and it was him," Aunt Cara said. Storm clouds floated over the three of them. Aunt Cara showed no emotion, and it was obvious she didn't fear me.

"If you ruin my hair, if one speck of rain gets on me, Carrie…" Aunt Carly warned. Her eyes were black.

I ignored her and began to float. They followed my lead.

War was to be had.

Lightning pierced the sky. The sound of thunder quickly followed. It sounded like a large tree branch hitting the ground, cracking into millions of pieces. A gale of wind ensued. Their hair became part of the scenery. In all my rage, they still looked unbelievably beautiful.

Aunt Carly looked ready to charge, but my Aunt Cara held her back with a cautioning eye. Aunt Cara still showed no emotion. "Yes, we could have said something," Aunt Cara began, "but you would not have listened, Carrie." The wind blew even harder.

"YOU KILLED HIS FAMILY!" I yelled. Lightning struck behind me. Aunt Cara paid no attention to my new trick. Aunt Carly was ready to fight, basically foaming at the mouth for the chance to hurt me. Aunt Chris remained calm. My eyes were black as coal. I could feel the ire building up inside of me. My demon was poised for action.

"Please, that shouldn't even count, it was so easy," Aunt Carly shrugged. "People die every day, Carrie; get over it. It was their time."

Aunt Chris intervened. "We were being hunted. People were becoming suspicious. It had to be done. We had no choice." She spoke calmly.

Aunt Cara told her story, "Clark was sick. I wanted to keep him. I loved him, Carrie. I had never before felt that way about a human. He was crazed for over thirty years. Your mother helped me with creating the illusion of him being well. None of the humans knew about his plight. He was dying and when he passed, everyone felt sorry for me. I never felt so connected to the human world after my change, but the residents of Howard Town came to my aid in my time of need. They supported me after Clark's death. I lost the love of my life." Aunt Cara's face looked sad as she spoke, even though her voice was emotionless. "Then the boys started to change and die. The powerful families in our little town, including the Greene family, started to investigate us."

"We respected Noah's family. They had been good to us," Aunt Chris stated with reverence.

Aunt Cara nodded to agree. Aunt Carly made a face; she didn't care for humans, period.

Aunt Cara continued. "The Greenes were very pious; and when the boys started to get sick and die, they figured out that we were different from humans. They had an idea about what we were."

"You didn't read that article, did you?" Aunt Carly inquired. "The headlines read, 'The Carter Witches Burned At The Stake: The Community is Safe Once Again.' I'm guessing no!"

My fury decreased a little. "What article?" I asked.

"They burned down the whole town, trying to kill us," Aunt Chris said.

"They tried to kill us in many ways," Aunt Cara continued. "The fire was one of them. We had to convince them to hurt themselves. It was hard because some of them were able to resist us."

My storm turned out to be a short one. The skies returned back to their beautiful blue. "We did convince members of Noah's family to kill themselves; but in all fairness, we were trying to convince the whole town to do the same," Aunt Cara allowed.

So we weren't invincible; we could be killed. I quickly removed that thought from my mind. I didn't want them to know what I was thinking.

"After trying to kill us and not being able to do so, they asked us to leave Howard Town and we agreed." Aunt Chris said.

My aunts slowly returned to the sand bed; I floated back to the ground, also.

Aunt Chris finished. "We were vengeful, I'll admit. We wanted to get everyone who tried to kill us. It was destined, Carrie. God had a plan."

"Noah's grandfather knew what I was but, Ingrid did not." I said.

Aunt Carly answered, "She wouldn't. She's legally blind. You have your mother to thank for that."

My illusion disappeared, and we were back in my room. I took my hair out of the bun and started removing the remainder of my clothes, the last reminder of my horrible day.

Aunt Chris stated, "We didn't just go around and hurt the humans…" She thought about what she was saying. "In that instance, it very was necessary." She ventured closer to me. "Cara and Celeste were very happy pretending to be humans. Carly and I wanted them to be happy, so we pretended as well."

"Speak for yourself, Christine. I know what I am and I never had a problem accepting it," Aunt Carly snapped. "I love being evil." She smiled. "It's what I am."

"What will happen if I tell Noah about me, about us?" I wanted some resolution. "That night my mother came to me, you took her away because she was going to expose your secret? If I tell Noah, will I be banished, too? Locked away in some hospital?"

"Do not tell Noah, Carrie," Aunt Cara warned. "There is a plan, a plan greater than you or I. Do not ruin this for us."

"First of all, we didn't technically take your mother; it was an illusion. And secondly, your mother wasn't banished. She made a choice," Aunt Carly insisted.

"I have no choice then. I must tell him." I was almost certain that needed to happen.

"He already knows there is something different about you, but he is too scared to ask. He is afraid all the rumors are true," Aunt Carly answered.

"He needs to learn about me from me," I stated.

"Well, what are you, an angel or a demon because you seemed to be confused?" Aunt Carly smiled.

"I beg you not to," Aunt Cara interrupted.

"Did you tell Clark?" I asked Aunt Cara. "Did my mother tell Caleb's father? Did she tell mine?"

They all stared at each other. They were having a mental conversation without me. I wondered how often they did that? I noticed all of their eyes were black.

"I need to be alone." I said breaking up their wordless conversation. They remained silent. They all just floated out of my bedroom door. Aunt Chris closed the door behind her. I finished changing my clothes; and for the first time since my change, I went to sleep.

I was five years old, chasing a rabbit in front of the main house. I looked happy. Mother waved to me from the patio. Aunt Carly was with Mother, both of them watching me. It was springtime, and everything was beautiful. I walked past the younger version of myself and smiled. I was beautiful. The weight of my family history and rumors hadn't aged me. I wasn't miserable...yet.

"You haven't lived up to your bargain, Celeste," Aunt Carly addressed Mother. "This is not what we agreed to." I walked closer to them and left my younger self at play.

"I never agreed, Carly. I built a family with William and Carrie. I can't just give her to you," Mother responded.

I didn't have any memories of my dad, but he was a part of my life? He didn't just die after being with my mother? We were a family? How?

I walked even closer so I could hear their conversation better.

"William? He will be gone soon, so no need to worry about that," Aunt Carly said.

"That's not what we agreed to." Mother snapped.

"I never agreed, Celeste." Aunt Carly said with acid in her voice.

Go ahead, Carrie, touch the tree, Aunt Carly purred. I looked back at my younger self. The younger me stopped playing with the rabbit and stood still in front at the blood tree.

I turned back to Mother.

"Carly, don't. She is an innocent. Your quarrel is with me." Mother's eyes grew back.

I didn't know what to do.

Should I go to help the younger me, or go to my mother and aunt?

"I'm sorry, Celeste, but she is your daughter; that fact alone makes her anything but innocent."

Go on! Aunt Carly coaxed.

Mother flew off the porch to grab the younger me, but it was too late. The young me had already touched the tree and fallen to the ground. I ran to my younger self and Mother.

"Carly, you bitch!" Mother picked up the young me and flew into the main house. She went to the living room and laid the younger me on the floor. Aunts Cara and Chris were there within seconds. Aunt Carly strolled in after them, sipping on lemonade.

"Wake up, Carrie. Come on," Mother ordered the younger me.

"Carly, what did you do?" Aunt Chris asked.

"Oh, I was just having fun." Aunt Carly waltzed up the stairs. "And I was so disappointed. She just passed out."

Then my younger self screamed and wouldn't stop. Mother, Aunt Cara, and Aunt Chris tried to control me, but couldn't. The younger me must have screamed for five minutes straight without stopping or taking a breath.

"Get back," Mother ordered her sisters.

Aunt Carly came downstairs. "Now that was the reaction I was hoping for."

My other aunts obeyed my mother's command. Mother's eyes turned white. The younger me froze, but I was still awake as I lay on the floor.

Mother hovered above the younger me. Her eyes went black. She didn't say anything. She just stared at the younger me. All of my aunts stood and watched.

"Is it done?" Aunt Cara asked.

"Yes," Mother said, defeated. She picked up the younger me and took me upstairs.

"How much of her memory did you erase?" Aunt Chris asked.

"Most of it. She won't even remember her father. She is yours now," Mother added.

I followed Mother upstairs as she carried the younger me. When I got upstairs, I was in my bedroom in our house in the city. There was an older version of me, sitting on the bed. I was right about the age my aunts took me from Mother.

"Carrie, things will be changing soon," Mother said as she pulled my hair back off my face and sat down beside me.

"Great," the younger, slightly older version of me said with heavy sarcasm.

"I know things have been rough—"

"Really?"

I remembered having this conversation as I watched.

"Things will get better I promise." She smiled.

"I doubt it. We live in Baltimore, you're a single parent, my father is a deadbeat, and your sisters are crazy. People talk about us, Mother. Did you know that? They say we are devils."

"Yes, I know. I'm sorry that you have to deal with that, Carrie."

"Why can't we move?" The younger me asked. "Get away from your sisters and the madness?"

"We can't. The craziness along with your aunts would only follow us," she reasoned.

The younger me placed my head in my hands. Mother patted me on my back. "Look, Carrie, I'm sorry-"

I snapped, "You're not sorry enough." I jumped off the bed and ran out of the room.

I woke up and looked around. I had on a white t-shirt and Sugar Daddy pajama pants I slipped on Christmas night. My hair was wild. I pulled it back into a messy ponytail. I looked outside at the blood tree. It was still bleeding.

Nothing new there.

A different smell came from outside. I could hear Aunt Carly in her room, singing and playing with her hair. Aunt Cara was reading. Aunt Chris was in the stables with the horses. I went to my balcony. There under the moonlit sky was Peter. He parked his car and headed toward the stables. Peter, the man Aunt Chris tried to convince to kill his wife after persuading her to have an affair with his best friend. I lightly stepped off my balcony and landed on the pavement below. I floated to the ground to get a closer look. There was something in Peter's face that intrigued me.

He was quite attractive. He stood five feet eleven inches and weighed about one hundred and ninety pounds, mostly muscle. He was built like a football player and had the blackest, smoothest skin I had ever seen. Despite the cold December wind, he wore a t-shirt under a light jacket.

"Christine," he barked in a deep voice.

My aunt flew from behind Sprinkles, my horse, the one I told my secrets. "Peter," she said pleasantly. She tended to the horses in a blue chiffon dress that fell mid thigh, wearing no shoes. "You have something to tell me." She was not surprised by his visit or his attitude because he definitely had one. I stood in front of the stables, not wanting to expose myself, but I was sure my aunt knew I was there. If nothing else, she could smell me.

"I love my wife," he started.

My aunt wasn't really paying attention to him. She started to tend to another horse of ours. "I know, but that is not the nature of your visit. There is something else you wish to tell me." She brushed the hair off the horse's face.

"I cannot do it. I love Ebony. She cheated on me, fine; I'll have to deal with it, but I will not kill her," he declared. He was strong in his conviction.

"Fine." Aunt Chris looked up at Peter for the first time during their conversation.

"So we are finished, Christine?" Now, he wasn't as sure of himself as he had seemed to be at the beginning of their conversation.

My aunt smiled again. "Whatever you say, Peter."

"The Bible says a man should love his wife—"

Why did Peter continue to talk after my aunt had been so understanding with his position? My aunt's eyes grew dark. The horses started to react wildly to the new atmosphere. She flew to Peter and stood in front of him. She was still calm when she spoke, but it was obvious she was not pleased. "Don't tell me anything about what the Bible says. I've read it front to back and back to front over a million times, human! You made your choice; you chose your wife."

Peter replied, "I chose God."

"Good for you," she replied. "Now leave."

Peter rushed past me. He was sweating now. *Not as confident as he was trying to portray himself to be.* He jumped into his Sonata and sped off.

Aunt Chris went back to grooming the horses. "Carrie, dear," she called. I walked into the stable, "could you fetch me the pail by your feet, please?"

There was a pail of carrots and other vegetables beside me. It was no more than three feet from her. She didn't need me to get it; she just wanted to talk. "Sure, Aunt Chris."

"How was your rest?" she asked.

"Different. How long was I out?"

"Only three days."

Only?

She continued, "Feeling groggy? Normally, if you want to feel completely rested, you may need to sleep for a month or two. The last time I slept, I slept for a year. It was great. I might do that again, real soon."

"So, that was Peter?" I asked.

292

She looked at me and smiled. She was so beautiful. She looked like she was doing some couture photo shoot for a fancy French magazine. "Umm hmmm."

"You were really mad at him."

"No, not really. I just hate when Christians think they know more about God and His word than I do. Self-righteousness will be the end of them."

"But he didn't do what you wanted."

"There are more out there who will. Peter was just one man; there are many who will do what I want. It is called free will, the greatest gift God has given man. There are many out there who will do whatever they must to achieve happiness, to make money, to be successful. The best part is that many of them don't even know they are sinning. To desire what your neighbors have, to lie to get that promotion, to steal to get that girl is all sin. The end never justifies the means. I'm not too worried about Peter; he will be back. They always come back. It's in humans' nature." She noticed what I had on. "I take it Carly didn't see you."

"No, ma'am. I would be dead by now." I laughed. Getting back to the topic, I asked, "So Peter loves God so much that he would forgive his wife even after what she did?"

"I would still be there for you, to love you through it."

Noah said he would love me through anything.

"Umm hmmm. Something to think about." She smiled.

Was God's love that great? Could His love cleanse anyone from any transgression? Could a man who loved God and his wife so passionately just accept her despite her crimes?

"We should go inside, Carrie. It's going to snow."

I waited as my aunt locked up the horses. She embraced me, and we began the trek up the hill. The dry leaves on the ground crumpled under our bare feet. "You know," she began, "sometimes we don't sleep well as demons. It is different; we may imagine seeing someone or doing something we didn't do, have fake memories. Did you know Carly used to have dreams of visiting her human family?"

"What?" I wondered if Aunt Carly saw the same baby I saw in my vision. It was just so unreal for me to think that Aunt Carly was capable of feeling any emotion.

"Human descendants, yes. She turned at a very odd age, twenty-one. She was married with three human children, two boys and a girl."

I tried to act surprised.

"She was a very devout Christian," my aunt added.

"Really? Carly Carter, a devout Christian?"

"She believed," Aunt Chris continued, "that the life she was living was the life that was meant for her. She was happy." We stopped at the bottom of the steps to the house. "Of course, she changed and had to leave her family, her husband, her sons, and her baby girl. She was truly sad. She wondered why God had forsaken her."

"Had He?"

No wonder she was bitter. Everyone whom she has ever loved was taken from her: her husband, her human children, and her demon sons. Not to mention the deal my mother didn't honor, and how Mother treated her in the past. Aunt Carly was superficial because what was the point in loving someone who was only going to be taken from you?

"No, God makes no mistakes," Aunt Chris affirmed.

I believed her.

"Why are you telling me this? I thought you didn't like telling me their stories?"

"I shared Carly's plight to say this. In a few days, a new year will began, a fresh start. Carly came to accept what God wanted for her, she discovered her true purpose. As hard as it is to believe her purpose was *this* life, her demon life that was the life that God wanted for her. There is good and evil in all men. There is no such thing as an entirely good person or an entirely bad person, and you are fooling yourself if you believe otherwise." She paused. "Once I had a vision about Cole being alive. He was grown with a family of his own." She smiled. "Did you dream when you went to sleep, Carrie? Did you experience anything or see anything?"

If she was asking, nine times out of ten she knew, so there was no need in lying. "No," I answered.

Liar. She didn't speak the word aloud. She opened the door for me. "A new start," she added.

"Aunt Chris, what was Peter about to tell you? About loving your wife? What does the Bible say?" I asked.

"Ephesians 5:22, 28-31: 'Wives, submit yourselves unto your own husbands, as unto the Lord. For the husband is head of the wife, even as Christ is head of the church; and he is the savior of the body. Therefore, as the church is subject to Christ, so let wives be to their own husbands in everything. Husbands, love your wives as Christ also loved the church and gave himself for it . . . So ought

295

men to love their wives as their own bodies. He that loveth his wife loveth himself. For no man ever yet hated his own flesh, but nourisheth and cherisheth it, even as the Lord the church . . . For this cause shall a man leave his father and mother and shall be joined unto his wife, and they two shall be one flesh.'"

"It is something to think about." I concluded.

Carrie, I know that is not Noah with his Christmas gifts in his hand, returning them? Aunt Carly questioned me.

I flew to my balcony; it was Noah. He appeared to be returning his Christmas gifts.

I'll handle it, Aunt Carly, I answered.

You better, she threatened. *Or I will.*

I found a pair of studded jeans and a plain white t-shirt. I ran my fingers through my hair and let it hang wild, put on my pink flats, then inspected myself before I went to the door to catch Noah before Aunt Carly literally ripped off his head.

I might as well look nice.

I didn't want to dress like my aunts, who at any given time looked like royalty. I wanted to be as casual as possible because nobody but my aunts walked about in haute couture all the time with the exception of maybe a super model or a movie star, and even they had off days.

Not my aunts, dressing down to them was not putting on any shoes.

I walked downstairs as if I was walking to my execution. I passed Aunt Carly, who was in the mirror in the living room. She was boiling. She shot me a look with her dark eyes. I paid her no mind. I had a horrible task to do, a task I didn't want to do.

"Noah, please come in." I opened the door before he could ring the bell.

He looked perplexed. "You guys are great at catching people before they ring the bell." He looked me dead in my eyes and said, "Carrie, we have to talk, Carrie."

I knew it. We hadn't spoken since that horrible Christmas day. I just didn't want to have this conversation.

"Of course. Please." I led the way upstairs.

Noah looked like, well, Noah. He was beautiful with his dark hair windblown in the late December breeze. January was just around the corner, a new start for him and an ending for me. His blue eyes were haunted.

"Okay," he said.

All three of my aunts were lined up in some kind of reception line like at a wedding, when the witnesses got to greet the new bride and groom and the whole wedding party; this, however, was not a warm reception. They didn't speak as we marched upstairs; they just stared at us. They moved in unison.

I imagined they were having their own conversation, one I wasn't allowed to hear. Aunt Carly scowled at the gift boxes. Her eyes weren't even close to green. My aunts' human façade wavered a little, and for the first time ever, I sensed fear radiating from Noah.

Noah didn't take off his black pea coat once we were in my room, signaling that he didn't intend to stay long.

"Yours," he said as he placed the boxes on my bed. He then stood by the door, prepared for a speedy exit. I floated to the window. His eyes popped out of his head for a bit, but then he shook it off. I saw no need to keep the lie going; it was the end of us anyway. I didn't know the first thing about breaking up with anyone, especially Noah, who wasn't just anyone. He was my best friend, my only friend. He loved me when I was just an ordinary human, when I was just his Care Bear. He never stopped loving me even when he should have.

Why couldn't I have this? Why couldn't I have him? But I knew deep down in my heart I had to end our relationship. The last thing I wanted to do was hurt Noah.

"Noah…" My pep talk in my head was one thing, speaking the words out loud was another.

Chicken! Aunt Carly antagonized me.

Get out of my head!! I demanded.

"Talk," Noah ordered. He didn't want to talk to me, and I couldn't blame him. Christmas was awful.

I was a coward. I couldn't just tell him the truth and blurt out everything. He would think I was crazy or evil, or both. No way was I leaving anything short of being his Care Bear if I could help it.

"I'm actually leaving Baltimore. I'm leaving Maryland," I managed to say. *Why did I sound so formal?*

This took him completely by surprise. "What? Carrie? What's going on? Are you leaving over what happened on Christmas?"

"My mother…" I said the first thing that came to mind. Noah's blue eyes pleaded for me to make sense of it all.

"I think I found my mother," I began. "And she is still not very well."

Noah sat on my bed next to his unwanted gifts. "So you're leaving to get your mother?" he asked.

"Yes." I sat down beside him.

"And you are bringing her back here, to get help?" he questioned.

"I don't think she wants to come back here."

"What happened to your mother, Carrie? I thought she was already in the hospital?"

"She was, I mean is. She was transferred to another facility." I lied and felt awful about it.

He searched my eyes for something, and I had nothing to offer him. "So what does that mean for you? Are you ever coming back?"

"I don't know."

"You don't know?" He jumped up. "What's going on here, Carrie? Maybe I can help you," he offered.

This was tearing me apart.

For me to be a soulless, heartless creature, *this* was killing me. Why did Noah have to be so...so Noah? Why couldn't he be a jerk?

Words started pouring out of me. "You see, Noah that is the problem: you can't. You can't help me. I am beyond your help. Your father and Pastor Cross were right. I'm not good for you. Know that! Know that you are special and loving. I wish we could be, but we can't. It is over. We are done!" My heart was beating like a drum. Before I knew it, I was floating and my eyes were black.

He stood by the door with his hand on the knob. He finally broke the silence. "I had a dream about you floating and eating everything in your kitchen. You looked just like that with those same black eyes," he said with recognition.

My eyes returned to green, and I lightly placed my feet on the floor. "That wasn't a dream, Noah." I said plainly.

I didn't want it to end like this, but shit happens. I wanted him to think that I was helping my mother like some humanitarian so he wouldn't have to know about my dark side.

"What are you?" he asked curiously.

I debated. *Tell him...*

Don't tell him...

Tell him...

Don't tell him...

"I don't..." I didn't know what to say. I didn't know what to do.

TELL HIM!

"Noah..."

301

My mind was racing. I was on the brink of what I could only describe as a mental breakdown when suddenly we were on the beach just like my Christmas day illusion minus the storm. Then we were in the rain forest.

"HOLY SHIT!" Noah barked. "What was that? Did you—" He gripped the hell out of the knob. "What in the... WOW! Did you see? How...how could you?" Of course he was tongue-tied. I was surprised that he didn't run away screaming, believing I was the devil.

"I can make certain things happen," I said.

"Like some *Children of the Corn* type shit?" He was pretty freaked out.

I wish. "Yeah, something like that. It's a mental thing I can do."

He found his footing. "You can make people do things?"

I nodded. I stepped closer to him, but he stepped backward and bumped into the closed door. I stopped. There was no need to frighten him anymore than necessary, so I kept my distance.

"You made me do things?" he asked cautiously.

"No." I haven't heard any Noah's thoughts, because he was amazingly an all-around good soul.

He held onto the doorknob for dear life. "But you have made other people do things?"

"Yes," I conceded.

"Bad things?"

I didn't want to say it, but I felt the need to be honest. "Yes."

He rested his head back on the door. "And your aunts..."

"Everyone in my family has this ability."

"So what Pop was telling me about your family... the Carters... the article... he was right?"

"I don't know exactly what he said, but if he said that my family was evil, then he was right," I again conceded.

He shook his head. "Carrie, you are not—"

I had to stop him. "Noah, you have to go. We can't be together and we can't be friends." I walked back toward my wall with my huge flat screen television mounted on it. "Leave now."

We couldn't be together. He would move on; he had to. Sure, he might be heartbroken, but he would find another. She would love him, and he would be happy again. I would be okay with that if in the end Noah was happy.

"Carrie?" I knew he had a million and one questions.

"GO!" I yelled. I knew my eyes had changed colors. He inched toward me. "GET BACK!" I barked.

Carrie, do you need— Aunt Cara started to ask me something.

"I need everyone to leave me alone!" I screamed and grabbed my head in agony.

Carrie, please don't be a drama queen. Aunt Carly just had to say something. *That Ingrid and Harry— You know what, I'm going to go over there and*—

"NO!" I called out. "Let them be!"

"Carrie," Noah started, "who are you talking to?" His face was pale and transparent. I could see the blood flow, or the lack thereof.

I don't why you just had to tell him, just sleep with him and get it over with, said Aunt Carly.

"Please, please, stop it! Get out of my head!" I begged and fell to the floor. I wanted desperately to be left alone.

"Carrie, what are you talking about? Should I get your aunts?" I forgot for a millisecond that Noah was still in my room. He inched closer to me.

"Noah, don't come near me," I ordered as I held out my arm to ward him away from me. "Go, please. It's for your own good." He didn't listen and continued toward me. I could smell him; his natural scent smelled so good. I was tempted to reach out, grab him, and kiss him.

I did, almost. He was within my grasp; I used all the mental energy I had to push him backward away from me.

I didn't push him back far, but it was enough. I had the power to move objects? I didn't know I could do that! I felt drained after performing that act. I didn't feel as powerful. I felt weak. I used a lot of energy to move him. I saw my reflection on my iPad screen; my pupils were all white. I fainted. Noah, though he was stunned at my mental ability to push him, still tried to come to my aid. With everyone in my head, it was hard to concentrate. I had an overwhelming headache. I balled up in the corner in my room between the wall and my desk.

"Carrie," Noah called as he reached to grab me again. "Your eyes?" It was a question and a statement. I just shut them as I lay helpless on the floor.

Carrie? Aunt Cara asked.

Carrie. That was Aunt Chris.

Damn it, girl! Drama! Aunt Carly insisted. *I knew allowing Carrie to go to dinner would be a disaster, but no, Cara, she just had to find out the hard way. Now look at her. I mean damn, she's really being annoying. Was it worth it? Oh, no, wait, it wasn't; she still is leaving and your plans are ruined!*

Carly, I'm sick of your insubordination! said Aunt Cara.

Insubordination? You don't really think you are stronger than I am, do you? Let's talk this out demon to demon; I will show you who is superior.

I wanted the fighting to stop. But, more importantly, I wanted everyone out of my head. If I could, I would have cried.

Aunt Chris interjected, *Please ladies, let's not do this in Carrie's space.*

"ENOUGH!" I screamed. "I can't take this anymore."

"Carrie, let me help you," Noah pleaded. I got up and stumbled onto my balcony.

"You can't." One lone tear drop trickled down my face. "Good bye." I said and then I leaped off the balcony. Noah, of course, unaware of my new skill set, ran over to the window to try to catch me, but I was already on the ground when he finally made it to the balcony.

I landed on all fours. I was going to fly, but I wasn't sure that I was strong enough. He disappeared from my balcony, probably running to catch me. I knew he wasn't crazy enough to jump. It was a good twenty feet from my balcony to the ground.

My aunts were already at the back door when I hit the ground. They displayed no emotion when I glanced back at them.

"Carrie is the strongest one of our kind," Aunt Cara said.

"Who or what did she move?" Aunt Chris asked.

"Noah." Aunt Carly sniffed the air. "She is who we thought she was. The prophecy is true. Esther can return, just as she said."

"Celeste will never let it happen. She would die first," Aunt Chris added.

"That can be arranged," Aunt Carly purred.

Aunt Cara nodded in agreement.

I stood up and walked to the blood tree. I touched the bark and felt the electricity. "I know this wasn't the life you wanted," I said to the tree. "I am sorry you know only pain. Thank you for showing me what I needed to know. Take care, Caleb. "

Noah finally reached the back door. I couldn't bear to look at him again; he would weaken my resolve. Noah frantically tried to push through my aunts to stop me. I flashed a look at the four of them standing in the door, and I took off as fast as I could.

"CARRIE!" Noah called. "You can't just let her leave!" he screamed as he tried to catch me, but I was down by the stables close to the main gate making my exit.

Aunt Chris simply said, "She has made her choice."

I had.

I was leaving.

To cure my demon.

Epilogue

Celeste

Present Day

Celeste was fatigued. She had been flying for days and decided to land and rest, ending up in some shantytown in New Orleans. The area was filled with abandoned FEMA trailers and tents. She thought this would be the perfect place for her to rest, since there weren't any humans around. She placed her bare feet on the ground for the first time in days. She walked over broken glass and drug needles. She felt the hopelessness that consumed this community after Hurricane Katrina. The stale smell of sin and death was all around her.

She noticed that the street lights were on. She wanted total darkness, so she focused her mental energy on crushing them. Her eyes turned white as she used her power to crush the bulbs one by one. After the last bulb was destroyed, Celeste collapsed to the ground, feeling drained. She fell onto a median strip covered with grass and closed her eyes.

Celeste remembered that Uriel was known for frequenting New Orleans. He once shared with her that his visits reminded him of a time long forgotten. Uriel was instrumental in the development of the culture of New Orleans. It was his home, and that was Celeste's reason for coming here. She knew it was a long shot, since no one had seen Uriel in decades.

She felt that Uriel was her only hope to regain her humanity and save her daughter. Celeste didn't want either Esther or Cara to use her daughter, and she wanted Carly nowhere near Carrie. She sniffed the air.

Someone was there.

At least four people.

Four sinful souls, she thought.

She leaped to her feet. The smell of sin was familiar to her, yet she could tell that she had never encountered these people before. It was an ancient smell mixed with the scent of someone younger.

Whoever they were, they were more than human.

"Announce yourself!" she ordered, speaking with authority. She was arguably the most powerful demon on Earth. She started to float and hovered at a height of eleven feet. She now wished that she hadn't destroyed all the street lights.

The creatures were close.

The wind blew some of the debris from the abandoned trailers toward her. Celeste turned, focusing on the scattered garbage. She floated back to the ground and slowly walked toward the dumpster.

As she walked, something or someone crossed her path.

"HEY!" she yelled. Suddenly someone leaped onto her back. Her eyes turned black as she flipped the person onto the cement.

"Fool," she growled as she stepped on the male who lay on the ground. She broke five of his ribs. "Do you know who I am?"

She examined the man, who was young and as well as beautiful. But something was different about him. He tried to free himself from her, but Celeste was too powerful.

"Be still," she ordered. She pressed harder with her foot, crushing two more ribs. She looked at his blood covered face. His eyes were a very light gray color, odd against his dark complexion. He had a crazed look of a rabid animal.

"A Blood Drinker?" Celeste was surprised. The Blood Drinkers had been all but erased. Malik, who was one of the Originals, and his son, Michael, were the only two Celeste knew of.

The male howled as he tried to claw his way from Celeste. "Blood," he moaned. "Intruder blood."

"Malik is in New Orleans?" Celeste asked him.

Just then, another person jumped from the shadows and launched herself at Celeste. The crazed woman also had light gray eyes and blood around her mouth. Before the woman came within two feet of Celeste, she crushed the man's neck with her foot and focused on the crazed woman with white eyes.

The female collapsed in midair.

There was only one way to kill a demon. Floating over to the woman's body, Celeste pulled her heart out of her chest and then yanked her head from her body with no effort. When she finished, she floated back to the man and did the same thing to him.

Throwing her trophies to the ground, she focused on them with her white pupils. Their body parts liquefied under her gaze.

Celeste wasn't safe here. She gathered the remaining body parts and buried them, not wanting to leave any evidence of her being here. She was very tired and wasn't moving as fast as she normally could.

"Celestial," a third person called out.

She didn't know this person.

It was another woman with the same gray eyes.

"How do you know that name?" Only the Originals and older demons would address her that way. "What is your name, demon?" she demanded.

"Celestial, is that how you address your Master?" Another woman, speaking ancient Sumerian, walked into the open space and addressed her. Celeste smelled the woman. Only a handful of demons could speak that dead language.

"Your Greatness?"

There was only one demon that had the power to possess humans. This had to be the work of Ezekiel and there were more than two Blood Drinkers in existence, so Malik had to be involved also.

The women spoke in unison, this time in English. "Yes."

Malik and Ezekiel were working together. Celeste refrained from using the proper greeting of an Original, which was "Your Greatness" along with their name. Though she was sure she was talking to Ezekiel, she didn't want to disrespect Malik. The Original Demons were very vain.

"You have killed two of our own kind," they continued. The

killing of a demon by another demon was a very serious crime. Celeste was in trouble. She had not only killed another demon, but she killed two demons protected by two Originals. Making a bold gambit, Celeste addressed Ezekiel by his full title.

"Your Greatness Ezekiel, I was unaware. I wish to apologize. I was being attacked, or at least I thought I was. When I asked the demon his name, he refused to respond." She slowly approached the two women, who represented Ezekiel and Malik, and kneeled. The ultimate praise to give an Original was to submit.

The two women looked at each other, moving in unison. Both had slender frames with beautiful porcelain skin, gray eyes, and auburn hair.

"Malik wishes to see you," they said. "Rise and come with us. You must rest in proper accommodations if you are to state your case."

Celeste did as she was told. If you wanted to live, you did not refuse an Original. She would have to tell them why she was in New Orleans and also have to admit that she killed two demons. Celeste knew she would be punished for her crimes. She mentally blocked herself from her family back in Maryland. She didn't want them to know where she was or to get the crazy idea to rescue her.

She rose to her feet slowly and followed the women who would take her to Malik and Ezekiel.

In person.

Book Discussion Questions

In _The Book of Carrie_ there are many interesting topics that are brought up. Here are some possible questions that you and your book group can discuss.

1. Are the words *normal* and *sane* relative terms as Celeste tries to explain to Carrie?

2. Describe Carrie's relationship with her mother. Is it a loving relationship? Why or why not? What about her relationship with her aunts?

3. Celeste challenges Carrie to describe a good person. Carrie has a difficult time with the task. What defines a good person?

4. Frances proposes an unthinkable request to Carrie. Do bad people deserve to die? What determines if a person should be put to death for their transgressions?

5. Carrie and Noah love each other unconditionally. Who loves who more and why?

6. Is it realistic to believe Carrie can change? Can she conquer her demon(s)?

7. Carrie's assessment of church, is it a fair one? Why or why not?

8. Is there such a thing as fate or are you in charge of your own destiny?

Meet the Author

D. Antoinette lives in Baltimore, MD., with her two amazing daughters and two imaginary dogs, Coco and Montriece. She enjoys singing (even though she can't sing) and displaying her awesomeness wherever she goes.

The First Book of Carrie is her first published novel.

To learn more about D. Antoinette or
to get the latest First Book of Carrie info, visit
www.IAmCarrieCarter.com
or contact her via email at
D.Antoinette0130.gmail.com